the rojocci papers

Freedom Within You
by
R. J. Graves, Jr.

This is a work of fiction. Names, characters, places and incidents are products of the author's imagination or are used fictitiously. Any resemblance to actual persons, living or dead, or to events and locales is entirely coincidental.

Cover design by: BETIBUP33 Designs

the rojocci papers
FREEDOM WITHIN YOU
Copyright © 2017 by R. J. Graves, Jr.
Published by R. J. Graves, Jr.
Pensacola, Florida 32503

Visit us at www.facebook.com/rojocci
www.therojoccipapers.com
ISBN-10: 0-9984073-1-3
ISBN-13: 978-0-9984073-1-9
Christian Fiction
$13.95 USD

Printed in the United States of America.

This book is dedicated to our
wonderful children.
And to our three, to date, precious
grandchildren,
who all make up our family.
Sarah, David and Robert
Kathryn, Matthew, Eloise and Madeline
Nathanael
Joshua and Lauren
Benjamin
Jonathan

Acknowledgments

Several people have helped me with many aspects of this book, none more than my editor, Susan C. Graves, whose tireless efforts and extreme attention to detail have been a wonder to behold. Heartfelt thanks also to Mike Parker, Kathy Coker, Sarah Whipps, along with Frank and Bernice Osborne, for their most helpful input and encouragement during the many revisions.

Although I will no doubt, inadvertently leave many others out of these acknowledgements, I do want to thank my friend, Doug Gehman, who first suggested and encouraged me to consider writing.

"It was for freedom
that Christ set us free;
therefore keep standing firm
and do not be subject again
to a yoke of slavery."

Galatians 5:1

-prologue-

It was a chilly day along the Gulf Coast of Alabama as we sat at a picnic table in late November 2016. Peeking through the lazily moving clouds every few minutes, the sun allowed us to warm ourselves in its brilliant rays. Several weeks had passed since our lunch together at the Cajun seafood restaurant where I had given him a copy of my initial draft of the book *Hidden Within You*. This time we met at a park in the quaint shrimping village of Bayou La Batre. Alan thought it would be more conducive to personal conversation than a busy restaurant. I acquiesced in principle. However, to be honest, I had been looking forward to enjoying the crawfish etouffee of our previous rendezvous.

Handing me the red-lined copy of my manuscript across the weathered wooden table, I flipped through it like a dealer readying a deck of cards. I could see he had written a smattering of remarks.

"Not many comments?" I questioned.

"No, not really," he replied.

"Great! I'm delighted to hear that. I'll make the changes and set about getting it published, hopefully by the end of this year."

Alan nodded his head and glanced out across the sun glistened Mississippi Sound. Soon, another cloud drifted over the water fading the bright blue to a battleship grey. He appeared to be deep in thought as if something was bothering him, though not in a troublesome way.

"I'm not sure what it is, but I feel something stirring in my heart. When I sense this, I've learned it's best to be patient and quietly wait until God makes it clear," he confided frankly.

I'm no longer surprised by the confidence Alan asserts when it comes to spiritual decisions. I think it's because he prefers to err on the side of faith, which often involves extended periods of waiting.

As he spoke, I noticed for the first time that this man with the kind eyes had aged since our first meeting over a dozen years ago. Maybe it was because the sun was hitting his face at an angle that highlighted his weathered skin and receding hairline. He didn't appear haggard. Rather, he sported a well-worn look, as with a favorite pair of jeans or shoes, worn but comfortable. Glistening in the sunshine, his hair was mostly silver now. He donned a pair of not-quite-round, tortoise framed glasses, which rode midway up the bridge of his nose, indicating those kind eyes had limitations. Alan was still wiry, even muscular, but as invariably happens to us all, he had grown older. Somehow, this revelation startled me.

We sat quietly for several minutes. I had learned from my many visits with Alan to be patient with these pauses. He never found them awkward, and I had become at ease with them too. Eventually he would pose a question or make a comment. It just took time. He was a thinker, who studied a situation and worked through the best way to say a thing before he launched into it. He had also disciplined his lethal quick wit. Undoubtedly, this had been learned over a period of several decades of offending, apologizing, and asking forgiveness. It was a course of study that required many episodes of shame and embarrassment, not to mention a healthy dose of humiliation. He once confided that he would rather suffer through a pound of humility than an ounce of humiliation. This was a statement I considered both wise and profound.

Sure enough, after several minutes, Alan turned toward me and asked, "So . . . would you like to hear about the dream?"

I was somewhat shocked but immediately answered, "Absolutely, whenever you're ready, I'm ready."

"Well, Annalisa and I have prayed about this for many weeks. However, each time we finished praying I had a check in my spirit. I couldn't put my finger on it, but I knew it was there, nonetheless. Now, I don't know about you, but I have learned to wait if I have a caution from one of two sources: my wife or my spirit. I try not to act upon some major issue without those two being in complete agreement."

With this, Alan paused and looked right into my eyes. I was sure, knowing most of what this man had been through over the last few decades that this lesson, too, had been acquired the hard way—by trial and error. As Betsy Taft had once told him, "You don't soon forget something that cost you dearly to learn."

Alan continued, "After discussing it with Annalisa, I discovered the caveat was only within my spirit. She thought I should share the dream with you and allow you to write the story, if you think it's worthy of pen and paper. However, you have to allow me to start at the beginning, well, almost the beginning anyway. You see, I determined that's why I had a check in my spirit—I hadn't told you everything leading up to the visit to the Morgan's cottage in October 1995. Granted, these are very private matters, but without the knowledge of those personal issues the dream won't have near the same meaning. So then, that's where I need to start. Okay with you?"

I nodded my head as I reached for my legal pad and pen. "Ready when you are, doctor." He glanced across at me and we both chuckled. Then he leaned forward, resting his arms on the rustic table and began his story.

one

Great power is only developed through much resistance. Freedom is power, not just in reference to governmental declarations or military prowess, but the freedom within the individual. It's the internal capability to accomplish what one desires, and also the might to do what one should. However, there is a strict prerequisite for one to be truly free. The secret is hidden within. There's no detour, no shortcut, no easy path to this liberty, only the struggle, the resistance, the fight. It stands as a formidable, nearly impenetrable fortress. But to the one who seeks to be free, who longs to be free, who must be free, it is but an ocean to be crossed, a mountain to be climbed, a moon upon which to land. It can be done.

For example, observe a graceful butterfly. To obtain the apparent carefree existence of fluttering from one bloom to another, the beautifully winged creature must first go through a great conflict—it must free itself from the restricting confines of a claustrophobic cocoon. This, to be sure, is no small struggle. An athlete, to break free from his corpulent form, must first endure many an exhausting effort in training. He must wrestle through daily decisions concerning every detail of his diet and lifestyle that would hinder his progress. If he perseveres, he is rewarded with the freedom of fitness, which affords him the opportunity to obtain his aspiration— the gold medal. The student, as well, must suffer many long hours of arduous study to obtain the liberty of an educated mind.

The American Revolutionary War is perhaps the most pertinent of examples; a people striving against grave odds to gain freedom for themselves through a long, grinding turmoil. The road to Yorktown, Virginia, and the glorious victory over General Cornwallis invariably led through the terrible crucible of Valley Forge. The struggle, the resistance, the difficulties, instills within a butterfly, an individual, or a nation the very qualities absolutely essential to being free. Without these characteristics experientially embedded, the rigors of freedom soon adulterate and overwhelm.

Alan Browne decidedly wanted to be free from his fears and insecurities, of this he was certain. However, the required struggle to obtain this deliverance was what he felt he absolutely had to avoid. He was convinced it would entail some great protracted internal conflict, and he didn't have the heart for that. So to encourage himself, he read biographies of others who had endured the prodigious battle within. These were stories of Biblical figures and historical persons, the heroes of the faith, who had come through great conflicts victoriously. He recently devoured such a book. An autobiographical work of a unique, if not peculiar, German minister named George Mueller. Mr. Mueller had founded orphanages in England, which cared for, educated, and trained thousands of homeless children. He was a poor man.

Nonetheless, he accomplished it all without ever asking anyone but God for a single shilling.

"It appears to me," professed Alan to himself as he laid aside the stirring book, "Freedom is more than a right. If I'm truly free, I have the ability or power not only to do what I want, but also to do what I know is right and good. Mankind, to be totally free, must not only have the liberty to do what they like, but also the power to do what they must. Mr. Mueller had that freedom, that power. And that kind of freedom in a nation, a church, a family, or even within a person's heart only comes through great struggle. Now, there's a life-long goal worthy of whatever is required to obtain it. However, it is beyond my experience."

Lounging back in the old swivel chair, his mind began to wander. He glanced around the makeshift woodworker's shop which he organized in the garage behind his home in San Ramon, California. Gazing at the racks of hardwood boards along the wall opposite, he put his feet upon the desk. Near to where he sat, stood a lengthy workbench where chisels, clamps, and crosscut saws hung in order on the wall above. The entire length of the rear wall of his shop housed another work bench with an electric compound miter saw. In the far corner stood his band saw and the latest of his acquisitions, a used, yet well-maintained drill press. In front of the rollup door was his most prized possession, a floor mounted table saw with the expansive outfeed work table adjacent to the rear. His livelihood might be bicycles, but his passion was working with wood.

He loved his shop and the way he felt when he was there. He seemed freer, less stressed. His thoughts were at liberty to be creative, to visualize new concepts and ideas. Placing his hands behind his head, interlacing his fingers, he spontaneously imagined his next project. He mentally worked through the material list, the cuts that needed to be made, as well as the glue up of the pieces. As though it was sitting there on the workbench in front of him, he could clearly envision the finished product.

"Man, thoughts are clearly dominating masters!" he announced while trying to recall what he had been thinking of before starting down the road to his now finished, imaginary woodworker's project. "First the thought, then the action," he pondered.

"Hmmm . . . where was I? Oh, yes, 'Through many tribulations we must enter the kingdom of God,'"[1] he quoted aloud trying to focus on what Mr. Mueller's book had highlighted.

Once again his eyes wandered around the shop as his thoughts commenced down the well-worn grooves in his mind like a car upon the icy ruts of a snowy road in winter . . . or like the newly appointed Apostle Peter returning to his fishing boat.[2] Default settings aren't easily overcome.

"I wonder if perhaps the freedom I yearn is actually the kingdom of God? And this same kingdom, which requires struggles to enter, He declared is within me."[3] Alan closed his eyes allowing this last thought to sink deeper.

"A struggle within me for a kingdom within me," he whispered several times.

"Well . . . whatever it is, wherever it is, I've got to find some answers," he admonished himself. "And sitting here ruminating on these boards isn't helping anything."

Catching a glimpse of his face in the shop window, he noticed a few more wrinkles than when he'd last studied it, and his thinning hair was almost entirely salt and pepper now. Reminiscently, he rubbed his upper lip where his once beloved mustache had proudly graced the open space between his nose and mouth. He had shaved it off years ago because the grey whiskers made him appear older. He realized he would have to shear his entire coiffure to achieve the same effect today. Recognizing he was still fit, though not his once sleek, sporty model, he decided he was more of a sedan, two doors, not four. Middle-age, he concluded, was a bummer—too old to be the lead dog, too young to sit on the porch.

"Man, oh man," he mumbled in disbelief as he plopped back down in his chair. "How did I get off on this train of thought? I'm not sure, but I think freedom and discipline might walk hand in hand."

It was late October 1995. Alan had been home now for a couple of weeks from his doctor recommended "decompression vacation" in Gulf Breeze, Florida. He had selected for his trip, after much discussion with his wife, Annalisa, a cottage owned by his neighbor Bill Morgan. The white sand beaches of the Northern Gulf of Mexico had been, in fact, absolutely gorgeous. The rustic cottage on the other hand, had been adequate for his needs, but without much appeal. Everything had seemed perfect, just what his doctor had ordered, except for the absence of his sweet bride and their three children, who he had missed from the moment he had boarded the cross country flight.

Alan had planned the vacation so he would have some type of physical activity every day. The last thing he had wanted was to feel lonely, and moping around the cottage would have had precisely that effect. For some exercise, he had brought along a bicycle, not his snazzy road racing machine, but the more comfortable touring bike. He'd checked everything, the restaurants, the route to the beaches, the shops to purchase gifts for his family, even the location of a local grocery store. He hadn't overlooked anything, except to check the weather forecast. Although he was born and raised a Virginian, he had lived in California for so long he hadn't really concerned himself with the weather. It appeared to him every San Ramon forecast was the same, "Night and morning low clouds and fog, otherwise sunny, high of seventy-eight degrees." Therefore, the inclement weather for this trip had never entered his mind.

Within a few days of arriving at the quiet coastal hideaway for rest and relaxation, he had discovered, through an early morning telephone call from Bill Morgan, that the weather in Florida isn't California. Unbeknownst to Alan, October was hurricane season, and further, there was a Category Three storm named Opal, which had a bead focused on his vacation spot. This had made for no small amount of consternation. Over the next three days he had, by the grace of God, passed through the storm. But it had changed him; God had changed him. Now, he was back home wondering how he would obtain solutions to his current, devastating situation. This had led him out to his garage, explaining to Annalisa he would be an hour or so.

"If only I could get free from all this debt," he mumbled. "This business has become such a burden. It used to be so much fun. I mean, I was making good money, had a great team of employees, and plenty of happy customers. But now all I think about are the bills, and how I can't get ahead of them. There must be a way. Somehow, there's got to be a way."

Standing up, Alan walked across to his workbench. He picked out a board of beautiful black walnut, about six feet long, and held one end up to his eye. He gazed down the length of the fine piece of lumber. To him it was gorgeous. It was straight, without the hint of a bow. He turned it perpendicular while he brushed his palm along its smooth finish, caressing it as he admired its perfection. He held it up and smelled the wonderful, earthy scent, like a connoisseur would a newly poured glass of expensive wine. Alan judged it to be absolutely sublime. He picked up another piece, but as he was beginning his assessing sequence his phone rang.

Alan flipped open the device. "Hello?"

"Hey, Alan, it's Joey Hinote, remember me?" Alan immediately recognized the voice as belonging to his new friend from Florida. He and Joey had been introduced on a bicycle ride the day before Hurricane Opal had made landfall. Afterwards, they met two more times before Alan left to return home. Joey and Alan had become fast friends.

"Hey, Joey, great to hear from you. How are things in Pensacola?"

"Good, everything is getting back to normal. Give it another month or so, and we'll be kicking and sticking like Popeye's chicken."

"What?!" laughed Alan.

"Ha, it means we'll be doing great," chuckled Joey. "Hey, Alan, you busy? You got a few minutes?"

"Sure, what's up, man?"

"Well, do you remember me telling you I had to move my folks into a retirement home a few months back?"

"Uh, vaguely. I think I remember something about a place out by the University of West Florida, right?"

"Yeah, that's right," replied Joey. "It's a real nice facility, very homey, and they like it up there. At least, I think they do."

"That's good, Joey."

"Anyway, now that they don't live there anymore, I've been trying to clean out their house. But I've been so busy with this new contract I picked up. Did I tell you about that?"

"No, what contract?"

"I got this amazing time and material deal with this huge hotel to refinish all their furniture. I mean, we're going floor by floor, room by room. It's going to take several months, so I'm really grateful. We delivered the first couple of rooms yesterday. So far, so good."

"Ah, that's great, man."

"Yeah, I needed the work. But hey, God always provides," proclaimed Joey.

"I hope so," Alan replied doubtfully.

"He does, Alan, His timing isn't always our timing, that's all, my brother."

"Thanks," Alan quipped softly.

"So anyway, I'm cleaning out my parents' house, okay? And they have more junk than you can shake a cat at."

"Shake a what at?" laughed Alan.

"A cat . . . shake a cat at," smirked Joey. "You've never heard that?"

"Nope, can't say that I have, but, okay . . . they have a lot of stuff. Then what?"

"We decided to start in the attic and kind of work our way down and out through the garage over the course of several months," explained Joey.

"Big house?" asked Alan.

"Oh yeah," replied Joey. "It's an old Southern clapboard farmhouse with a wraparound porch; at least it wraps around three sides anyway. The first floor has big rooms, you know, a parlor, a dining room, and a kitchen, as well as a small bathroom and stairs leading to the second floor. The second floor has a hall bath at the top of the stairs and three bedrooms with tiny closets."

"Does it have a big attic?" asked Alan.

"Yep, that's the kind of creepy part," responded Joey.

"Creepy part?"

"Oh yeah, baby. In the back of the closet in my parents' bedroom is a door. Behind the door, is a set of very narrow and steep stairs. One flight leads upward to the attic and the other to the kitchen below. I'm not sure, but I think it must have been for the servants of the original owners back in the 1800s."

"What makes you think that?" asked Alan.

"Well, because there are platforms, like bunkbeds in the attic, six in total. I think that's where they must have slept. It's got high ceilings, you know, exposed rafters . . . and bats!"

"Bats?" inquired Alan.

"Yeah, when we were young that attic used to scare the sweet tea out of my brothers, sister, and me. We would hear noises in the attic in the middle of the night and were convinced there was somebody up there who was going to come down those stairs and get us."

"I thought you said the stairs came to a door in your parent's closet?"

"I did. It became their room in the latter years. But in the early days, my brothers and I got the largest room, the one with the door opening to those stairs. Alan, I can still remember some of those creepy feelings like it was yesterday," confided Joey unashamedly.

"Yeah, I too have noticed how memories last a long time and have the unique quality of popping up just when you least want them to," remarked Alan.

"No kidding, like while you're going through your parent's stuff in their attic!" laughed Joey. "Did I say creepy?"

"Yes, you did," chuckled Alan.

"Okay, enough of that. So anyway, I'm up there in their attic digging through making piles of stuff: one pile for storage, one for giveaway, and another for the dumpster. I had noticed a big trunk and had left it for last, dreading having to go through every single item in its interior. I mean, Alan, this is one of those old travel trunks. It's huge, man."

"Yeah, what was in it?" asked Alan curiously.

"Stuff, papers, you know, letters, tax returns and junk like that. In fact, you want to know something? My father supported his entire family in 1959 on a mere five thousand seven hundred dollars. Can you believe it, a growing family of seven on less than six thousand a year?"

"Wow, things sure have changed," exclaimed Alan.

"You ain't lying, brother. But that's not all I found. There were bundles of letters, some from as far back as the 1930s and a few even older. Letters my grandparents had saved. In the midst of this postal heap, down toward the bottom, was a smaller packet tied with a piece of ribbon. I thought it looked out of place, so I pulled it out of the trunk and sat down on the bottom bunk. The light was dim, and it was quite stuffy up there, but what I saw made my eyes brighten and my breathing quicken."

"What was it, Joey? What did you find?" begged Alan.

"As I untied the ribbon that bound the letters together, one fell on the floor in front of me. I glanced down but not wanting to drop any more, I turned my attention quickly back to the rest of the letters still in my hands. However, as my mind caught up to what my eyes had seen, I recognized something familiar. There, on the back of the letter lying on the floor at my feet, was a hand printed word scribed in a diagonal fashion. I literally did a triple-take before my mind believed what my eyes were seeing."

"Was it **rojocci**?" blurted Alan.

"Yes, it was," assured Joey, "and all the other envelopes had the same handwritten symbol."

"Whaaat?! Really? How many, Joey? How many posts do you have, man?"

"Twenty-seven."

"Wow, that's unbelievable, man!" shouted Alan all the way from California. "That's fantastic! Have you read any yet?"

"Yeah, I've read them all. Uh, by the way . . . you know how **rojocci** is an acronym? Well, I know what all the **rojocci** letters stand for now: 'receiving of Jesus overlooked cherished Christian insights.' I know it's not the way I was supposed to discover them , but I was kind of exploring, you know?"

"Ah, don't worry about it, Joey. What were the messages in the envelopes? Any new revelations or anything?" pleaded Alan with his most influential tone. "Wow, Joey, twenty seven of them, that's incredible."

"Most of them are how-are-things-going-with-you kind of letters. But there are a couple indicating that my Dad, and maybe my Grandfather, along with this guy from Minnesota were trying to track down some sort of a meeting or conference that was organized way back in the 1800s."

"What did they find?"

"Well, that's just it, Alan, they never actually come out and state what they discovered. It's almost like they didn't want anyone else to know or something. I mean, they didn't even tell me, and I'm their son and grandson. Kind of hurts my feelings."

"Nah, don't think of it that way. They knew you would find the letters, so they didn't feel the need to reveal it to you when you were younger. Besides, maybe they lost interest, didn't have the money to go exploring, or something. Don't let it get to you, man, okay?"

"Yeah, I guess so. Thanks, Alan."

"So tell me, what did you find within those envelopes?"

"Well, like I said, not much . . . except toward the end of the 1960s when they stopped writing. I think perhaps the guy in Minnesota, his name was Marvin Leipzig, died or something. The last letter is dated September 17, 1968. However, in the two previous letters there is indication of this meeting, you know, the one in the 1800s. I think it must have been some sort of **rojocci** fellowship conference or something."

"No, couldn't have been, they never met together. It was just loosely held by the principle of what the acronym represents. I've never heard of them having an actual meeting," argued Alan. "The whole intent of the colonists who founded it was for it to be an inspiration to individual Christians to continue seeking the Lord and His kingdom, not to start another denomination or something."

"Hang on a second, Alan. Let me get those last two letters," stated Joey.

Alan played the Jeopardy Game Show theme song in his head while he waited for Joey. As the pause continued, he whistled a second refrain.

"Okay, I'm back," breathed Joey.

"Did you have to run down the street to find them?" joked Alan.

"Ha, very funny. They were in my bedroom and I'm sitting outside my workshop in the backyard, so it was a bit of a jog," defended Joey with a chuckle. "I haven't been riding my bicycle much lately. I'm getting way out of shape."

"Me too," lamented Alan. "So what do they say?"

"Uh . . . this third to the last letter gives an indication of the meeting. Something they called the 'Conference of Unity' along with the dates but no location."

"What were the dates?" pried Alan.

"Uh, August 17-21, 1866." The phone went silent as both Alan and Joey tried to figure what the significance of those dates could have been.

"Alan?"

"Yeah, yeah, I'm thinking."

"Well, there's a map with the second to the last letter. A partial map anyway but absolutely no mention of any of this in the final letter."

"What's the map of?" inquired Alan.

"I don't know. It's only a small piece of a larger map. The edges are torn on all four sides. There's a city or town in the middle circled in red ink."

"What's the name of the town?"

"Looks like Pfeiffer Station," replied Joey. "Do you think the 'P' is silent?"

"I'm not sure. What state is it in?"

"There's no indication on the map as to what state, Alan."

"Hmmm . . . okay, what other towns are nearby? Maybe we can figure it out that way."

"Uh, there's several, the biggest is Kenton. There's also a Dunkirk to the north and Mount Victory and Ridgeway to the south. To the east is a place called La Rue."

"Okay, I wrote them down. Look, I've got to run. There's so much going on here right now. I really want to follow up with you soon though. How about next Saturday morning, you going to be around for a phone call?"

"I ride with the group in the morning, but I'm usually back by eleven or so. We could talk after ten a.m. your time, which would be noon here. Work for you?"

"Perfect. Talk to you then. And Joey, we'll figure out where this Pfeiffer Station is on the map. I'll put my daughter Julie on it. She'll have an answer in a matter of minutes," assured Alan.

The following week was a blur of activity while Alan fought desperately to stay on top of the money issues regarding his three bicycle shops. Try as he might, they just kept getting farther and farther behind. He knew the end was near, and those thoughts always created an unbearable heaviness within him. He hated it but felt helpless to do anything about it.

He was so consumed by his situation, he completely forgot his commitment to telephone Joey. In fact, he didn't remember to have Julie research the location of Pfeiffer Station either. Two Sundays later, while sitting in the family room that afternoon with Annalisa, his phone rang.

"Hello?"

"You, okay, Alan?"

"Ah, man, I'm so sorry, Joey. Life has been a bit tough lately." Alan held his hand over the phone and whispered to Annalisa to get Julie. "How you doing out there? Everything going well?"

At that moment Julie appeared, and Alan once again put his hand over the phone. He quietly instructed her to get the sheet of paper off his desk that had a list of towns written on it and to try to quickly determine in which state the towns were located. She nodded her head like she was on a secret mission and vanished as quickly as she had appeared.

"We're all well here, my brother. This furniture refinishing project has me buried. We were doing great at three rooms a week, but now they want five rooms completed each week. Man, I need some help. This pace is brutal. I'm literally working six days a week, ten to twelve hours every day."

"How much longer until you're finished?"

"Well, there are eighteen rooms per floor, and there are eight floors in this hotel. We've finished one and a half floors so far. The problem is they have three more resorts they want us to do. Two are a bit smaller, but the other is almost twice as large. When it rains it pours. You know what I mean?"

"Yeah, I do, although in a different way, that's all," replied Alan candidly.

"Hey, I'm calling to see if you determined where the town of Pfeiffer Station is located?"

"Uh . . . yeah, hang on a second."

Just then, Julie marched back into the room, "Ohio, Dad." He motioned for her to come in his direction while he answered Joey.

"It's in Ohio," he declared confidently as he pecked Julie on the cheek. "Thanks, honey," he mouthed with a smile.

"Ohio? Alan we should plan a trip up there as soon as I get through these three hotel projects. You up for that? Say sometime in the spring?"

"I don't have the funds for a trip right now. Maybe we could try sometime in the future. Sorry, man."

"No problem. Let's see what next year holds. You never know, maybe God would free us up a bit. I sure would love to do a bit of **rojocci** exploring."

The two friends ended their phone call shortly thereafter with the commitment, one way or the other, they would continue to stay in touch. And they did exactly that. They talked over the holidays and again in late January. Strangely, neither called the other in February. However, it was the phone call in March when Joey discerned something was terribly wrong with his California friend.

-two-

"You gave God a black eye!"

"Who said that!?" Joey was incredulous and close to getting angry. "Who would pronounce such a condemning verdict on you and Annalisa?"

Alan and Joey had been talking on the telephone for nearly twenty minutes when Alan shared this bombshell. It had been an incredibly difficult season at the bike shops. This coupled with the financial pressures he was enduring had allowed him barely enough time to catch his breath, or have a conversation with a friend. However, today he made time. He went out to his woodworker's shop in the garage where he could talk privately. There wouldn't be any disruptions from the children and no inquisitive looks from Annalisa while he sang the blues of his anthology to his friend.

It was early March 1996 and Alan was broke. He was scared, exhausted, and ready to give up. The last few months, since arriving home from his rest and recovery trip, had been a blur, a dreary, murky, discouraging blur. In an effort to lift his mood, he called his friend Joey, who lived in a tiny Floridian burg called Hurst Hammock where the

Perdido River meets the bay with the same name. Joey had been through a business failure a number of years previous and was trying to encourage Alan to persevere through his season of difficulty.

"Look, Alan," Joey exhorted, "Who would make that kind of disparaging remark to someone who is hurting, to someone who is already feeling distraught? I mean, what kind of person would make such an accusation? Who does he think he is anyway?"

"He's our minister," Alan replied in a monotone.

The phone line was silent. Either Joey was about to explode or he had just passed out. Alan wasn't quite sure which to expect. Finally, after almost a full minute, Joey's voice, at a much higher octave than Alan had ever heard, called out all the way from the Central Time Zone, "Whaaat?! That guy deserves to be . . ."

"Now wait a minute, Joey," Alan interrupted. "In his defense, you don't know the whole story. Let me tell you what happened, okay? It may well be, but I don't think it's all him. I mean, it's a tough job being a member of the clergy. In fact, I've attended four churches in my lifetime, and up until a few months ago I've had nothing but praise for every one of those guys. Those are not easy positions, you know. I have the utmost respect, admiration, and have benefited so much by their ministries. It's not that he's a pastor. It could be anyone in the position of influence. But something started to get off balance here lately, I mean, in our church. He's not the same guy or something. So it's not all his . . ."

"Sure, okay, tell me what happened," Joey's tone gave evidence that it really didn't matter what Alan was trying to tell him because in Joey's mind it was wrong for anyone to give such an indictment upon another's life. To him it reeked of judgment, and he wasn't fond of those who leaned toward being judgmental. Yet, he too was judging, and he knew it, but in this case he felt justified.

"Well," Alan started, "it all began around the time of the birth of our second child, Richard. With this newest blessing from God, we could no longer fit in our two bedroom townhouse in Moraga. So shortly after his birth, we started looking for a larger place. We thought a single family home with at least three bedrooms and two baths would be nice. You know, something we could grow into because Annalisa and I both wanted more children. After several months, we found a home in San Ramon that had a lot of potential. I say potential, meaning it needed a lot of repairs and updating. But hey, I used to be a carpenter. I was certain I could do most of the work."

"Did you buy it?" asked Joey.

"Not at first, but after several viewings and some negotiations the sellers accepted our final counter offer. Thirty days later we were homeowners. It was a perfect location for me, being on the north side, close to Danville. It was about halfway between my bicycle shops in Lafayette and Pleasanton. Later, I built my third shop less than three miles from our new home. The remodeling of our house took over a year of nights and weekends, but we finally got it finished and we love it. However, I ran up the balances on our credit cards in the process. I wasn't overly concerned, since business at the shops was good. I mean, in those days, we were really making excellent money."

Alan continued, "We tried to sustain attendance at our church in Pleasant Hill, but the long drive was becoming too much to handle with the kiddos and working on the house. So we sampled churches much closer to our new home in San Ramon. After a couple of visits, we found one where we really felt welcomed. We loved the people, and they seemed to love us as well. The pastor gave deep messages from the Bible, and even the Tuesday evening Bible study we began attending was a nice balance of fellowship and in-depth study. We felt blessed to have found just the right place."

"A good church is such a blessing," added Joey.

"It sure is," agreed Alan as he moved forward with his narrative.

"Within a year or so, I was asked to lead the singing one Sunday evening. It seemed to go well, and they must have liked the way I led the worship because I was asked to lead again. A couple of months later, one of the ministers left to shepherd another church. The pastor asked me if I would present a sermon for that particular Wednesday evening service. With trepidation, I prepared and delivered a sort of illustrated message, using some props and visual aids I had brought along for enhancement of the topic I was sharing. Through a number of circumstances, and before I knew it, I was leading singing every other Sunday and Wednesday evenings and on the alternate dates I was teaching."

"Wow, I didn't know you were a pastor," exclaimed Joey.

"I wasn't," quipped Alan. "I only helped out when I was needed, although, I was grateful to be using my gifts. I had always felt somewhat of what people say is a 'calling'. I mean, I guess I had always wondered about being a pastor but never thought it would ever happen. Regardless, that was a very encouraging time in my life. Using my spiritual gifts was very fulfilling, and there was some semblance of order in our lives, even though other things were starting to spiral out of control."

"What do you mean?"

"It's kind of difficult to explain," Alan hesitated and then continued. "In my mind, I had this perception that I needed to continually expand the bicycle shops. If I stopped growing them, I was sure they would, uh, I would fail. It was a continual pressure I felt and still do. But I fear it's too late now. Unless God does a miracle, I will have to close all three shops and lose all I've worked so hard to accomplish. It's been devastating, Joey, absolutely brutal. I feel lower than I have ever felt in my life and completely helpless to do anything to stop it. And as of this past Thursday, I don't have anything else left that used to bring me some sense of accomplishment or satisfaction."

"Don't feel that way, Alan. It's only for a season. Even if you lose everything, have to live somewhere you're not excited about, and have to start a new life, even that's temporary. Remember . . . the battle is in your emotions and in your mind. Tell me, what happened this past Thursday?"

"Thanks Joey, I know it is, but it doesn't make the fight any less severe. I feel like such a failure, and with this latest declaration on Thursday, by a man I really respected, I've been in a tailspin I'm not sure I can ever recover from. In fact, that's one of the main reasons I called you today. But before I get to that, let me finish my story, okay? I mean, do you have time?"

"Sure, I don't have anything going on today until later this evening."

"Uh, what time is it there?"

"It's quarter after three, so we have plenty of time," assured Joey.

"Okay, let's see, where was I? Oh yeah . . . so I'm doing all this speaking, leading worship, and teaching some Sunday school classes, as well as the occasional Bible study. I mean, I'm really involved. Then, the pastor asked me to be on the church Board. I was beginning to think I might be in line to be the next pastor of this body of believers or something. All the while, the bike shops were taking up more and more time and were glissading into a deeper and deeper financial crevasse."

"Alan, I can understand why you feel like you're ready to crack."

"Well, that's not near the extent of it, Joey. It gets much, much worse."

Just then the door to the garage flung open. "There you are!" Annalisa accused with a smile. "What are you doing out here? Who are you talking to, Alan?"

"It's Joey, honey."

"I like you too, Alan, darling," laughed Joey.

"Ah, man, I didn't mean you, Joey. I was talking to my wife. Can you hang on a minute?"

"Sure, sweetheart," mocked Joey kiddingly.

"Thanks, dear," laughed Alan as he covered the phone with his hand and looked up at Annalisa. She was looking down at him with her arms akimbo, although, unlike Alan, she wasn't smiling.

"Who is that?" Her voice rose in pitch and volume as it ended the question.

"It's Joey Hinote in Florida. He's the guy I had the meeting with the day before I left to come home, remember?"

"Hmmm . . ." Annalisa didn't look convinced.

"Come on, honey, he and I had lunch at the restaurant with the funny name. Don't you remember? I think it's called The Oar House. I've talked with him a couple of times since I got back from my trip."

With a frown on her face, Annalisa leaned forward toward Alan like she could see right into his heart. Then reaching down, she grasped his shoulders with her hands pulling him forward. "Dinner's in an hour," she whispered, kissed him on the cheek, and headed for the open garage door. Before closing it, she glanced back at Alan and stuck her tongue out. As she shut the door, he could hear her giggle.

"You still there Joey?"

"Yeah, everything okay?"

"Oh yeah, no problem here." Alan laughed. "But let me finish my story, okay?"

"Sure, go ahead, my brother. You were saying it gets much worse and something about what happened Thursday."

"Yeah, yeah, I'll tell you about that in a minute. First, let me bring you up to date. I was working my tail off trying to keep the shops above water, but I was getting further and further behind. It's been awful Joey. Then, we had our third baby. The bills were piling up at home. And after I opened up my third shop, I started losing money in my business. Three shops costing me money, and three kiddos spending money. I've been stressing so long now, if I have a minute when I don't feel the pressure, I check my pulse to make sure I'm still alive."

"I know exactly what you mean," replied Joey.

"Then on top of all that," continued Alan. "I was beginning to have some health issues or at least symptoms anyway. I started visiting my doctor more than a few times each week. One day, he finally told me to see a psychiatrist. I'm not kidding; he actually said that to me. Boy, what a slap in the face. A real wake up call, you know what I mean?"

"Wow, your physician told you to see a shrink? That's messed up," teased Joey.

"Yeah, I sure am messed up. That's the perfect word to describe me," Alan spewed. "Somewhere along in this timeframe, Annalisa shared with me the unexpected news that she was pregnant again. I was absolutely about to break. I mean, the egg shell was cracking and my yoke of comfort was about to spill out all over the place.

"Wow, Alan, that's tough."

"That's not all, Joey."

"Really?"

"Yeah. Things were getting so bad that my doctor told me to go away for two weeks for some rest and relaxation. I think he used the word 'decompress'. What a perfect word. I was so compressed I was sure I was going to explode one day. You know, like a ticking time bomb that could have a rapid, involuntary decompression at any second! Therefore, I decided to go to our neighbor's cottage in the peaceful, stress free setting in Gulf Breeze, Florida. And what do you think happened? Hurricane Opal happened! However, during that visit, in my most stressed out state of mind, I had this marvelous experience with the Lord including a very vivid dream the night the storm blew ashore. Don't get me wrong, I'm really grateful for God touching me. But no sooner do I get back than, boom, here we go again."

"More bad news?" questioned Joey quietly.

"Yeah, I'll say it was bad news." Alan's voice gave indication that he was still at nine and three-quarters on the ten digit stress scale. "Well, shortly after New Year, I think it was the day after we last talked, we had a visit to Annalisa's doctor where they performed a routine sonogram. Immediately following, he told us there was something wrong with our baby. I mean, Annalisa was only three and a half or four months along, but they could tell something wasn't right. Her doctor said the little boy probably wouldn't make it to full term, you know, to nine months. We were crushed. Cut to our core. Absolutely broken."

"I'm so sorry, Alan," consoled Joey.

"Thanks, man, you're a good friend. There really aren't words to describe how I felt then, and how I struggle now."

After a brief pause, Alan continued. "So we drove straight from the doctor's office to our pastor's house; he had kind of been my mentor. We really needed someone to pray with us, to offer some words of comfort and hope, you know, to help us get our bearings. We sat down in his study and through tears told him the whole story. When we were finished, I asked him to pray that God would heal our unborn son. You know what he said?"

"Uh . . ." Joey was figuring the obvious answer coming to his mind couldn't possibly be the correct one.

"He chastened and rebuked me. He made us feel like we had brought this on ourselves, that we had sinned in some grievous way, and now God was punishing us. It was the first conversation I had with him where I recognized he held the position that nothing bad ever happens to good people."

"What on earth?" barked Joey. "Virtually every person in the Bible had awful things happen to them. Does he think they are bad people? Hey, what about Jesus? He had some pretty terrible things occur in His life, right?"

"Yeah, I agree, Joey. But I was absolutely incredulous. At the time, I didn't know what to say. No one had ever told me if I was in Christian leadership, nothing difficult should ever happen to me or my family. I was shocked, humiliated, and angered all at the same time. We sat there in utter astonishment. I was, for what may be only three or four times in my entire life, utterly speechless. He continued his admonishment, uh . . . chastisement for several more minutes, though I can't remember a single word of what he said. Then, he told us he wouldn't pray for the healing of our baby."

"Now, I'm speechless and angry!" barked Joey.

"Well, wait a minute, there's more."

"What? I hope this gets better?" interjected Joey.

"No, no, it doesn't. It actually gets far worse. That's why I had to call you, Joey. I need someone to talk to about this whole situation. I knew I couldn't tell this story to anyone here in California. They would know exactly who I was talking about. I cannot bring myself to that . . . and yet I have to talk to someone, or I'm going to lose it, man."

"Sure, Alan, I got you, my brother. Talk to me; I'm listening."

"Thanks, Joey. So we went home feeling more condemned, more worthless, more discouraged than ever before. I mean, we were completely dazed and confused. I remember calling it shell-shocked. We couldn't tell anyone about our situation at first. We were grappling with it and confused ourselves, pondering whether we had actually committed some unpardonable sin of some sort. It was like walking around with a scarlet letter or something. I mean, it was devastating. We couldn't help but wonder if we had caused our baby's deformity. We never let ourselves even mention our baby's condition. It was . . . agonizingly painful," acknowledged Alan softly. "Words are a terribly poor conveyor for expressing sorrow."

"I understand," agreed Joey.

"Then about four weeks ago, the heartbreaking day arrived. It was on a morning just like any other. I remember it was quite chilly outside. I had awakened early and was in the kitchen when I heard my precious Annalisa's muffled, yet anguished call coming from the bedroom. I will never forget, as long as I live, the sound of her distressed cry for help. It wasn't loud enough to arouse the children but contained enough emotion and, more importantly, urgency that I knew this was an emergency and she needed me immediately."

Alan's voice began to break as his eyes filled with tears. "I can still hear her sweet, frightened voice beckoning me to hurry. I turned the corner into our room and saw her lying in bed with a look of fear and agony etched upon her face. She motioned for me to close the door. I did and then turned around as she threw back the comforter. There was so much blood. I dropped to my knees beside her and laid my hands on her head and quickly prayed with all my heart for our Lord's help. Then I gently asked if she was okay. She replied that she woke up having some strong contractions. I quickly grabbed some towels. But sadly, before we could really do anything to prevent it, our little boy was born. He wasn't alive. We were inconsolable. We couldn't stop sobbing. Through much weeping, I carefully cleaned him up, cut the umbilical cord, and washed and tidied up Annalisa while she held our tiny one. Only the three of us in our room, it was a preciously devastating time. We named him Christopher Kyle, wrapped him in a baby blanket, and put a newborn hat on his head to cover the spot that had caused his stillbirth."

"I'm so very sorry, Alan. That is so sad, my brother."

"Yeah, I don't think I'll ever get over this. For no apparent reason at all, I sit down and cry my eyes out. Sometimes this happens several times a day. It doesn't seem to matter where either; in my car, at work, at a restaurant, on my bike, watching television, with no warning, I just start sobbing."

"Maybe with some time and God's help things will get easier," comforted Joey. "How's Annalisa doing?"

"Like me, she's broken."

"God will heal you both."

"I hope so," he sniffled. "Anyway, we kept the kids home from school, and after I got everything straightened up and in the washing machine, we invited them into our bedroom to meet their precious little brother. You talk about strength, those kids are amazing! Man, I love them! After we all had a good cry together, Julie organized the family, including me, into a real team. She had us all scheduled so Annalisa wouldn't have to lift a finger. It was such a blessing to see how much they love their mother and were anxious to do whatever they could to help." Alan paused for several seconds as he choked back his tears.

"You okay?"

"Yeah, it's hard, man. I think it will be this way for a long time," confided Alan.

"God will heal you guys. Hold steady, my brother. He will do it."

"I hope so, Joey. It's so . . . well, later I, uh . . . anyway, I took Annalisa and the baby to the doctor's office, so he could check her out. She was fine and needed no extra attention, which came as a huge relief to us both. However, he encouraged us to be patient and understanding with one another because the majority of couples who lose a child end up getting divorced. He stated how several studies had shown they are unable to comfort one another because they are deeply grieving themselves. He commented that each individual moves through the grieving process differently, and when each one doesn't respond in the same manner, they think the other one doesn't care. Those were very sobering words to hear."

Alan paused to compose himself. "I dealt with the funeral home, and we surrendered his tiny body to them later that afternoon. It was enormously difficult. Parents aren't made to see their children die. It should be the other way around; the parents are supposed to die first. We broke down again right there in the lobby of the doctor's office after the funeral home folks left. Our nurse gave us a room where we could continue to grieve in private. And boy did we. It was a few minutes before five o'clock that evening when we were finally able to return home to our precious children. It was a Thursday."

"Again, Alan, I am so very sorry." Joey's voice was very quiet and sympathetic.

"Thanks, Joey. I really appreciate it."

"Really, my brother, I feel terrible for you guys."

"Thanks." Alan continued his story. "So we woke up Sunday, and Annalisa told me she really wanted to attend the church service that morning. After several attempts from me to dissuade her, and several assurances from her that she would be okay, we decided to go. We were sure that our brothers and sisters at church would want, or perhaps even need, to comfort us as much as we needed their comfort. What a blessed time of fellowship and worship. It was like Heaven had opened up its windows, and His love and comfort descended upon us like a warm, gentle waterfall of peace and joy. You could actually feel the love of God in that place. Then . . . the pastor moved to the pulpit to give the sermon. He had entitled his message 'Are There Consequences For Sin?'"

"He did not!" Joey's voice held more than a hint of anger.

"Uh, yes. Yes he did. And it was an utterly difficult message to sit through. I'm not sure, maybe he thought we weren't going to be there and had prepared it accordingly. But we were there, and it was deplorable. A few folks, at varying points in the sermon, actually got up and walked out. We sat there though, through the whole miserable thing. Well, miserable to us anyway."

"That's unbelievable, Alan."

"Yeah, it's un-be-stinking-lievable."

"What?"

"Oh, nothing. I mean, yes, we were in a state of shock. We drove home in silence. We both felt so condemned, so discouraged, so depressed. I mean, there we were four days after losing our son, and we found ourselves having to endure a sermon, in the midst of a couple hundred people, which had apparently been prepared using us as an example. It was devastating."

"Look, Alan, I don't want to tell you what to do or anything, but you need to leave that church immediately and find somewhere else to attend. There is something going on there that you and Annalisa do not need to be a part of at this point in your lives. Seriously, my brother, it's not healthy. You guys are way too vulnerable right now. I think if you stay there, you may have some serious emotional consequences that could be long-lasting."

"Yeah, I've had thoughts like that too, Joey. But all our friends are there. They're our support group. We really need them right now. I don't think we can leave. We're really hurting and those folks love us. And frankly, we need their love. You know what I mean?"

"I hear what you're saying, Alan. But listen, if you stay there under that severe message for much longer, it will have some long lasting effects on your self-esteem. You're hurting, it's understandable, but because you're so deeply wounded you're very vulnerable to influences, and more importantly, you're unable to defend yourself . . . and Annalisa."

Joey continued, "I'm no counselor or anything, but there are serious things going on here. Remember what her doctor said? Many couples end in divorce after experiencing what you and Annalisa have been through. Think of your children too, they are at a very exposed place right now in their lives. I know you're hurting, my brother, but you have to be strong. I promise you this, Alan, I'll be praying for you several times each and every day."

"Thanks so much, Joey. I'm really struggling with not knowing what to do. I mean, there are a lot of folks at the church who we are close to and are very dear to us. I can't leave them. I feel a sense of responsibility to them, especially if this thing with the pastor gets any worse."

"Worse?" Joey's voice was ascending to a higher pitch. "I don't think it could get any worse than it already has. I don't think it could get any harsher than what has already been said."

"Well . . ."

Joey interrupted, "Don't tell me!"

At that moment, the garage door swung open and Richard popped his head in, "Mom says dinner's ready in five minutes, Dad. We're having some kind of taco salad thing."

"Okay, son, tell Mom I'll be right there."

"Do you need to go?" asked Joey.

"Yeah, but I really have appreciated our talk. I need a friend right now. This is incredibly difficult, and I don't know what I should do. This last thing that happened pretty much sealed the deal for me, but I don't want to go off half-cocked. I want to be sure it's God who wants me to leave and not my emotions, you know, my anger, my bitterness, or anything. We could find ourselves in somewhat of a precarious place. I don't want to jump out of this pressure cooker and into one that's even more pressurized."

"Yeah, I can understand, Alan. That's wisdom brother," assured Joey.

"Thanks. Look, I need to go, but before I hang up, I want to tell you this last bit."

"There's more?"

"Well . . . the pastor called us to a meeting three days ago."

"Uh, oh."

"Yeah, uh, oh is right. I thought maybe he wanted to apologize, or clear the air, or something. So there was part of me that was actually looking forward to getting things settled. I figured he would say what he needed to say, and we would have a chance to say what we needed to say. You know, like adults sitting down and working through our issues together. We set a time, and Annalisa and I met him at the church in his study. It was four weeks to the day since we had lost our Christopher Kyle. We were still deeply hurting. Well, after prayer and some pleasantries, he turned in my direction and with a frown made a thoroughly disturbing remark. I didn't say a word for fear that I would literally lay into him. I was certain, if I opened my mouth, my quick wit, hurt, and resentment would take over and within seconds I would have pronounced more judgment upon him than any one person deserved. I mean, I had a boat load, no, a cargo ship load of animosity stored up toward him, and I was ready, as we say in cycling circles, to unleash the beast! I'm not proud of it, Joey, but believe me, I can lower the boom when I'm pushed . . . and I was shoved way too far that day. But instead, gratefully, I reached over, gently grasped Annalisa's hand, stood up, with no expression on my face, and the two of us walked out."

"Really? That was probably the best thing you could have done, Alan. Good for you, my brother. To get in some heated argument with accusations flying and thoughtless words spewing wouldn't have been good. You did the wise thing. You took the high road. The spirit of accusation comes from the enemy. You don't want to be compatible with that. He is the accuser of the brethren, and he accuses us before our God day and night.[1] I think that's in the Book of Revelation somewhere."

"Thanks, Joey, I'm trying."

"Yes, you are, brother, and don't give up. Hey, before we hang up, I had a thought I wanted to share with you. I mean if you're open to hearing it."

"Sure, go ahead."

"Do you remember why The **rojocci** Fellowship was established in the first place?"

Alan hesitated and then conceded, "Yeah, so we Christians wouldn't surrender our God given rights of a personal relationship with Jesus Christ and allow another to act as our conscience, like an intermediary telling us what we can and can't do or something."

"That's what I was thinking too while you were sharing your story with me. You see, you're just like me, Alan. I knew better too. I had given another person too much sway in my life. It's so easy to do; it's like the default setting on a computer or something. I don't even have to tell it what to do, the machine always returns to the same setting. Precisely like human nature, you know what I mean?"

"Yeah, sorry to say, I sure do. And the enemy is an expert at dealing with our nature because he's been tricking mankind for centuries. No, actually it's been much longer, for millenniums." Alan's voice had a hint of disgust, as he now recognized he had been duped, not by any human schemer, but by the old crafty hater of mankind, the enemy of all that is good and right, by the wretched devil himself.

"I hate that guy," confessed Joey with an equal amount of repugnance.

"Me too. I hate the way he always pits one of us against the other. He's a master at it. He makes us think someone else is to blame when he's actually behind the scenes, just like the nefarious puppet master that he is, laughing his sinister head off at the two humans getting angry with each other. I'm getting mad sitting here talking about him. He's a liar and a thief and a killer and a destroyer of lives[2] . . . and he enjoys it!"

"Yeah, you got that right, Alan, good point. Let's commit to pray for each other so we aren't again deceived by him any time soon. Remember what we talked about? It all begins with a thought, right?"

"Yes, yes, yes, thanks for the reminder."

"Hey, Alan, I know you need to get going for dinner, but do you mind telling me what your minister said to you guys? The last thing he declared that kind of put you over the top, you know, right before you walked out. I mean, if it's too hard for you to repeat, I'll understand and all. But I'm going to be praying every day for you, Annalisa, and your kids. I'll be praying that the Lord heals all of your hurts and sorrows, especially those the two of you bear. I'm confident He will and in a way only He can. However, when you are able, let me know what the pastor . . ."

He said, "It's been four weeks. Sign the receipt and get on with life."

-three-

The conversation during dinner that night was lively as each one of the children had several items they felt needed to be discussed. Alan and Annalisa, seated at either end of their dark hardwood dining table, smiled across at one another. It was strained but sincere, at least to the degree each could muster. After dinner, he helped with the dishes, scurrying the children off to their rooms to complete their homework assignments. The two wounded mourners were silent as they accomplished their tasks by rote. Over the past month, both had been hurting so deeply that neither had anything with which to comfort the other. At times, Annalisa would quietly weep, and Alan would caress her back and shoulders to let her know he cared. Alan too, on occasion, would suddenly and unexpectantly have tears fill his eyes. Evenings were always the most difficult.

Once they finished the dishes, the house was quiet and still. Alan suggested they sit in the courtyard, so they could enjoy the beautiful starry sky. The early night air was cool without the hint of a breeze. They sat across from one another at the round umbrella table that graced the brick paver patio. Neither uttered a word. Several silent minutes had passed when Annalisa cleared her throat,

"Ahem."

"Yes, honey?" asked Alan.

"I didn't say anything."

"Yes, I know, but you're thinking about saying something." Alan was gently prying open the closed lid of his dear love's broken heart.

"Alan?" Annalisa spoke so softly he could barely hear her. "Do we have to go back there again? I don't think I can sit through another one of those sermons. I mean, these last few weeks have been pretty rough."

"I know, my love, I know. That's why I wanted us to sit out here, so we could discuss what to do without the children hearing us. Joey thinks we should leave."

"I do too, Alan." Annalisa's tone was firm but free of any anger. She wasn't indicating anything that resembled resentment or acrimony. No, she was hurt. And she felt the pain at a depth she had never experienced before.

"Yes, I know you do, and I think we need to leave too. I just don't know when." Alan was really wrestling with what exactly he was feeling. He had come to know their pastor as a real man of God, yet these last few months had contained a multitude of mixed messages. He wasn't quite sure of anything anymore.

"Honey?" he continued softly, "I know some things were handled poorly, but I'm not so sure it's entirely his fault."

"What? How can you say that, Alan? After all he's done. How can you say something like that?!"

"Hold on, dear. I know you're hurting, I'm hurting too. That's precisely what I mean though. Maybe we aren't able to see things clearly because we're grieving so deeply. Perhaps, we should wait a bit. I'm sure we'll see things differently given some time." Alan paused to let his words sink into her wounded heart. He had learned that words take more time to permeate the heart when they must travel through many layers of fresh hurt and calloused pain.

"Listen, my precious love," he continued. "Is our great God and Father the Sovereign Ruler over all the earth and the affairs of mankind?"[1]

"Yes, of course He is." She was beginning to see where Alan was going with his question, and she felt a tiny flicker of hope kindle within her.

"Is there anything you can think of that He doesn't either cause or allow?"

"Hmmm . . . nothing I can think of."

"Do you believe He loves us?"[2] He let the smallest hint of a smile curl upon the edge of his lips.

"Yes, you and I both know He loves us more than we could ever think or imagine." Annalisa actually had a half smile on her face, and her eyes were starting to arch upward.

"Well then, my sweet bride of nearly sixteen years, He has either caused or allowed all of these things over the last several months to happen for our good because He loves us. It is so difficult to see what good could possibly come out of all of this, but somehow it will. He'll do it. He will . . . and I'm declaring this, the only way I know how—by faith."

"Alan, for the first time in months I feel some hope in my heart."

"I'm so glad, my sweet wife. I'm feeling hopeful too. Thank God for hope! You know, it's a powerful force. In fact, it's one of the big three: Faith, Hope, and Love.[3] I was thinking about this only yesterday. Did you know there's a chapter in the Scriptures devoted to faith?"

"Yes, it's Hebrews chapter eleven," Annalisa smiled.

"How about love, where's its chapter?"

"Ha, it's the thirteenth chapter of the Book of First Corinthians," she affirmed with a half giggle.

Alan encouraged, "Very good, you wise young woman, you. But here's the tough one, where's the hope chapter? Hope is such a powerful force, virtually equal with faith and love, three mighty engines, indeed. Now, these two have their own chapters in the Holy Scriptures, but where is the chapter dedicated to the other power of His three dynamos? Where is hope's chapter?"

Reclining in her chair, Annalisa rested her head on the back and looked straight up into the clear night sky. This was, in fact, a wonderful exercise for the two of them to work through together. They had been deeply wounded: first, by the news of their baby's defect, then, by their pastor's response, further, by the death of their precious baby Christopher Kyle, followed by the brutal sermon, and finally, by the insensitive proclamation by their pastor to get on with life. Yes, they were hurt, cut to the core, and without any glimmer of hope until a few minutes ago.

Annalisa looked back at Alan. She had tears in her eyes, "Oh, Alan!" she cried aloud.

He jumped up from his chair and dropped to his knees next to her as they threw their arms around one another.

They wept together. The flood gates of her heart, which had been so tightly bound up and locked down, blew open. The tidal wave of hurt and pain gushed out through those precious, wonderful tears. He kissed her several times on the cheeks and forehead. Then, through the sobs, he thanked and praised their Father in Heaven for all He had done, was currently doing, and would continue to do concerning them. This moment stretched on for several minutes before a peaceful calm and assurance, which emanated from within them, settled as a glorious blanket of encompassing love.

Alan offered her the sleeve of the flannel shirt he was wearing to wipe away her tears. She willingly used it and pleaded a "sorry" after finishing. Alan, looking down, chuckled at the black splotches left by her smeared mascara.

"Thanks, honey."

She smiled at her adoring husband, cradling his face in her two hands. "What would I do without my strong knight in shining armor? Where would I be without you, Alan? You have such a wonderfully gentle way of allowing God to speak to me. Don't get me wrong, you are a magnificent leader, at least you are to me. But I love the way you don't force anything. You let me have the wonder of discovery. I will always love you for that, my amazing life partner."

"Oh, I'm so glad the Lord met you, my love."

"Me too." She paused long enough for him to look into her eyes, "It's the whole book isn't it?"

"What's the whole book?"

"Faith has its own chapter. Love has its chapter. But hope is the whole book. The whole Bible is full of hope, isn't it?"

Alan was slowly nodding his head.

"I love you, Alan Michael Browne."

"I love you more, Annalisa Michelle Browne."

"That's not possible."

"Oh, yes it is," he laughed as he drew her into his arms once again.

A heavy, thick fog blanketed the entire area the next morning, but inside the Browne home there was a new clarity, a new hope, and a new lightness in the air. Yes, they had suffered the loss of their precious son, and there was still a great deal of uncertainty at church. However, they both sensed a freedom from the sting of hurt, and from the pain, whether caused by another or not. Alan was right, Annalisa concluded, as she finished her morning shower. They had given way too much sway in their lives to another person, at least another person who wasn't the Lord. Losing their beloved baby son would still hurt, she realized, but not nearly as much as if they hadn't elevated this man up on a pedestal, making him nearly equal with the Lord Himself. It's like Betsy had advised them many years ago, "When one of the spiritual gifts is given a place of prominence over the other gifts, things tend to get out of balance. 'Only the Lord should have preeminence.'"[4]

After breakfast, as she was drying her hair, Annalisa wondered if this was one of the reasons the early colonists had formed The rojocci Fellowship way back in the 1700s. The whole situation at their church seemed so insidious to her, like the fog in the Bay Area, which creeps in slowly while everyone is asleep. Then in the morning, when one awakens, it's so thick people can barely see a few yards.

"Yes," she thought. "We were kind of sleeping but were still awake. We weren't making our own choices or decisions. However, by not making them, we really were making them. We determined not to decide and therefore, we decided. It wasn't him . . . well, not to the degree I thought it was. No, it was us. By not questioning his actions, by not speaking up, by not taking a stand, we actually allowed, no we chose, his influence to reign over the multitude of checks we were feeling in our hearts. We were the ones who gave him greater sway. He didn't do it. We did."

That evening when Alan arrived home, Annalisa grabbed him by the hand and marched him out to the table in the courtyard patio, their favorite outdoor spot to spend time alone. She related to him all she had discovered earlier, and how she believed it was God's Holy Spirit who had led her. She wasn't trying to convince Alan of the authenticity of her insight because she knew he felt the same way she did. But she was delighting in the fact that His Spirit had spoken directly to her regarding their situation. This was every bit as pleasing to her as the revelation itself.

"Yes, I believe that's true, honey," Alan reassured. "I allowed him more room in my life, our lives, even our marriage than I ever should have. There were nights, as I was trying to fall asleep, when his words kept swimming around in my head. I would lay there awake for hours."

"I know, Alan, I had similar thoughts sometimes. But whenever he brought up some new concept I didn't grasp, like in a sermon or at prayer meeting or something, I would say to myself, 'Oh, he's studied the Scriptures so much more, he's so much more mature, and so much wiser than I am, so put that pot on the back burner. I'll understand what he means later.' Well, later never came, and all my pots are boiling over."

"Yeah, I agree. I have felt the same way for several months. My stove top is a mess. But let's be clear here, we're not saying it's our fault our son died, right?"

"No, heavens no. For me, what has happened in my heart, with this new revelation, is now I have hope. Before, I thought I, we, were some kind of random victims. Nothing made any sense. It's like I thought our treacherous enemy, the devil, was a loose cannon on a rocking ship in heavy seas. Wherever the cannon was aiming when he pulled the trigger was where the bombshell would land. And this time it happened to be on us."

"Well . . ." interrupted Alan.

"Wait a second. Let me finish, okay?"

Alan nodded as Annalisa continued her explanation of her marvelous insight and new found freedom within her. "I was reading the first few chapters in the Book of Job this morning."

"Why, sweetheart? That's a difficult book to read even if you're feeling good about yourself."

"Wait until you hear what God showed me. Now, you remember the first couple of chapters, right, Alan?"

"Yeah, pretty much."

"Well, remember the enemy came into the throne room, and God asked him, 'Where have you been?', or something like that. The devil replied that he had been wandering around on earth among the sons of men.[5] I'm paraphrasing here, but you follow what I'm saying, right?"

"Yes," nodded Alan.

Annalisa stared right at Alan and questioned, "What was he doing amid the people on earth?"

"Uh . . . I don't know, wreaking havoc. I mean, Jesus says the enemy comes to steal and lie and kill and destroy,[6] so I guess he was doing something like that. Why?" Alan had a perplexed look on his face as he gazed back at Annalisa across the patio table in the dimly lit courtyard.

"I agree!" resounded Annalisa. "I think he was telling lies to folks; he was working death and all kinds of destruction. Yes, he was wreaking havoc, like you said. Did God already know this? Did He know what the enemy had been up to?"

"Sure, He did. He knows everything."

"Then . . ." Annalisa paused waiting for Alan's full attention. "Then, my dear husband, what were the next words out of our Heavenly Father's mouth?"

"What?" smiled Alan. He was so pleased with this new joyful Annalisa that he wouldn't dare steal her thunder.

"God asked the devil, 'Have you considered my servant Job?'"[7]

"Yeah, so?" Alan was still smiling.

"Dear, who brought up the topic of Job to whom?"

"Uh, God brought it up to the enemy."

"Why?"

"Uh . . . I'm not sure, maybe for some kind of refinement process or something."

"Alan, we read in the first chapter that Job was a righteous man, head and shoulders above everyone else, or something close to that anyway.[8] Did God love Job?"

"Yes, of course He did."

"Then why?" Annalisa reiterated, "Why would God suggest to the enemy, who does nothing but steal, lie, kill, and destroy, to consider His servant Job?"

Alan was no longer smiling but was silently pondering while staring at Annalisa. She now was the one who wore a grin on her face.

"Alan?"

He cocked his chin once in her direction acknowledging he heard her.

"It's because God loved Job so very much. Our Father in Heaven brought up the topic of His servant Job to the enemy because He loved Job. He desired to have a deeper relationship with Job. He wanted to be closer with His servant. It's true, Alan. Think what He did with Abraham, uh, Abram. Great difficulties, right? I mean, what did Betsy always say to you? Wasn't it something like, 'Great hardships make great hearts?' I'm pretty sure that's what she said, anyway. Look at Abraham. He nearly had to sacrifice his own son, but God called Abraham his friend . . . His very own friend! Think of Moses, Elijah, or even Daniel. These all had great difficulties they had to endure, yet look at the depth of relationship they had with their Father in Heaven. Well, suppose He wants the same for us, honey?!"

Alan picked up his chair and moved it over next to Annalisa and sat down. Then, turning toward her, he softly affirmed, "He does want the same for us, my precious love. I think I first recognized it while at the Morgan's cottage last fall in Florida. Do you remember that storm, Hurricane Opal?"

Annalisa nodded in acknowledgement.

"Well, I never told you everything about what happened there. You see, I had an incredibly vivid dream the night of the storm. Ever since that night, I feel there has been a huge shift in my relationship with our Lord. It's like He's a great vortex drawing us ever nearer to Himself. Maybe He has always been doing it, and I only recently started noticing. Regardless, I sense there has been the beginning of a huge change in my life. That much I know for certain."

"I can feel it too, Alan. It is obvious something has changed within us these last few months."

"Yes, so much is fluid. It's like change is our normal. I think of all that's happening with the shops. Honey, I can't keep them open; there's too much debt. God will have to do a serious miracle, and do it real quick, for us to avoid losing all three in bankruptcy. I know He can do anything, but the business is in dire straits."

"He can and He will, Alan. I know He will. He has healed a deep hurt in my heart. If He can do that, He can do anything."

"I hope you're right. I mean, I know you're right, but we may not have seen the last of difficult times."

"That's what I discovered this morning, Alan. The pain and suffering is confirmation that He loves us and is drawing us closer to Himself. Come on, honey. You know, it's like you have told me so many times before, 'For a runner to be *good* he has to endure pain and suffering. But for a runner to be *great* he must not only tolerate, he must love pain and suffering. Pampering never produces greatness.' You also told me, 'You have to have a heart for the stretch or you'll never win.' I always wondered what you were talking about. But now I think I understand better because of what we have been experiencing in these very natural, physical circumstances these last few months. These adverse conditions are developing deep within us, in our hearts, an eternal relationship that is and will be so much more rewarding and fulfilling than anything we could ever lose here on earth."

With that final statement of her renewed faith and hope, Annalisa flopped back in her chair and raised her hands toward Heaven. She began praising God and telling Him how much she loved Him. Alan sat next to her thanking the Lord out loud for all He was revealing to the two of them through their very real adversities. After several minutes, they both quieted down, basking in this new freedom they felt within their hearts. Alan broke the silence.

"Uh, honey, there's something else to consider."

Annalisa looked at Alan. "Yes?"

"Yeah, well, I got a couple of phone calls today. I don't want to tell you who called, but I will share this much, both calls were from folks at church. They both asked the exact same question."

"What did they want?" Her voice gave evidence to the curiosity in her heart.

"Uh, they both wanted the same thing," confided Alan.

"What?"

"They asked if I would consider becoming their new pastor."

"Whaaat?!" Annalisa's voice reached an octave that Alan had rarely heard. When he had, it usually meant something similar to disbelief and amazement all at the same time.

"Yeah, they said if I would agree, they would call a business meeting this Saturday and vote our current pastor out and call me as their new pastor."

"Oh my word, Alan, what did you say?"

"Well, it was incredibly hard because I recognize that I really want to be a pastor, and if not the pastor of our church, then a pastor somewhere, eventually anyway. But I knew I couldn't take them up on their offer."

"Why not, sweetheart?"

"Because I will not be a party to a lynching. Suppose we're all wrong and he's right, I mean, in God's eyes. I couldn't live with that looming over my head for the rest of my life."

"Alan, it's not a lynching, a hanging, or anything. It's the people deciding they have had enough, and they want a different leader, that's all."

"I'm not so sure, my love. I really think there are some serious spiritual forces at work here, and I don't want to be on the wrong side of the battle, do you?"

"No, of course not, you know that. But if the congregation wants to change leadership, then they will change leaders, and someone will become the new pastor. Why not you? You've told me for years, honey, you thought the Lord had called you to be a shepherd of His people. Here it is, your opportunity. He's placed it in your hands, and all you have to do is take it."

"I don't know if I'm ready for that quite yet. Look at Moses, David, or even Jesus. They experienced great hardships in leading and shepherding God's people. It's a very difficult lifestyle. Do you think we could handle more than what we are already dealing with now? It's not something I would ever presume to take upon myself. God comes calling, not me."

"What do you mean, Alan?"

"Well, take Moses for example. He didn't presume to take the role. God called to him from the burning bush. How about David? He was anointed king by Samuel early in his life, correct? But Saul was King at the time. Saul chased David and tried to kill him several times."

"Yes, and David could have killed Saul too, like in that cave."

"That's right," Alan continued, "But why didn't he kill him?"

"Ummm . . ." Annalisa glanced down at her lap then up at Alan. "Because he didn't want to raise his hand against God's anointed."

"Precisely. So what did David end up doing?"

Annalisa shrugged. "I can't remember."

"David fled Israel until God made him ready for the kingdom and the kingdom ready for him. Then, years later, he was installed as king. And don't forget what David's son Absalom did. He turned the heart of the people and stole Israel away from his father David. Remember what happened to him?" Alan widened his eyes, staring right at Annalisa. "I don't want that end."

"Neither do I, Alan."

"Well, I was thinking and praying on the way home this evening. In both of those cases with King David, who Scripture teaches was a man after God's own heart, he made the decision to leave Israel. He didn't try to fight for what was rightfully his. Instead he trusted his well-being to the God who was able to deliver him. Both times the kingdom was his to take or to keep. Both times he deferred to others and departed rather than causing division. Can you imagine? What an amazing man of God." Alan paused.

Annalisa was staring right at Alan eagerly anticipating the next words to pass through his lips. "Yes, Alan?"

"Sweetheart, I think it's time for us to leave our church. Not with any malice or contention, but a quiet departure that expresses love to our pastor and the others. I believe the best way to accomplish this is by writing a nice letter of appreciation for him and his ministry to our family. We can articulate that it has become apparent that it is our time to find another church in which to serve. By doing it this way, we won't be exposing the others who may want to oust him. Hopefully, we can remain friends with him and anyone else who may want to, knowing we are all part of the family of God. What do you think?"

"It sounds good to me. I've been ready to leave for months."

"Okay, let's write up something appropriate, not with even a hint of bitterness, but with love because he has shown kindness to us in the past. It's only been the last two years or so that things have changed. Then, I'll take the letter and my keys to the church building and leave them on his desk early Sunday morning before anyone arrives. Afterwards, I think we should disconnect our phones."

"Perfect." Annalisa chirped. "I feel really good about this, Alan, don't you?"

"Well . . . I hope so. It's hard telling what lies around the next corner, my love. It has been comforting having an older brother in the Lord, like our pastor, close by for counsel."

"What do you mean 'around the next corner'?"

"Now, you know we're in a real financial pickle. It's no secret we may lose everything. In fact, I got the mail out of the mailbox tonight when I arrived home. We don't have enough money to pay those bills this month, sweetheart. Like we've talked before, I think we need to put our home on the market, and sooner, rather than later, perhaps in no more than a week."

"I knew this was coming, Alan, but so soon? Can't we wait until the end of the school year?"

"The school year ends in about a month. By the time we get this place ready, the soonest it would sell is next month. Plus, it won't close for another thirty days after that. So we wouldn't actually be moving until mid-summer at the earliest."

"Okay, let's get things moving. Oh, Alan, this is going to be so hard—first, losing our son, then, leaving our church, now, selling our house, and moving, all in the same year."

"Don't forget, closing the shops and filing for bankruptcy. At some point, we'll have to cross that dizzying bridge."

"Oh, not all that in the same year, Alan. God's vortex must really be drawing us closer. I wonder how much longer? How long has it been? When did this start?"

"Well . . ." Alan paused and looked down at the brick pavers. The same brick pavers he laid himself four years ago, during one of the hottest weeks of that whole summer. He glanced up at the new roof he had installed on the garage, and around to all of the stucco walls the entire family had painted together over spring break a few years back. They had put a lot of hard work into turning this run down house into a beautifully comfortable place they were proud to call home. Now, they were going to lose it. The thought of it all was almost too much for Alan to bear. Annalisa interrupted his downward spiral.

"Alan," she pried, "How long has it been?"

"How long has what been, dear?"

"How long have we been enduring these difficulties? Remember, you said something about a shift or something."

"Oh yes, I'm sorry. It seems to me it has been over a year and a half. But something really shifted in me since the visit to the Morgan's cottage in Florida. I think that's when something in the spiritual realm changed, like an awakening or something. Maybe it's a huge paradigm renovation within my heart. Whatever it is, it appears to be impacting everything on the outside too. Anything we may have felt was secure, it seems, He is shaking. The more it gets shaken, the more we will be certain of the things that cannot deteriorate. However, that which is not solid is surely collapsing all around us. We have a whole lot to be thankful for, my love. Although, there appears to be a bit that's crumbling as well."

"I know, Alan, but I sense it's a good thing," she confessed. "At least that's my hope."

"Really?"

"Yes. I think so." Annalisa's voice sounded more confident than her eyes revealed.

"I hope so, too. I mean, yes, I think it is. But it doesn't make it easier to swallow. Especially when some of these issues have been a huge part of our lives for many years. It's not like they're bad things or evil things. However, perhaps they are not providing the best conditions for our spiritual growth. Maybe it's because they are matters that keep us burdened or enslaved and we don't even realize it. How would we know how much these encumbrances keep us from an intimate relationship with Him, until we don't have them in our lives anymore? Remember the week we backpacked on the John Muir trail? I was amazed at how I actually got used to carrying my forty pound pack. After a few days, it became part of me. Maybe that's what we're not seeing as long as we continue to haul this current life around with us."

"Alan," whispered Annalisa, "It's scary, but I've had many of the same thoughts that you're expressing. I mean, suppose this isn't some great devastating loss, some punishment, or discipline for our sin, or something. Perhaps it's actually our Father in Heaven drawing us nearer to Himself because He loves us. Maybe He's nudging us toward a deeper walk with Him than we've ever experienced before."

"You know, honey, I believe something very dramatic happened at the Morgan's cottage starting with the night the hurricane hit. Something changed within me, I mean, something real deep, something spiritual."

"Alan?" She was using her soft, sweet voice he so adored.

"Yes, my love," he replied as he reached over resting his arm on her delicate shoulders.

She smiled, glancing up at him, "Tell me about your dream that night at the cottage."

-four-

With the night air getting rather chilly, Alan suggested they continue their conversation in the warmth of their home. Besides, he knew sharing the dream with Annalisa was incredibly personal, and he didn't want someone inadvertently overhearing while he described it to her. Alan had learned that spiritual matters can sometimes be very private, not meant to be communicated with everyone, at least not with one who is not of kindred spirit. Annalisa was most definitely of kindred spirit. However, the timing had never seemed to be right to reveal his cherished spiritual treasure with her. Tonight was different. The chemistry was right.

Spiritual insights and revelations, Alan had discerned, were like valuable pearls. What may seem precious to him, may not necessarily be to another. He had found where the Lord had warned in the Scriptures not to toss these pearls before swine. They may trample them under foot as worthless, and turn, and tear you to pieces.[1] He was sure the Lord had made this clear to him personally as well. He had, on several occasions, experienced that trampled upon feeling before. It was similar to the time, back in 1976, when the new Bi-centennial Cross Country Bike Trail had just been completed. He mentioned to a close friend that he had a dream of riding his bicycle across the country. The friend mocked and ridiculed him like he was some cycling fanatic who must have a death wish. The criticism hit its mark. Alan never accomplished his dream. Though he would never consider people swine, there were a few individuals he had met over his lifetime who could teach the hogs a lesson or two in advanced trample-ology.

Over the years, he also had discovered many folks were uncomfortable in discussing matters of the Holy Spirit, thinking it perhaps strange, mystical, or impractical. Others, he found, feared the topic might cause a division of some sort, so they avoided it altogether. But it was beginning to dawn on Alan, that a life led by the Holy Spirit appeared to be the most practical of all lifestyles. Many times he had reminded himself "God is spirit[2], and He must have created humans with a spirit so we can commune together." However, realizing not all would agree with him, he had chosen to keep the majority of what he was discovering about spiritual things to himself. Even Annalisa was not made aware of some of it, like the dream he had one night at the Morgan's cottage. They had made it a point to not keep secrets from one another. Although Alan had learned over the years that proper timing is invaluable when sharing something new, important, or unusual with her. And his vivid dream certainly met those criteria.

"Would you check on the kids, honey, while I dish us up some lasagna?" called Annalisa from the kitchen as Alan locked the French doors in the dining room.

"Sure, my love, I'm starving. It's almost nine o'clock. We were out on the patio for nearly three hours." Alan's voice sounded surprised.

They sat down together at the kitchen table. Then, Alan reached across and held Annalisa's hand while he prayed. After they had closed with the "amen", Alan started right in on the lasagna as she served them both some salad.

"Thanks, honey."

"You're welcome. How are the kids?"

"Julie's in her room doing homework. Richard is in the living room looking out the front window. He thinks there's a hawk or owl in one of the trees across the street waiting for the Morgan's cat. He wants to see the fight and who will be the victor."

"Oh, honestly, Alan." Her tone was a mixture of humor and disappointment.

"He told me he had finished his homework," affirmed Alan.

"Well, I'll check on that after dinner. And where's Emma?"

"Our sweet Emily is having tea in her room. Uh sorry, I mean, in a Moroccan palace with several dolls, or rather royalty, of varying sizes and nationalities."

Annalisa laughed, "Sometimes that girl cracks me up. Where on earth do you think she got such an imagination?"

"Are you kidding me?" crowed Alan.

Annalisa glanced across the table at her astounded husband. "You're right about that, Alan Michael, she's exactly like her daddy," she snickered.

"Me?" he retorted. "That kid is one hundred percent pure Annalisa Michelle Browne, just in a smaller package." They chuckled together as they each realized that Emily was the apple that hadn't fallen far from their tree.

"Let's leave the cleanup for the morning," suggested Annalisa. She knew they were both anxious to continue their intimate conversation. Alan agreed and after they tucked the children in, they headed off to the sanctuary of their bedroom. The room featured a high peaked ceiling with rustic beams and a single, five-blade ceiling fan suspended from a pole. Sitting on the loveseat, Alan glanced out the ample triple casement windows that framed a picturesque view of Mount Diablo. Annalisa plopped down on their comfy queen size bed with the mission style oak frame. The bed sat upon a huge, hand woven, Mexican rug, which covered a portion of the buff tile floors. Matching the rest of the home, the trim was plain and along with the two panel solid doors, was painted a high gloss off white hue. It all had a cozy Southwestern feel, in style, if not in palette. Annalisa preferred whites, creams, and beiges, with a splash of color here and there. Their sanctuary exemplified her tastes.

"Well, Alan?"

"Yes, I know . . . let me first state, this is an extremely personal matter, and I really don't want you to share it with anyone else, okay?"

"Of course, honey."

"I mean, if anyone does the telling, I want it to be me."

"I know, dear, my lips are sealed." Annalisa was smiling as she crossed her heart and turned an imaginary key in front of her mouth, indicating the vault was locked.

"Not funny," chided Alan.

"Sorry," she muttered as she lay back on her side propping her head up with one hand.

"Okay. Well first, please remember all I was going through when I headed down to the Morgan's cottage. I was really hurting. Still am. But what I'm trying to say is . . . I desperately needed our Father in Heaven to do something and, uh, well . . . He did."

"I'm so glad He did, Alan."

"Yeah, me too. So, uh . . . there I was with Hurricane Opal churning out in the Gulf of Mexico and heading right for the Morgan's cottage with me inside. Frankly, I was scared. I'd never been through a hurricane before, so I didn't know what to expect. Without electricity and therefore, no lights, it was deathly dark in that tiny, claustrophobic bungalow. It felt like a tomb. I was sure there wasn't any air inside; it was hard to even breathe. And noisy, man it was deafening. The storm was so loud, and it lasted so long, I thought I may be losing my mind or something. Did I mention I was afraid?"

Annalisa just nodded her head so as not to interrupt her husband's story.

"Well, I told you about how I had cried out to the Lord and how a few minutes later I thought I heard Him speak, not audibly, but in my heart or mind, right? I mean, at the time I thought I actually heard His voice. That was kind of frightening too, but in a different way. So I jumped up and ran outside on the porch, but then I quickly realized I was standing in the full onslaught of the storm and was sure I would be killed. My fears followed me everywhere I turned."

"Yes, I remember, honey, that was awful."

"After I came back inside and had calmed down a bit, I had this impression to read in the Book of Hebrews. Over the next few hours, with the storm so boisterous it was hard to think, I reflectively read in Hebrews until I found this wonderful insight in chapter four. The verse revealed to me that we have both a spirit and a soul.[3] I was astounded because I had always believed we only have a soul. After a few more minutes of discovery, I started thanking and praising Him for all He was doing and for this new revelation in particular. It was such a precious time, honey, just absolutely amazing. I sang and praised and shouted and thanked and praised and sang some more. I did this until I felt extremely tired. Then, I laid down right there on the floor by the kitchen table. I was soon asleep and dreamed a most vivid, marvelous wonder."

At this point, Annalisa sat crossed legged and inched herself forward, right up to the edge of the bed, directly across from Alan. He paused until she got settled and comfortable, holding a pillow in her arms as it rested on her lap.

"Now remember, honey, this is a dream, so some points aren't crystal clear like it would be if I were awake. You know, they're kind of hazy or something. However, shortly after I awoke, I did write down the dream to the best of my recollection. It was kind of surreal at times, that's all. So please be patient with me, okay?"

Annalisa nodded.

Alan turned a page in the little notebook he balanced on his knee.

"Well, in the dream, I found myself in a long beautiful corridor with very high arched ceilings, walking in the direction of an extremely bright light. It was actually more of a presence than a light. I was advancing toward it, and I hadn't noticed before, but there was this guy, uh . . . more of an angel than a guy, strolling next to me in the same direction. I'm pretty sure he was an angel, but at the time I wasn't positive. I glanced up at him; he was over a foot taller than me. Looking down, he nodded his head once. However, he didn't say anything. He quickly turned his gaze forward again. I wasn't scared or anything. I think I was more intimidated than anything else. I mean, he was an impressive figure."

"What color was he?" begged Annalisa.

"What color?" Alan scrunched his face puzzled by his endearing wife's peculiar question.

"Yeah, was he like golden or silver? Or maybe he was clear, like you could see through him or something, you know, like transluscious."

"You mean translucent?"

"Whatever. What color was he, Alan?"

"He was neither, uh . . . or all of the above. He looked like a person, a man. He looked like people you would see on earth, only he was wearing a bright white robe."

"Really?"

"Yes, my love. Now, let's see . . . we were walking side by side toward this bright light, more brilliant than I have ever seen, at the end of this enormous hallway. It was magnificent. There were all sorts of vivid colors, gold and silver too. It was so incredibly beautiful."

"I thought you said there wasn't any gold or silver?"

"Honey . . . if you keep interrupting we'll never get through this."

"Sorry, Alan, go ahead."

"As we neared the end of this grand hall or passageway, I noticed there was a large number of people standing in pairs, similar to the way I was walking with this guy beside me, except they were all stopped. It was like they were waiting for something. I turned to the guy, uh angel, and asked if he knew what all those folks in line were waiting for."

"When we stopped at the end of the double line, he turned to me and spoke in the most gracious voice I have ever heard. It made my heart melt when I heard it. There was so much love in the tone, as though it had been soaked in love for centuries. I literally was reduced to tears standing there next to him. There is absolutely no pride whatsoever in Heaven." Alan's voice broke as he replayed this humbling scene for Annalisa.

"What did he say to you, sweetheart?"

"He simply stated, 'It's not what, my friend. It's Who.'"

"Oh, Alan." Annalisa's eyes were as round as saucers and bigger than Alan had ever seen them before.

"Yeah, 'Oh, Alan' is right. I immediately came to realize, with that simple seven word sentence, I was in line to see the Lord Himself, in His very throne room. My mind jumped into hyper drive; you know, like in the *Stars Wars* movie. I wasn't ready to stand before the King of Kings and Lord of Lords. I needed to find a way out of there and quick!"

Holding up one finger as she jumped out of bed, Annalisa ran over to the door. She flipped the switch, turning on the ceiling paddle fan. Then she ran back, jumped onto the bed in the exact same spot, and put the pillow back in her lap. She leaned forward ready for Alan to continue.

"Honey, what was that?" he complained.

"I could see you had little beads of sweat forming on your forehead, so I was helping you out. It must have been intense, Alan, if you're sweating just telling the story."

"Yes, it was incredibly intense. So much so, that I asked the guy who I now confidently knew was an angel if there was any way I could, uh . . . kind of, postpone this visit. I told him I really needed to go back to earth and clear up a few things before, you know, going in there. I must have convinced him because after much cajoling from me and no words from him, he simply held up his hand. I immediately stopped talking. I mean, after all, when an angel holds up his hand . . ." Alan paused to let the seriousness of his situation sink into her thinking.

"Then he shared with me, 'You have been granted permission.' In a split second, I was back on earth. Everything was the same as before I had stood in line with the angel, with the exception that I had a desire to do something different with my life. I mean, to do something more worthy, more in service to others than selling and repairing bicycles. I felt if I could serve others more, this might be the way I could gain approval the next time I stood in line at the throne room."

"What do you mean, Alan?"

"I'm not sure, honey. It's a dream. Anyway, like I mentioned before, sometimes it's not crystal clear. Regardless, I found myself back on earth and convinced that

I should sell the bicycle shops and pursue a job of public service, like a firefighter, a policeman, a nurse, or something. I think it was sometime in the late 1960s because people were talking about the recent assassinations of Martin Luther King, Jr. and Bobby Kennedy as well as a big rock concert near Woodstock, New York. Working as a policeman, I began trying to do the best I could to serve and protect my fellow citizens. However, try as I might, I simply wasn't cut out to be in law enforcement. I found it to be more of a lifestyle than a job. Then, while taking a nap one day, I awakened in the grand hallway leading to the throne room again. I started walking toward the light. It was a peculiar thing, uh, sensation . . . well, kind of like I was drawn to it. No one told me to go there, but it was always drawing me nearer. In fact, it's the same feeling I experienced in the Morgan's cottage after I woke up. Anyway, I was walking toward the light down the long corridor and . . ."

"Was the angel there too?"

"Yes, my love. I looked up and he was there right beside me."

"Same angel?"

"Honey," chided Alan. "Yes, same angel, he didn't say anything though. It was very much like the first time. I'm not sure, there didn't seem to be a whole lot of superfluous talking in Heaven. There was always lots of singing and music, but it was kind of in the background, soft and really beautiful. Not like elevator music, no, these melodies actually passed through you. And as they did, it was like your spirit was a sponge soaking it all up."

"Wow, that's amazing," whispered Annalisa with a reverent tone.

"Yes, I've never experienced anything like it."

"The melodies of Heaven."

"Hmmm," nodded Alan as they both sat quietly. After a minute or so he continued telling his dream. "Well, the closer I got to the end of the line the more nervous I started to feel. Then, the one next to me, the angel, glanced down at me, and with that marvelous voice of love simply stated, "Peace to you."

"I started weeping again. Heaven was too much for my human emotions to handle. Without thinking, I started pleading with him again for another chance. I believed I hadn't shown near enough love for others to be accepted in this majestic place. I begged him to allow me one more return to my life on earth and promised to try even harder this time."

"In his quiet, calm voice he softly replied, 'It's not necessary for you to return.'"

"Please, give me one more chance," I begged with tears streaming down my cheeks.

"He held up one hand, for what was no more than a second or two, and then looked down at me, 'It has been granted to you.' In a split second I found myself quitting my job as a police officer and deciding to get some training to become a missionary."

"What? Really?"

"Remember, my love, this is in my dream. Yet it was so real; I felt sure it was actually happening. I perceived I was in a classroom in a college somewhere learning about people groups, languages, and customs. It was very hard to understand. I couldn't grasp the concepts. I was beginning to think I wasn't supposed to be a missionary. The next thing I realized, I was living in South America working as a missionary's helper, a kind of apprentice, alongside the likes of Peter Elliott, Nate Saint, and others. At first, it seemed so wonderful. But after a few months, or at least I think it was months, they asked me to go with them while they tried to reach a tribe of Auca Indians near a river sandbar they had nicknamed Palm Beach."

"Wait a minute, Alan. Do you mean those missionaries that lost their lives to those Indians back in the 1950s?"

"Yes, honey, all five were killed by the Aucas. It was awful. I've read Elisabeth Elliott's book *Through Gates Of Splendor* three times. In my dream, I was with them all, though I never really saw any faces. It's like I just knew it was them. You know what I mean?" Alan glanced at his adoring wife to assure himself that she was closely following what he was describing.

She nodded her head and smiled.

"Anyway, I was trying to help all of them, including their families, as much as I could. I wasn't much help, and they didn't ask me to go with them to Palm Beach that particular day. However, before the terrible news of their deaths broke I was back in Heaven walking down the magnificent hall toward the throne room again. I glanced to my left and there he was, the very impressive angel, walking by my side."

"Same angel?"

"Yes, and this time I was stuck. No more extra chances, no begging and pleading for another shot at life. I sensed that this was my time, and I couldn't delay it any longer. I was soon in the throne line with the tall angel standing right next to me, and my turn was coming up quick."

"What did you do, Alan?"

"What could I do? I prayed my heart out. Before I knew it, I was face to face with God. I mean, I never saw His face; I more sensed Him really, but He most definitely was there. I realized it was because of His great mercy and love that His face was hidden from me. The enemy was there too, hurling out a list of all the awful things I had ever done, right down to the smallest of selfish acts and thoughts I was sure nobody knew. Then, like a harsh prosecuting attorney, that wretched accuser barked out his declaration.

"He's guilty! Guilty as the sin he has committed. Condemn him to the Pit. He is mine, not Yours. For You to be a God of justice, You must declare him GUILTY!"

"Honey, I was fully expecting to hear the verdict from the throne to be in full agreement with the evil one's horrible accusations. I mean, if you could have heard how convincing he was. Oh, it was so dreadfully terrible. The entire time he was accusing me I was nodding my head in agreement. I deserved the worst. I was worthy of the Pit — that terrifying darkness where I would be lost from the presence of my loving Father forever, not just a day or two, but forever, FOREVER!. I was certain that all my actions, all my thoughts, all my life had condemned me. I was absolutely positive that even my life as a policeman, as a missionary, wouldn't be able to save me from all I had done. I cringed.

My heart sank in utter despair knowing at any second the gavel would drop, and I would be led off to the horrifying, black darkness, away from the marvelous, resplendent Light. I was trembling, waiting for that verdict, those terrifying words. The anxious seconds hung like an eternity. Do you know what I heard next?"

At this point, Alan completely broke down bawling uncontrollably. Annalisa jumped off their bed and onto the loveseat close to her beloved husband. "It's okay, Alan, our great God loves you. He loves you so very much," she consoled as they gently rocked back and forth in one another's arms. Alan nodded his head silently, wiping the tears from his eyes.

"I know, my precious love. You know what I heard instead of a verdict condemning me forever to the Pit?"

"What? What did you hear my wonderful husband?"

"I heard the most remarkable voice of love. Words cannot describe the sound. They don't come close to conveying the wonderfully beautiful and melodic intonation. It was like the loveliest symphony, more magnificent than any music ever heard on earth, combined with the most awesome, majestic, yet serene waterfall. It was frightfully terrible and comfortingly peaceful all at once. And then, He softly, yet boldly . . . claimed me as His own!"

Alan started weeping again. After composing himself he continued, "My joy and love for Him was absolutely rapturous. It sprang forth like a river that could no longer be held back by the mightiest of dams. I fell to my face on the floor and worshipped Him with all my heart as it all burst from deep within me. I sang, praised, and thanked Him. I couldn't hold back a single word, even if I wanted to, which I didn't. They were words too deep to explain, to define. I have no idea where they came from, yet I knew I was praising my great God and Father, the King of Kings. Oh, His name is truly wonderful! He is truly wonderful! It was all absolutely glorious, honey . . . so absolutely glorious!"

Alan turned to Annalisa, who herself had tears freely flowing down her cheeks. The two held each other tightly, slowly swaying back and forth as they sat on the loveseat together softly singing a song of praise.

"Then, honey," he whispered in her ear. "I felt a gentle tap on my shoulder as I lay there in the throne room. At least, I thought I was in the throne room. But when I looked up, I was in a gorgeous countryside setting with no one around except my new friend, the angel. He leaned down and helped me up to my feet on the brilliantly green grassy slope."

"I told you," he gently admonished, "going back wasn't necessary. Now listen, the Father wants to make sure you understand it's solely the blood of the Lamb that covers and atones for your sin,[4] not your efforts trying to get yourself clean and acceptable. It is only the broken body and shed blood of His precious Son, the Lord Jesus Christ, which cleanses you from all sin and redeems you for Himself. Remember, it's only by the Son's grace through faith that you are saved. It's not by your doing. It's by His doing. It's His gift to you, to all."[5]

Then he expressed very softly to me, "He who is forgiven little, loves little; likewise, he who is forgiven much, loves much.[6] Let this be your guide. Now, may the grace of the

Lord Jesus, the love of the Father, and the fellowship of the Holy Spirit be with you always."[7]

"When he began to bless me with these words, he laid his hand on my head. I closed my eyes and bowed. After he removed his hand, I waited a few seconds before I opened my eyes. When I did, I looked around for him, but he was gone."

Glancing down at his notes, Alan paused for just a few seconds before continuing, "I found myself in front of what appeared to be a small building with singing coming from inside. I proceeded in through the front doors. It was a tiny congregation worshipping and praising together. They made such a wondrous sound. It was so beautiful that I moved around this semicircle of worshippers and began singing with them. Although I never saw the Lord, He was surely there. Each one of the people worshipping knew their place of participation in this assembly. It was so beautiful, so simple, sweetheart, that I lifted my hands toward Heaven and sang with all my heart. The next thing I knew, I was waking up, flat on my back, on the kitchen floor of the Morgan's cottage. I still had my hands lifted upward, and I immediately noticed the silence."

"What silence?"

"After getting up off the floor, I went outside. The sun was shining, and I realized it was a new day, and the terrible storm, Hurricane Opal, had passed."

"Wow, Alan, that's so incredible. I have had such heaviness these last few months. It's been a huge burden I've been carrying around in my heart. Do you know what I mean?"

Alan nodded his head in agreement.

"However, while listening to your dream I actually felt like I was there with you. When he, uh, the angel, told you there was no need to return to earth, I felt a tiny release in my heart. I mean . . . you know? It's like a bit of that burden was lifted and removed. Then, when the Lord claimed you as His own, even though you deserved the verdict of Guilty and the Pit, I felt like He was telling me, 'Annalisa Michelle Browne, you are My own, too!' Oh, Alan, I sense a new life, a new spring bubbling up within my heart. Tell me again what our precious Lord's voice sounded like."

"It's hard to describe because it sounds so wonderful. In fact, wonderful doesn't come close to accurately representing what I heard. There's really no resonance like it on earth. His voice kind of sounded like a combination of the most beautiful symphony and the most glorious waterfall. In one ear it was so terrifyingly frightful and in the other ear so majestically beautiful."

"Why is that, Alan?"

"Because He holds the keys of death and of life.[8] The absolute power of the entire universe is in His mouth, and when He speaks all are completely silent. Life and death are in the power of His tongue.[9] Hey, I just thought of something, maybe that's why there was so little needless talking there . . . all were listening."

"Did you see any choirs or the elders on their thrones or anything like that, honey?"

"Well, no, it was a dream. Granted, it's a spiritual dream, but a dream nonetheless. It seemed real to me though. And because of it, or rather, because I have sensed the Lord drawing us closer, I have had a real strong desire to read and study His Word every day. I mean, I'm really ruminating on it. I feel like my spirit has been so parched, lacking the water of the Word to saturate it. As a result, when I drink, I guzzle it down completely."

"Yes," agreed Annalisa. "But don't you believe that your dream was from God?"

"Yes," agreed Alan with a bit of hesitation. "Yes, I do, although, having never experienced something like that before, I'm not one hundred percent sure. You know, it's a dream."

"Well, I am," confessed Annalisa. "The Scripture says that you will know them by their fruit,[10] and I have seen some marvelous fruit in you lately, Alan."

"I think time will tell, my love. However, for now, I sure have appreciated sensing the realness of God in my life."

"Me too, honey. Let's see what He does."

"But don't tell anyone, okay? Not just yet anyway." The hopeful couple prepared for bed and after praying together, fell asleep in one another's arms.

The next morning dawned like so many in the San Francisco Bay Area, with dense fog. After breakfast, Alan headed off to his largest bicycle shop, which was located in Danville. His schedule for the day would take him to the Lafayette shop by eleven o'clock or so, and then on to the shop in Pleasanton, leaving there around six o'clock. The day had all the pressures he had come to expect of his struggling business. However, there was a cautious optimism, a new lightness in his heart, almost, dare he admit, an expectation that God was indeed going to do something on their behalf.

But what would He do? How would He accomplish it? By what means and when? These were all thoughts Alan mulled over and over in his mind throughout the day. These weren't his only concerns. No, he also considered preparing the house for sale, getting it closed, and paying off their personal debt; at least he hoped the proceeds would tidy up most of their household financial obligations.

"Hope, there's that word again. I do have hope, Father, some hope anyway." As was his habit, he half-talked-half-prayed while he drove to the Pleasanton store late that afternoon. "Thank you for hope, my Dear Father in Heaven. Thank you. I know you're working; I just can't see it yet. You will reveal what You are doing when You are ready. Only help me to trust You, okay, Lord?"

Arriving in Pleasanton later than normal, Alan worked through a few responsibilities with his manager. Then, he began to ponder a different configuration for the sales floor. He was thinking something new might boost the lagging sales numbers in this, his smallest shop. Having just sat down with some sketches he had drawn, the phone rang.

"I got it, Dave" Alan called to his manager, who was working on a bike in the repair stand.

"Cycle Sport and Fitness, Pleasanton. How may I help you?"

"Alan Browne, please?"

Alan thought the voice was that of an older man, with a hint of a New York or perhaps New England accent. "Speaking," he answered.

"Mr. Browne, Bill Barker's my name. I own more than a dozen bicycle shops throughout the Bay Area. I have very seriously been considering the Interstate 680 corridor for my next move. I understand you have stores along this freeway in Pleasanton, Danville, and Lafayette. Is that correct?"

"Yes, sir."

"Mr. Browne, have you ever considered selling your shops?"

-five-

Annalisa had just taken their dinner out of the oven when Alan arrived home from an arduous day at work. He made a bee-line for the kitchen. Approaching her from behind, he wrapped his arms around her and gave her an extended kiss on the cheek.

"Go get cleaned up. Dinner will be on the table in five minutes," she crooned as she leaned back into his arms.

He turned her around and gave her a long, deep kiss. She kissed him back. Then he held her at arm's length and stood there grinning.

"Okay, Alan, what's going on?" She was smiling, but curiosity was written all over her face. "Come on, spill it."

"If I had a million lifetimes to live, sweet bride of my youth, I would want to live them all with you. You are the love of my life, honey."

"What brought this on, Alan?"

"Whaaat?! How about, I love you too, my handsome and manly husband?"

"I love you too, Alan. Now, what brought this on?"

"Ummm, I don't know . . . uh, what's for dinner?"

"Oh, no you don't, Alan Michael. You can't use those redirection tricks on me. I'm not one of the kids, you know. Come on, tell me what's going on!"

Continuing to pepper him with questions, she was convinced he was, in fact, withholding some exciting news. At one point, she grabbed his arms and began shaking them while she bounced up and down with anticipation. As usual, Alan found this extremely humorous, and was the main reason he enjoyed teasing her. He was howling so hard it was difficult for him to speak. She jumped up and down even more due to this inadvertent delay in revealing his secret. Sometimes a similar scene would play out for several minutes, and in one case years ago, nearly half an hour.

"Please, please, Alan, what is it? Please?!" Her face was a picture of everything he loved about her. Those deep brown eyes arched fully upward as her smile lit up the entire room. It nearly spread completely across her face creating the tiniest little dimples in each cheek. Her shoulder length auburn hair, still pulled back in a ponytail from her afternoon exercise session, was bobbing up and down, keeping cadence with her petite frame. Her voice hit that highest of octaves that fully delighted Alan.

"Okay, okay," he laughed. "Let me catch my breath a second." She had mostly quieted down yet was still pulling back and forth on his arms. After a few seconds, he settled down enough to regain his composure.

"Well?" She begged. Annalisa had stopped yanking his arms but obviously remained anxious about what Alan was concealing.

"I received a phone call today," he announced in a monotone. "It was from a man I met briefly, a number of years ago, at the California Bicycle Shops convention in Sacramento. His name is Bill Barker. He didn't seem to remember meeting me though, but that's okay."

"What did he want, Alan?" She was much calmer now yet still full of curiosity and anticipation.

"He wanted to know if I had ever considered selling my shops."

"Whaaat?! Are you serious? Really? He really wanted to buy the bicycle shops?" Annalisa's face was filled with a mixture of surprise, delight, and amazement but also held a hint of disbelief.

"Now, hold on a second, honey," petitioned Alan.

"How much did he offer you? Was it for all three or just one? Two? Was it for two?" She now had ahold of his arms again and was beginning to pull up and down on them.

"Wait a minute." Alan's tone was slightly firmer this time. "He didn't offer me any money, well . . . not yet anyway. You see, that's not how things are done. This was only an initial contact to see if I had any interest. Besides, Dave was in the shop, so I really couldn't say anything on the phone. I got his phone number and told him I would call tomorrow."

"Oh, then what's all the suspense for? Why didn't you just say he was calling to see if you would consider selling your shops?"

"Ha, that's exactly what I said!" Alan was near blurting out a sarcastic remark but was able to stop himself. Nonetheless, he was thoroughly enjoying her naiveté.

"Are you laughing at me, Alan?" She was pointing one finger in his direction with an expression that was borderline irritation. It wasn't anger, but she was looking annoyed.

"Honey, no . . . well, I mean, uh . . . you're sometimes, uhhhh . . ."

"Alan?!"

"Look, sweetheart, you don't understand, that's all. Business deals take a bit more time to work through than a simple offer and an acceptance. The exciting thing is this: Mr. Barker is interested in buying the shops. If he offers us enough money, we'd avoid bankruptcy and all the nastiness that could involve, including the emotional stress I'm sure neither of us needs right now. That's the news I was thrilled to tell you."

Alan paused to let that soak into his life partner's fragile heart. "You okay, my love?"

She looked up into his slate blue eyes and with one hand brushed his sandy brown hair off his forehead. "But it's good news, right?"

"Yes, it means God may be answering our cry for help, sooner, rather than later. And yes, that's fantastic news!" Alan was smiling as big as he knew how, to try and convince her that the good news is what he had been laughing about and not his wife.

"Okay, I think I comprehend it a little better now. That is wonderful news then, dear. Go get cleaned up for dinner."

Alan started to turn away toward the hall bathroom when he felt a slap on his rump and heard her comment, "You're getting quite a bit of grey hair, honey."

As he continued on, she could hear Alan call from the hallway bathroom, "We'll finish this later tonight!" Annalisa giggled as she served the dinner and placed it on the dining room table. She smiled knowing full well the intent behind his playful comment.

The next morning Alan wanted to telephone Mr. Barker as soon as he had finished breakfast, but to avoid appearing overly anxious, he thought it wise to wait. Calling sometime around eleven o'clock, he decided, would demonstrate the right mix of respectfulness and eagerness. To hinder any rumors and the employee problems that would undoubtedly follow, he purposefully headed out to the woodworker's shop in his garage. With pen and notepad ready, he dialed the number.

"Bill Barker, who's calling?" Alan decided the accent was definitely from New York or perhaps Boston.

"Mr. Barker, it's Alan Browne. I own Cycle Sport and Fitness. You called me yesterday evening." Alan was trying to sound bold and confident though he was feeling timid and unsure.

"Yes, Mr. Browne, how are you today?"

"I am well, sir, and you?"

"Fine, fine, just fine. Please call me Bill."

"Yes sir, and please call me Alan."

"Okay. Well, Alan, can I assume from our little talk last evening that you are interested in selling your three shops?"

"Yes sir, I mean, under certain conditions anyway."

"Sure, sure. Then tell me, Alan, how's business?"

"Uh . . . it's pretty good, I guess. I mean, we're real busy and all."

"Good, good, I'm glad to hear that. Are you free next week for a lunch meeting? I was thinking over here at the San Leandro Marina. You ever eaten at Horatio's, Alan?"

"Uh, yes, sir. My wife and I had dinner there a couple of years ago. I had a stuffed flounder dish. It was excellent."

"Fine, fine, how's Tuesday look for you? Say one o'clock?"

"Sounds perfect."

"Great, great, and, Alan, don't forget to bring your latest financial statement. Have a good day." With that, Bill Barker ended their brief conversation.

Hanging up the phone, Alan could feel a heaviness creeping into in his chest. The last comment from Mr. Barker carried a bucket load, which was rapidly becoming a heaping pile, of dread. Alan was beginning to convince himself that this deal could never work. The financial statement would surely reflect the dismal shape of his bicycle business. Once Mr. Barker saw it, he'd quickly determine Alan's shops weren't worth a penny. Sitting in his woodworker's shop, the dark cloud of doubt and despair began to mushroom above him. By the time he picked up the phone to call his accountant, Junior Alvarez, he was certain that selling his bicycle shops was, most likely, an ill-fated dream.

"Junior? Hey, it's Alan. How you doing, man?" Alan was attempting to sound cheerful and positive.

"Alanza, how many times have I told you the "J" in Junior is silent. It's pronounced like an "H", man. Come on, it's Hoo-nior not Junior, got it?" Alan could hear the smile in Junior's voice.

He had met Junior on one of his bicycle shop's sponsored rides a few years back. It was a ride up one side of Mount Diablo and back down the other. The course was an absolute Sufferfest, at least for several of the lesser seasoned riders, which included the likes of Alan and Junior. Actually, they had introduced themselves about three quarters of the way up amidst the heavy breathing and extreme muscular pain. Both thought the other's name sounded funny when expressed through their labored exhalations. Then, once on the downhill and back to somewhat normal breathing, the two riders found one another's company thoroughly enjoyable. They became fast friends and training partners, frequently greeting each other with the same routine—Alan mispronouncing Junior's name, and Junior calling Alan, Alanza.

Two years ago, Junior had become a CPA. At the time, Alan's current accountant was considering retirement, so Alan and Junior had a discussion regarding Alan's downward pecuniary spiral. The following month, Junior became Alan's accountant and advisor for all things financial. Junior was the first one to suggest the possibility of selling one, two, or all three of the bicycle shops. At that point, Alan wasn't at all open to his good friend's sage counsel. However, within the last eighteen months, he had become convinced this was a more attractive option than bankruptcy.

"Junior, you're not going to believe this!" Alan's tone revealed that Junior was actually going to like what Alan had to say next.

"You're finally going to do the Lake Tahoe century ride with me?"

"What? No, no, it's something else, you know, business." Alan was trying to tone down his enthusiasm a bit.

"So you're not going to ride . . ."

"Hang on a second. I mean, this has nothing to do with riding. I just got off the phone with a guy who is interested in buying my bike shops."

"What? That's great, Alan. I still think it would be a good move for you and Annalisa."

"Yeah, well, I'm not so sure. But if it can get me out of this pickle I'm in, I think I'm open to giving it a try, at least with certain conditions. Look, he wants to meet me next Tuesday for lunch, and here's the tough part . . . he wants a current financial statement."

"Ooooh . . . I'm not sure that's going to be helpful for you, Alan. The numbers aren't looking good. You would really have to explain the situation to him and emphasize your service business. I mean, that's the only thing you have that is somewhat positive. Your debt looks bad, man. Junior's tone was very sobering to Alan's already clouded heart.

"Hey, Alan, why don't I go with you? I can steer him through the discussion to see the potentials and not the liabilities, you know, your debt."

"No, I think it's a lunch where he and I can get to know one another and discuss initial concerns. It probably won't get detailed or anything. Besides, I'm sure it will only be the two of us."

"Okay, as long as you're confident you can handle him. Hey, why don't you drop by my office on Monday afternoon around four o'clock. I'll have your financial statement complete, and I can kind of coach you through it, okay? Look, bring your bike. We'll do that Livermore/Del Valle loop I've been telling you about. It would be good to get in some miles. What you do say?"

"Yeah, that sounds good, Junior. It would feel good to get the blood pumping, and it's always good to burn off some stress . . . and man, do I have a dump truck load full of that."

"Hey, mi amiga, you riding with the group Saturday morning? I hear we're doing that Palomares Canyon loop. Great ride, you in Alanza?"

"Nah, man, I need to stick close to home. Annalisa's still hurting, and I wouldn't feel right taking three to four hours to go riding. But soon, I hope."

"I'm sorry, Alan. I know this has been tough on you both. I don't think my wife and I would be handling it as well as you two. You guys have something deep down that most folks don't have. Uh, I've got to run. I'll see you Monday at four, right?"

"Yep, I'll be there."

"Great, tell Annalisa I said, hi, okay?"

"Will do. And, Junior, thanks for your help."

"No problemo, muchacho," laughed Junior. "See you Monday."

Over the next few days, leading up to his meeting with Mr. Barker, Alan made time to think through every possible scenario that could present itself. He wanted to be prepared to squelch any negative tactic this would-be-buyer could possibly present and completely convince him that his shops were a good investment. Monday afternoon Alan met with Junior, who coached him on several possible strategies that Mr. Barker might try to employ in an effort to negotiate a cheaper sales price. By the time Tuesday morning arrived, Alan felt like a Special Forces soldier readied for any maneuver the enemy may throw at him. With this mindset, he drove to Horatio's restaurant and his meeting with the man Annalisa had jokingly labeled "The Barker". Earlier she had cautioned her overwhelmed husband, "Mr. Barker is just that, a barker. And his bark is worse than his bite."

Arriving at the restaurant right on time, Alan was met at the door by a young lady dressed more like a runway model than a business woman. She was tall, blond, and wearing a dress, which appeared to be more suited to dancing than to work; although her shoes, Alan noticed, were not at all conducive to the dance floor. He guessed they made her four to five inches taller than her actual height.

"Mr. Browne?" she asked without even a hint of a smile.

"Yes," he acknowledged. "I'm Alan Browne."

"I'm Tina Billingsley, Mr. Barker's personal assistant. Mr. Barker is waiting in our private meeting room. If you would follow me, please." Her voice was soft but curt and very business-like.

As they turned the corner and passed through an open door, Alan immediately discerned two very important facts: this was not a private meeting with Mr. Barker, and he was way under dressed. Both of these he found very intimidating. He extended his hand to shake the out stretched hand of Mr. Barker, who was standing among four other people – three men and a woman, all of whom were wearing suits and ties.

"Alan, Alan, how are you? Good to meet you in person."
Mr. Barker's voice was boisterous and every bit as much in-
your-face as his presence exuded. He was a rather large man,
nearly bald with a wisp of grey hair combed straight back.
Alan guessed him to be in his late fifties. He was wearing
gold glasses, and when he grinned Alan caught a glimpse of a
gold trimmed tooth. He wore a total of four gold rings, two
on each hand. One was a pinky ring displaying an enormous
diamond. Twice as Mr. Barker adjusted his glasses, Alan
noticed he was wearing a gold wrist watch, highlighted
with diamonds, which matched the rest of his accessories.
He obviously liked the way gold and jewels made him
appear.

"Let me introduce some of my associates who will help
us work through the details of this little purchase of ours.
That's . . . if we can work out a deal," laughed Mr. Barker.
With this last comment, he slapped Alan on the back and
moved him forward to meet the others.

"Alan, call me Bill, I insist. Now, let me introduce my
Business Manager, Edna Foster. She's been with me since
way back in Philly."

Alan gave a slight bow toward Edna as he glanced up at
Bill. "So you're from Philadelphia?"

"Yes, yes, born and raised there, even graduated from
Temple. Moved to the Bay Area when I was twenty-seven
for a business opportunity and have rarely been back East
since. No reason to, California is where the action is."

"Uh, yes sir." This whole situation was becoming a bit
overwhelming for Alan.

"This is my personal attorney, Mitch Delphos, and my CPA, Tom Jones."

Alan shook his hand and looked at Bill, anxious to ask a question.

"I know what you're about to ask, Alan, but don't. Tom hears that question all the time. Besides, you don't want to hear him sing. You can trust me on that one." At this comment, the room erupted in laughter as Bill slapped Tom on the back.

"Finally, meet my Director of Operations, Bruno Giordano. Okay, okay, let's all sit down, shall we?"

The table in the center of the room, no larger than Alan's living room, was round with six chairs along one side of the curve and a solitary chair on the other. Alan sat in the single seat. As he glanced across the battlefield, he took note of how Bill's troops were aligned. His personal assistant, Tina, sat immediately to his left, with pen and paper at the ready. Edna, his Business Manager, was on his right. Next in line to Edna was the attorney, and beside him Bruno, the Operations guy. On the other side of Tina, was the quietest of all the opponents, the CPA, Tom Jones. Alan was trying to size them up as much as he was trying to remember their names. Less than a minute after they had taken their seats, a waiter walked through the open door.

"Welcome everyone. My name is Daniel, and I'll be serving you today. Can I get anyone something to drink?"

After the drink orders were placed, Bill started right in with the business of the day. "Alan, did you bring your financials?"

"Yes, sir, but I only have two copies. I didn't realize . . ."

"Fine, fine, let me see what you have there."

Alan stood up and handed a copy of his business financial statement to Bill. Without even a glance, Bill shuffled it to his personal assistant. "Tina, honey, tell the restaurant manager, oh, what's his name, we need six copies. Tell him it's for me."

Bill continued, "Now everyone, while Tina is getting those copies made, let me tell you all about Mr. Alan Browne. He moved here in the late 1970s and went to work for that small shop in Lafayette. Remember Rudy's Bicycle Shop? Well, Alan bought that from the original owner and a couple of years later purchased that little struggling shop in Pleasanton as well. My guess is business was pretty good in those day, eh, Alan?"

Alan nodded his head but said nothing. Bill picked up where he left off. "But then you built that big shop in Danville three years ago, right?"

"It's been about two and a half years."

"Okay, okay, two and a half. And that's where things got a bit tight for Alan. I've been trying to wait him out, hoping I could snatch up his shops when he filed for bankruptcy. But he never did. Somehow he hung on. That's very impressive, Alan. Now here we are, with you still owning something that I would very much like to have. It would, how do you say, complete my circle of the Bay Area, at least in bicycle shops." Bill had been tapping the tips of his pudgy fingers together but suddenly stopped, enlacing them as one weaved fist.

"Could we say we have David stopping Goliath?" joked Bill. "Hardly."

R. J. Graves, Jr.

At this point, everyone in the room, with the exception of Alan, chuckled as if they knew something he didn't.

"You see, Alan, the bicycle shops are only one of many businesses I own. I have a chain of grocery stores in Northern California. I own an OTR trucking company and a stone quarry that provides gravel to a host of counties, including those in the Bay Area. I manufacture a line of sports clothing and also own a factory; the products of which are shipped around the world. I even own seven movie theaters.

"So here's the deal, Alan," Bill smugly grinned across the table directly at Alan. "I am prepared to make you a fair offer for your three shops. You can take it or leave it. However, if you don't accept it, be forewarned, I will build my own shops close by and run you out of business. Nothing personal you understand, just good business." Bill's gold trimmed tooth sparkled as he made this last comment.

With that, Bill reached into his inside suit pocket and pulled out a sheet of paper folded over lengthwise and slid it across the table toward Alan.

Alan picked up the offer but before opening it asked, "What about my employees? They depend on me for a job. I want them to be taken care of."

"Of course, of course, I'll need them too. Who would run the shops without them? Oh, and you'll find we need you also, for up to ninety days at a handsome salary. Now, how about some lunch? You hungry, Alan?"

"Uh . . . I think I need to go work through all of this. You've already given me quite a bit to digest. If you know what I mean?"

"Sure, sure, but how about a bite to eat for the road? A soldier can't march on an empty stomach." This last comment, once again, had everyone in the room laughing, except Alan.

"Uh, Bill, would you please give me twenty four hours to think this over. I need to talk it over with my accountant and, uh . . . my wife."

"That would be fine, fine. You go on home and talk it over with the little lady," Bill gibed as he stood up. The rest of those in the room stood as well. Alan met him at the door and shook his hand, thanking him for the meeting. He then shook the hand of each of the rest of Bill's armada before opening the door to head out.

"I'll call you by noon or so tomorrow, okay, Bill?"

"Great, great, look forward to hearing from you, Alan. Have a safe trip back over the mountain."

"Thank you, sir." Alan quickly walked out of the room which had been his battle zone. He dared not stop to review the paper Bill had slid across the table until he was sure he was out of eyesight. In fact, he had driven all the way to Castro Valley before stopping along Redwood Road to open Bill's offer.

"Well, let's see what we have here." Alan expressed aloud as he glanced around to assure no one was watching.

At the top of the page was the simple title "Offer to Purchase". The first two paragraphs appeared to be mostly legalese. Then, his eyes fell upon the purchase price along with some exclusions and conditions. His eyes widened while he calculated the numbers in his mind. A smile started to spread across his face.

"This may be enough. Lord. I think You may have worked yet another miracle in my life. I think this may be enough to get us out with a little left over."

Next, his eyes moved down the page to the final clause concerning his employment for up to ninety days as part of Bill's transition team. The weekly salary was indicated along with a few conditions for employment.

His mouth dropped wide open as he gleefully laughed out loud.

six

On the way back over the mountain to San Ramon, Alan called Annalisa, who had been at home praying for him. He wanted to assure her everything went well and that he would be home shortly to discuss the details with her. Next, he tried to reach Junior. He got his answering service and left an urgent message for him to return his call as soon as possible.

What a difference the ride back from San Leandro was compared to the drive he had made an hour ago in the opposite direction. Alan kept trying to calculate the figure Bill had offered in relation to the debt numbers he had almost memorized. He continued to come up with the same answer each time. "I really think it may be enough."

Upon arriving home, he and Annalisa moved straight to their sanctuary, the master bedroom. She had prepared him a sandwich, chips, and a glass of cold milk. She was obviously anxious, but unusually patient as Alan took a bite of his favorite hoagie: turkey on sour dough including provolone, lettuce, tomatoes, a splash of oil and vinegar, along with several dashes of oregano. He then took a long swig of milk. Afterwards, he rested back on the loveseat and with a deep sigh confessed, "That was tense."

"I would guess so. Did he make you a good offer?" she questioned with a mixed look of trepidation and excitement. "Do you think it will be enough to pay off the debt on the shops?"

"Okay, honey, so here's the deal," Alan explained with a half-eaten sandwich in one hand and chips in the other. "This Bill Barker is a savvy businessman. He owns all kinds of companies, not just bike shops. He told me he has been eyeing our shops for years. Then, he kind of threatened me."

"He threatened you?"

"Well, kind of, anyway. He mentioned, so calmly, so matter-of-factly, if I didn't sell to him, he would build his own shops and put me out of business."

"What did you say to him in response?"

"What could I say? I didn't say anything. I believed him!" Alan stuffed the final bite of sandwich in his mouth and then continued, "It's not like I could bully him back. This guy has more money than I could ever dream of and evidently knows how to use it."

"Sweetheart, don't talk with your mouth full."

Alan placed one hand over his mouth and mumbled sarcastically, "Don't bully me."

Annalisa playfully slapped him on the shoulder and laughed, "Me, the bully?"

Alan smiled, nodding his head while he held up one finger as if to say, "Hold on a second until I finish chewing."

"What kind of a man is he, Alan? I mean, do you think he's a crook or anything?" Annalisa had a very concerned look on her face, like she had been considering these questions for quite some time. "Does he wear a lot of gold jewelry or diamonds or anything like that?"

Alan was still holding up one finger trying to swallow the oversized last bite of his sandwich. He almost had it down when she asked another question.

"Did he have anybody with him, I mean, like hitmen or something? Were you right? Is he from New York? Do you think he's like an organized criminal?"

Finally swallowing his sandwich, Alan took a quick swallow of milk to help wash it down. "Whoa, now wait a minute, sweetheart. You've got yourself all worked up making him out to be a mob boss or something. I don't know anything regarding his personal life, but there was no indication he's part of some crime family or something. I mean, come on, honey, an organized criminal, really? He's a businessman and evidently a good one because he's been very successful. Now, let me tell you what he offered us, okay?"

"Okay, I'm anxious to hear what happened at your meeting. So he did offer you something? Do you think it will be enough, Alan?"

"Well, it looks like it might be, but I'm only going by what I can remember of our situation. I really need to discuss this with Junior. I called him and left a message, but he hasn't called back yet."

"Well, what do you think, Alan? Will it be enough?"

"Yes, I think so. It appears that Bill Barker somehow knew exactly what we needed to pay everything off and offered us just a little over that amount. I'm guessing we may have . . . oh, I don't know, maybe twenty left over, after all is said and done."

"Only twenty? Why, Alan, that's not enough to take our family out to dinner. You've owned those shops for more than sixteen years. After all that work, sweat, pain, and suffering, you'll only have twenty dollars left? That's not fair! Besides, don't you think that's cutting it way too close, honey?" Annalisa was frowning partly due to the fact that she thought this Bill Barker, whoever he was, was taking advantage of her hard-working husband, but she was also wondering why Alan was smiling while she wore a scowl.

"Thousand," Alan announced quietly as if it were a secret.

"Thousand what?" She was still frowning. "Oh . . ." She grasped her hand over her mouth. Once a few seconds passed, she questioned through her fingers, "Dollars? Really? Left over after everything else is paid?"

"Yes, my love, I think so anyway. However, I'm doing these calculations from memory. I may be off a few thousand or so. Despite not having our actual numbers in hand, I do think we would at least have a little something left over. I mean, not enough to buy another business, or house, or anything but maybe enough to get a fresh start somewhere."

"What do you mean, somewhere, Alan?"

"Honey, come on, we've talked about this before. California is incredibly expensive. It will be nearly impossible for us to buy another house here. But look, let's talk about that later. Let me tell you what is in the rest of the offer from Bill Barker, okay?"

Annalisa wasn't happy about the very real possibility of leaving her home state. She was born here. Her family and friends all lived here. Everything she knew was here. It was all so familiar, so comfortable. And what about their children, their schools, their friends, their soccer teams, they were all here too. This would be incredibly hard on them as well.

However, deep down in her heart, she knew Alan was right. She slowly nodded her head trying to show Alan she was interested in the rest of the deal, but the fresh dose of reality he had just dished up was occupying her thoughts. "Change," she pondered aloud. "Why does everything always have to change?" Then, upon her heart lighted a song they had sung many times at church. She recognized there's only One who never changes. Life would always include change, but Jesus never. A smile slowly broke across her face.

"I think one of the biggest lessons in life is something I am starting to understand."

"What's that, honey?" he questioned, tilting his head to one side.

"It's the lesson of letting go. It's a hard one, Alan. And I think it is one we learn all throughout life here on this earth. Think about it . . . my life has been filled with so much more peace since I've relinquished bitter feelings against others who have hurt us. I really feel something like freedom in my heart, freedom from past hurts and freedom to love someone who may have hurt me. I've also been learning about surrendering my expectations. Boy, those expectations can literally tie me up in knots. But as I've been trying not to expect things from others, from situations, or even from God, I'm finding I'm so much more at peace. It's like I'm a happier, more content, and more grateful person. I think all of life may be one big lesson in learning how to let go. You know what I mean? It's a course of study I'll continue to work on right up until I let go of my very last breath here on earth . . . and step into eternity with Him."

Alan slid onto the bed next to his sweet bride, and the two of them laid down side by side with Annalisa resting her head on his chest.

"You are such a wise, godly, young lady. Where did you get such insights, my precious love?

"From looking into the Scriptures and living life with you, honey. And from . . . well, losing our son. We'll never be the same again. I know that for sure. But I think therein may lie the joy in our sorrow, you know?"

"You see," she continued. "While you were at the meeting with Mr. Barker I thought seriously about some things. I considered whether I am actually happier because we have all of this stuff. I mean, you know, does it in any way contribute to my joy and my peace? If it does, then what will I be like, on the inside, in my heart, if these things are taken away from me? It was very sobering. On the other hand, what might I gain, if I am able to let them go? As hard as it is for me to contemplate these things, I acknowledge it would be even more difficult to follow through with them, you know, to actually give them up. However, I think there is great benefit to me, to us, to our kids, and maybe even to others, if I'm able to do so."

"Wow, honey," exclaimed Alan. "Those are deep thoughts."

Annalisa continued, "Listen, suppose all of these material items are like shackles on our hearts. If we lose it all, we may be free of it, but I think I would be angry or bitter. I'd feel like we had been dealt a raw deal, like it wasn't fair or something, you know? But suppose . . . just for a minute, I am able to give it away before it's taken from me. What might be the sensation in my heart then?"

"You know," added Alan, "when I worked for my cousin Dan, in Virginia, remember Dan the Man? He did business with a millwork shop in Luray, out in the Shenandoah Valley. I can't remember the guy's name. I think maybe it was Stephen. He and his family had made a vow to live meekly. I don't think it was at the poverty level, but they lived humbly. That's for sure. Honestly, I have never met a more pleasant family. They seemed so content, so gracious; I was really impressed with their kids, too. Later, I asked him about his lifestyle. He told me when he and his wife prayed to receive the Lord Jesus Christ into their hearts, they felt impressed to lead a quiet life and to work with their hands. To them, this meant living close to the ground, you know, humbly. He thought it was better to give something away since you couldn't take it with you anyway. I think there's some wisdom in that."

"Well, I don't know about you, Alan, but I'm not ready to give up this house, this home of ours quite yet. Maybe I could start with something small, you know, like my extra clothes I rarely wear that hang there in the closet month after month, year after year. What do you think, honey?"

"I think that's a good approach to a solution. Start small and go bigger as we feel confident this is the direction God would have us go. Let me pray for us, okay?"

Annalisa, who was still lying next to Alan with her head resting on his chest, nodded her agreement. Alan prayed the Lord would make His direction clear for their future, including what, if anything, they should relinquish, as well as when they should move, and even where they should relocate. When they had finished praying, Alan pulled his wife close to him drawing her up in his arms.

"You are such a strength to me, my love," he whispered in her ear. "I really don't know what I would do without you, nor do I ever want to find out."

"Me either," she smiled. "I definitely have to die first."

"Oh, no you don't," he laughed. "I'll be the first to go. I don't want to live one day of this life without you, no way."

The two held each other in their arms as they lay on their bed. "I sure love you, honey," she whispered. "It would be nice if we could stay in our home and not have to move away. I think that would be, perhaps, the most difficult of all these things we are considering."

"Me, too, I think it . . . hey, wait a minute. I didn't tell you the rest of Bill Barker's offer for our business. Somehow, we got sidetracked or something. But there's another really good part I haven't told you yet."

Annalisa sat up, somewhat kneeling next to Alan yet resting on her legs. "What part, Alan?"

Bill has a condition in his offer that I must work for him for up to ninety days as part of his transition team. There's a salary that goes with the position."

"Really? What kind of salary? I mean, how much will he pay you?"

"It pays fifteen hundred dollars a week . . . for up to ninety days. That's a potential earning of about nineteen thousand dollars, if he needs me for the full term of the agreement."

"Wow, Alan, that would almost double what you think may be left over from the sale of the shops. Maybe we could still stay here in our home?!" At this point, she was bouncing ever so gently upon their bed, hoping the motion could somehow churn up the answer she was hoping to hear.

"Maybe, honey, God can do anything," he consoled. "But I don't think it will be enough to keep us in our home, or even buy us another one, if we sell. I most likely won't have steady employment, and you know our credit looks pretty bad right now. I'm not even sure we could find someone who would rent us a house. Although, like we have been talking, we can give it away, in other words, sell it, or we can have it taken from us in foreclosure. I choose, sell it. What do you think?"

"Yes, I agree. It's so excruciatingly painful. However, nowhere near as bad as losing our Christopher Kyle. Yet in the close aftermath of that terrible loss, this seems to be dredging up some pretty awful feelings I would just as soon forget. Oh, Alan, I know it's better to give it up. But I really don't think I'm ready."

"I know, my sweet love, I know. Me too, and it pains me to even think about what will happen next week, next month, or even next year. I'm genuinely worried about our future; where we'll go, what we'll be doing, how we'll live?

Let's take one day at a time, okay. And from where we sit now, at three forty-nine in the afternoon, I think we're going to make it through today . . . looks like it anyway. Then tomorrow, we'll deal with tomorrow, okay? Maybe it won't be nearly as terrible as what we are envisioning. Maybe our great God will have mercy on us."

"Yes, and I would rather depend on Him than any other," she affirmed. "I think He actually enjoys helping those who have no place else to turn but to Him. Remember what the speaker at church told us? You know, that guy from, I think it was somewhere in Mississippi . . . remember what he said how God enjoys writing the last chapter. How a story, a situation, or even a life isn't over until God is finished with it. And He loves to put wonderful finishes on His works. Remember that, Alan? After Sunday church service, we had him over for lunch. What was his name?"

"Yes, great guy, really down to earth. His two sermons were refreshingly practical. I really appreciated his messages. I think his name was Teddy something. Was it Teddy Wilbeam? Yep, that's it, Reverend Teddy Wilbeam from Wiggins, Mississippi."

"How did you remember his name?"

"Well, after he spoke at our church, he visited with us here, and then I took him to the airport later that evening. We had plenty of time before his flight, so we stopped for coffee. I really enjoyed him. He had such a unique way about him, a very sensible approach to life. He told me, 'Always leave room for God'. We wrote letters back and forth for over a year, but gradually discontinued. I wonder what he's doing now?"

"He was a pastor, wasn't he?"

"Yes. He shepherded a small nondenominational church a few miles outside of a town there in Southern Mississippi. I think he described it as a congregation of about two hundred and twenty or so. Man, honey, I sure would like to do something like that. I mean, shepherd a small group of people. But I don't have any credentials, seminary training, or anything. I do have a little experience but not nearly enough to pastor a church."

"You could shepherd a church, Alan. You would be really good at it too."

"Oh, I don't have the confidence, my sweet love. I'm not as mature as I look," he smirked.

"Maybe that's one of the main reasons we're going through all of this," she reasoned. "Maybe God is training you to be a man of God. A man like Job was, not at the beginning of the Book of Job, but at the end. A man, who hadn't only heard about God and could have told you information about Him, but one who had actually, by real life experience, known God. Now, that would be a valuable individual, a highly esteemed shepherd of His people."

Laying back down next to Alan, Annalisa rested her head again on his chest. "I can hear your heart beating," she smiled. "It's not beating nearly as fast as when we first laid down."

"I think it's because I have such peace right now, sweetheart. I feel so hopeful, like all that we have been and are still going through is going to really be of service to others, you know, will help others someday. So that makes it kind of worth the suffering or something. It's still painful, but not as much because I believe God will use what we are enduring for our good."

"I think I know what you mean," she whispered. "At some point, we'll get to comfort others with the comfort that God gives us through these times.[1] And as a side benefit to us, we get to let go of all sorts of potential hindrances. You know, the stuff that keeps us from living like He may want us to live."

"Hmmm . . ." moaned Alan.

"What is it, honey?"

"Well, I'm not sure. It's the smallest check within my heart or my spirit maybe. I need to see if it's the Lord's Spirit prompting me. I'm not sure what it is, but it's something."

"Let me know if you would like to talk about it later, okay? Meanwhile, I think I may take a short nap. I'm really tired."

"Me too," agreed Alan. "I think I'm a bit drained emotionally."

The hopeful, yet weary, couple dozed off, snuggled up close to one another. It wasn't a deep sleep, which afternoon naps rarely provide, but at least it was restful.

Startled out of his unconscious state, Alan glanced at the clock before answering his phone. It was two minutes before five o'clock; they had slept for nearly an hour. He gently moved Annalisa, who was now awake but groggy, and grabbed his phone.

"Hello?"

"Hey, Alan, it's Junior. How'd it go today, brother?"

"Oh, man, thanks for calling. I need to sit down with you as soon as possible. I have an offer from this buyer Bill

Barker. I need to know exactly where we are financially, so I can get back to him with an answer."

"Okay, great, is it a good offer?"

"I think so, but I really need to sit down with you to see where we're at, and if this will cover everything or not. Can I come by the office this evening?"

"No, that won't work. My wife and I are going out to dinner, and then she wants to see a romantic comedy movie. I won't be back until after ten or so."

"Well, that's okay with me. I can meet you that late. I mean, this is real important."

"Alan," Junior's tone was more direct. "Just because the movie gets out at ten doesn't mean our evening is finished. If you get my drift?"

"Oh, yeah, right . . . uh, sorry about that, man."

"No problemo, hombre," laughed Junior. "How about tomorrow afternoon, two o'clock at my office? Does that work for you?"

"No, I told the buyer I would have him an answer within twenty-four hours, and that would make it about one-thirty or so. Don't you have anything in the morning? The earlier the better."

"Alanza, you told the buyer of your business, your three bicycle shops, which are in somewhat of a contorted financial plate of spaghetti, that you would give him an answer, to what will be a huge life-changing decision, within twenty-four hours?! Hombre, have you lost your mind? I can't give you an accurate number on that short notice."

"Come on, Junior. I really need your help," pleaded Alan.

"Look, Alan, you're a dear friend. I mean, I consider you like a brother, but I would need more time to get you that number, or at least anything that would remotely resemble an accurate figure."

The phone was silent.

"Okay, can you meet me at the office at seven in the morning? I have a very important appointment at ten, but maybe I can get close to a number for you by then, maybe."

"Thanks, Junior. I really appreciate this, man. See you at seven, and by the way . . . have fun tonight!"

"Oh, you know I will!" chuckled Junior. "Hey, bring that offer letter he gave you. I really need to see it. Mañana iguana."

"See you at seven and thanks again Junior."

Alan lay back down on their bed next to Annalisa with his head resting on the pillow. "Wow . . . that was a bit scary. I was so afraid it wasn't going to work out," he exhaled deeply. "Woof."

"Yeah, I can feel your heart pounding."

"Well, it's incredibly important we get that number together tomorrow morning. I need to give Mr. Barker an answer by one o'clock or so. I sure don't want him to withdraw his offer."

"Oh, he's not going to. He needs your shops to accomplish his goals. He would be shooting himself in the foot if he rescinded his offer to you."

"Hmmm . . . maybe you're right, honey."

"Alan, tell me something, please," she was using her soft voice, which he so adored.

"Yes, my love."

"Before we fell asleep an hour ago, you mentioned something you thought God may be speaking to your heart but had a check in sharing it. What is it? What's troubling you?"

"Well, it's not really troubling me," he assured her. "It's more of a hazy thought, kind of like when you're trying to view a tree through a thick fog; you're not quite sure what kind of tree you're seeing. You know what I mean?"

"I think so."

"I can see how important it would be for someone to be a clear channel, for God to effectively use them. Especially for someone who is a shepherd of God's flock. It would be imperative to be free and not be tied up in knots on the inside. It would be essential for him to have worked through many, if not most, of the issues of his heart. I don't mean, you know, only cars, furniture, a house, or those issues on the outside. I mean, those things that hinder him on the inside, in his heart. It would be critical that he had a freedom within him, don't you agree?"

"Yes, I would love to attend a church with a pastor like that," she nodded.

"Me, too, especially after all we've been through recently. Well, if at some point, God calls us for that same purpose, or even for a higher walk with Him, it seems to me He would have to do that work in each of us. And I think we're only at the beginning of that freeing process. To me, when someone prays to receive Jesus as their Savior, they are in fact saved. However, it appears they still have all types of lifestyle issues to work through. Yes, they possess personal salvation, but they don't live like it in many areas of their lives yet. It seems to me He leads them, uh . . . us through this life using all kinds of varied natural circumstances and events to help set us free from what hinders us from walking with Him, and therefore limits our ability to love and serve others. Honey, like we're discovering, some of those hindrances are on the outside and some are on the inside, hidden within our hearts."

"Do you mean," questioned Annalisa, "He would have to work a greater level of liberty in our hearts, so we can more fully love and serve both Him and others? If that's what you're saying, then that may be the greatest need we have, a growing freedom within ourselves."

"I mean precisely that. Maybe a lot of what we are going through has to do with issues that crimp and stymie us. However, it may be natural things causing the impediment, yet . . . it must be a spiritual transaction that attains the freedom within. He uses the natural to accomplish the spiritual, like he did with Job, David, Daniel and others. This is something that's so very deep that it could perhaps take years to accomplish, my love."

"That's okay, Alan. I'm not going anywhere without you. 'We'll hold steady,' said one lump of clay to another," she smiled as she kissed him on the cheek.

"We will be faithful to Him," he assured her. "That may be the test that lasts a lifetime. Remember, He loves us, and He wants us to be successful even more than we want to be. I believe our loving Father in Heaven is accomplishing a deep work in us both—a freedom within me, and a freedom within you."

~seven~

Early the next morning, Junior and Alan quickly and systematically worked through as many of the numbers as time allowed. It was extraordinarily important to be as accurate as possible, all the while considering the time constraints. When they were at a point where both of them felt confident they had uncovered all costs, liabilities, and inventory, Junior totaled up the figures. Alan paced back and forth across the office floor.

"It'll work," announced Junior with a smile, looking up from his computer. "Barely, but it will work. My advice would be to close on this deal fast before you amass any more losses. You know he'll present you with a contract. I would accept it with one condition, you finalize it within thirty days. That will give you the opportunity to tidy everything up before accruing any further debt."

"Okay, that's a good idea. I'll state it as a condition. How much do you think will be left over?"

"Well, depending on the closing date, somewhere between twenty-five and thirty."

"Really? Are you sure? Oh, man, that would be so helpful. I think I could actually breathe again."

"But remember, the longer the actual transfer of title delays, the more bills will continue to pile up, and the less money you will have left over from the sale. Trust me; it is in your best interest to get this closed sooner, rather than later. Think of it like the meter in a taxi. The farther the trip to your destination, the longer the meter keeps ticking. This is you, Alan. You're in the taxi, and you have to pay the bill when you finally arrive at your destination: the closing table. Got it, mi amigo?"

"Yeah, yeah, I understand, Junior." This time Alan pronounced Junior with an emphasized English "J" sound.

"Ok, Alanza, just so you recognize the gravity of your situation," cautioned Junior while he patted the stack of papers with the palm of his hand.

Driving back home with those words ringing in his ears, Alan decided to telephone Bill Barker shortly before one o'clock. He thought the time, until then, would be best spent in strategizing how he would handle the important call. He wasn't sure why he was so suspicious of this buyer. Maybe it was Annalisa's line of questions the day before. Maybe it was the setting where the meeting took place. Maybe it was Bill's armada, as Alan had labeled them. Maybe it was all of the above. Whatever it was, Alan was leery regarding today's phone call.

After having lunch together around noon, he and Annalisa spent some time in prayer before Alan headed out to the desk in his woodworker's shop. He was back, seated at their kitchen table, inside of five minutes.

"Couldn't reach him, honey?" questioned Annalisa as she sat down with him.

"Yes, I did. The call was over in less than two minutes. I couldn't believe it. Sixteen years of work, done, finished in ninety seconds. Somehow it's so sad to me. I mean, I know it has to be done, but it seems so sad . . . and it makes me feel so very sad."

"It's going to be alright." She reached across placing her hand on top of his. "What did he say, Alan?"

"It was incredible. We exchanged greetings, and I mentioned my two conditions regarding jobs for all my current employees, and that we close within thirty days. I told him I didn't want this to drag on for months. He replied with his, 'Fine, fine', and then asked me if I was good to move forward with a contract. I responded with a, 'Yes sir', upon which he told me a contract would be delivered to our home address by special courier no later than noon this Friday. That's the day after tomorrow! I expressed my appreciation, and he nonchalantly explained that I will have until five p.m. on Monday to have the executed contract on his desk in Oakland, stating, 'We'll close twenty-one days from Monday.' He then said, 'Have a good day. See you Monday.' And he abruptly hung up. That was it."

"Wow, that guy is so sensitive. Isn't he?" Annalisa remarked sarcastically.

"No kidding."

"I feel like calling him and letting . . ."

"Now, honey, I'm sure to him it's only another business deal. He doesn't care about all our heartache and hard work. It's a dollars and cents thing, uh . . . dollars, anyway. That's all it is to him. It's money and how to make more of it. He wants the Freeway 680 corridor, and we happen to have that wrapped up with our three shops. Well, at least from Lafayette to Pleasanton. Therefore, I guess it's good for us too. I mean, we won't have the continual concerns over money, or more accurately, the lack of money. So yeah, that's a good thing. It's just so sad."

"I know it is, Alan, but keep your eyes on Jesus, the Author and Perfecter of our faith.[1] Remember, He is for us not against us.[2] He'll see us through this; He will."

"Thanks, my love, I know He will. It's when you are in the midst of it, well, as you know, it's not easy."

"Yes, I know, but try to focus on what Joey told you about our emotions being one of the two biggest battlegrounds." With this, she gave his hand a gentle squeeze.

Alan glanced at his sweet bride allowing the slightest smile to acknowledge he had heard her. He turned to look out the window and let out a quiet sigh, "Hmmm . . ."

The contract did, in fact, arrive by special courier Friday morning. Alan drove straight to Junior's office to have him look it over. Everything appeared straightforward, and after reviewing the document of several pages Junior gave Alan the thumbs up. Saturday morning Alan, Annalisa, and the children visited with her parents, so Alan could get Dad William's advice on the contract from a legal standpoint. His attorney father-in-law was impressed with the thoroughness of the instrument. After Alan answered a few of his questions, he too acknowledged it was a sound agreement.

The remainder of the weekend Alan spent thinking and praying about the contract, his employees, and the future of all involved, especially his family. He arrived at Bill Barker's office at quarter after eleven Monday morning with the signed document. The meeting lasted no more than two minutes. In fact, they stood in the reception area as Alan, fighting back his emotions, handed it over to Mr. Barker. It may have been a piece of paper to one man, but it represented years of hard work trying to obtain a dream to the other.

"Fine, fine," remarked Bill Barker with a wry grin, again revealing his gold rimmed tooth. "Thank you, Alan. I'll have my attorney contact you in the next week or so to set up the closing time. I won't keep you. You have a nice day."

Alan was so taken aback and discouraged by the emotionless nature of the transaction, he hadn't even noticed the parking ticket under his windshield wiper until he was driving back over the mountain toward San Ramon. He pulled over onto the shoulder of the six lane freeway and turned on his emergency flashers. Reaching across the windshield he lifted the ticket from under the wiper. Settled back behind the steering wheel, he glanced down to view the amount of the fine. Suddenly, the flood gates unexpectantly blew wide open. He bellowed out a cry that had been building up inside of him for months. He began sobbing uncontrollably. The tears poured down his cheeks soaking the ticket, which lay in his lap. The dam had finally been breached and all it took was a minor twelve dollar parking violation.

Since the terminal diagnosis that their unborn child had a birth defect and wouldn't live, the flood waters had been cresting at the very rim of the dam, threatening to overflow. In reality, this had been building for years with the enormity of business problems piling up. But the awful report concerning their baby was what initiated the cracks in the dam. Now he was sitting in his vehicle, on the side of a major freeway, crying like never before. Again he glanced down at the ticket in his lap and marveled at how such a small issue could precipitate such a huge surge, this flash flood of emotion bursting from the depths of his being. It had been accumulating for way too long. Finally, in this conspicuously awkward location, his blessed relief had inescapably arrived.

Startled out of his emotional stupor by a rap on the driver's side window, Alan hastily wiped his hands across his face. He swung around to see the gold star on the uniform of the helmeted California Highway Patrolman, who was staring into his window from behind mirrored sunglasses. Alan had been too engrossed in his circumstances to notice the motorcycle with the flashing red and blue lights as it had pulled up behind him. However, now he couldn't miss the intimidating iconic image motioning him to roll down his window.

"Driver's license and vehicle registration, please." The stern male voice was deep and very business-like.

Fumbling around for his wallet, Alan continued drying off his face. He hurriedly found his registration and handed it out the window to this frightfully formidable figure. He then held up his billfold, which contained his driver's license for the officer's review.

"Take it out of the wallet, please, sir."

Immediately removing it from the leather sheath, Alan held it up for the lawman's scrutiny. Within a few seconds, the items were given back to him.

"What seems to be the problem, Mr. Browne?"

"Uh, nothing, sir."

"Why are you stopped along a busy highway?" His tone was still very formal.

"Well, that's a long story. You see, I got this parking ticket and . . ."

"Let me see that, sir."

"What were you doing in Oakland, Mr. Browne?"

"Uh . . . well, I, uh . . . was, uh . . ."

"Mr. Browne, why are you sitting in your car, obviously distraught, stopped on the side of a busy freeway? Do you need any help, sir?"

At this point in Alan's life, that was an extremely loaded question. He could go on for hours answering that inquiry. For him, the question with the shorter explanation would be, "Where don't you need any help, sir?" However, he just glanced over at the concerned officer and simply quipped, "Yes, sir . . . I need a new life."

Then, Alan noticed a small black leather strap attached to the gun belt of this inquisitive CHP official. To his pleasant surprise, he was sure, in the tiniest of letters running vertically along the length of the piece, was the word, **rojocci**. Alan leaned his head out of the window, tentatively pointing one finger at the thick tassel.

"Uh, officer, what's the word stamped on the short strap, right there?"

"It's **rojocci**, why?"

"Because I'm a part of the fellowship too and have been for nearly twenty years."

"Really? I only joined about six years ago. Some of the older guys I work with are in it as well. None of us for as long as you though."

The patrolman's tone had changed from quite cold and professional to quite warm and friendly. "Yeah, it has really kept us going. Sometimes this life of law enforcement isn't easy. It helps to be a part of a group where you are challenged to keep searching, to keep growing, to never quit no matter what. I couldn't do this job without knowing my fellow **rojoccians** were praying for me."

"**rojoccians**?"

"Yes sir, that's what we call each other."

"I've never heard of that before. I like it," smiled Alan.

"Well, the guys at the station made it up. We have Bible studies once a week and pray for each other. It sure does help with my walk with the Lord."

"It sure does. Thank you, officer."

"You're welcome, sir. Hey, do you mind me asking you a question?" The CHP leaned down to the window as he faced the oncoming traffic.

"Sure, go ahead," replied Alan, who was now feeling somewhat better about life and this situation with law enforcement.

"Do you know what the second '**o**' stands for?" he asked through a sheepish grin.

"Yep, it stands for the word 'overlooked'."

"Overlooked? Mr. Browne, thank you, sir. Now I only have two more letters to discover, and then I'll have the whole meaning."

"No, thank you, my friend, uh . . . my fellow **rojoccian**. You have helped me tremendously. More than you will ever know."

"Really? Well, I'm glad to be of assistance. You know, sir, one final word if I may . . . you mentioned that you needed a new life. I have found, for myself, I have to let go of my current one before I'm able to obtain the new one that's already waiting for me. Have a good day, sir, and safe travels."

The two shook hands, and with that they parted ways. Alan watched his mysterious **rojoccian** brother swing his motorcycle into the left lane and swiftly disappear around the next curve in the freeway.

The CHP officer's words rang in Alan's ears for several weeks. It appeared to him that he was unquestionably passing through a dark, stormy season of letting go. He wasn't at all sure what the following season would look like or even how long this one would last before the new buds of promise, the new life, would began to appear. But one thing he and Annalisa knew, the current cloudiness brought with it some rather severe winds of adversity. And those winds were rocking their little family's sailboat relentlessly. Alan had yet to learn the secret of tacking. By nautical definition, tacking is using the same winds that are pushing one backwards, to propel one forward. It is similar to an eagle in a storm, who instinctively knows the secret of using the

R. J. Graves, Jr.

turbulent winds to soar ever higher, to a new freedom, a new vista, a new altitude far above the turbulence below.

The next few weeks were a blur of activity, stress, and emotion for Alan and Annalisa. They closed on the sale of the bicycle shops, readied their home to be placed on the market, as well as prepared for the end of the school year ceremonies for their children. Working at the shops for the new owner, Alan sensed his time there was short. Annalisa felt particularly low, knowing their children wouldn't be attending these schools again. In fact, here it was the end of June, and she didn't even know what they would be doing next week. The continual uncertainty was taking its toll on her already sensitive emotional nerve endings. Adding to the tension, she had to assure the house was spotlessly clean. For at any moment, the phone could ring announcing yet another realtor's imminent arrival to show their house to a prospective buyer. For her, the stress was never ending. Just yesterday, she told Alan she was at the point where she would prefer to sell the house immediately, than have to go through another week of the uncertainty of not knowing when it would sell.

A few days later, Bill Barker informed Alan that his services were no longer needed. He had let Alan go exactly like he had done everything else, quickly, abruptly, and without emotion. Just like that, Alan was without an income. It was Friday, June 21, 1996. For the first time in nearly twenty years, Alan was officially unemployed. Once he arrived home that afternoon, he checked the balances in his bank accounts. They held barely thirty-four thousand. But now the clock was ticking, and with each tick another few dollars seeped out from his diminishing reservoir. The dollars that paid their home's mortgage, utilities, insurances, car payment, gasoline, food, clothes and more, were slowly leaking. They were draining continually downward like Junior's taxi cab metaphor had warned.

This all added to Alan's already fragile emotional state. He and Annalisa had frequent talks together trying to make some sense of all the change. So much so, Alan became convinced it was the only topic they could talk about. Finally one day, two weeks after being terminated, Alan exploded in a fit of anger. He shouted at Annalisa, at the children, and in a huff kicked a plastic clothesbasket sitting in the hallway. The booby trap became firmly lodged on his foot, halfway up his calf, looking more like a device for catching crabs than for hauling soiled laundry. This frustrated him all the more as he stormed out the back door, clothesbasket-boot and all, heading for the asylum that was his woodworker's shop. Once there, he continued his tirade flattening a box of nails with his old framing hammer, and finally, hitting a scrap piece of lumber on his workbench. He watched it, as if it were in slow motion, while it flew across the garage and straight through the closed back window, shattering glass all over the floor.

At that precise moment, he heard the garage door slam shut. He swung around to see Annalisa standing there with her arms folded, hips cocked to one side, "What in the world was that, Alan?" Her tone was a mixture of anger, impatience, and surprise. "Huh? What on earth were you thinking?!"

"I didn't intend for it to break the window. I was only blowing off some steam . . . .uh, frustration really."

"I'm not talking about the silly window, Alan!"

"I know, honey. I'm sorry. I just don't know what to do any more. I feel absolutely useless. I used to be a leader, a speaker at church, and an employer. People looked up to me, they respected me, and asked my opinion. Some even asked for my advice on struggles they were having in their marriages and with their children. And now, I'm nothing. Worse . . . I'm a middle-aged nothing. Nobody even thinks about me. It's like God has put me on a shelf to shrivel up and die."

"No, He hasn't, Alan. We're going through some changes, that's all. I know it has been difficult for you lately; it has been for me too. But shouting at us, breaking windows, and destroying laundry baskets isn't going to help anybody."

"I know, honey, I'm sorry. I need to get back to work. But I've been looking, and I can't find anything. Seems no one wants to hire an ex-bicycle shop owner who's in his forties. And this sitting around waiting for our house to sell is driving me batty."

"I understand, dear, but I've been doing it longer than you have, and I haven't kicked anything yet. Although to be honest, I've thought about it . . . more than once. Maybe we need a break? You know, get away for a weekend or something. That may be just what the doctor ordered, Alan. We haven't had a vacation in almost two years. Well, except for the time you were in Florida at the Morgan's cottage."

"That was no vacation. You can trust me on that one. There was a hurricane, for crying out loud," complained Alan.

"Yeah, I know, but at least you were able to go away. The kids and I haven't gone anywhere, not even to the beach, or the mountains, or, dare I say, Lake Tahoe?!"

"True," conceded Alan. "But we never had the money."

"What's our excuse now?"

"Oh, I don't know about that. We need the money to live on until I can find another job, open a business, or something."

"I'm not suggesting a month in Europe, Alan. Only a few days away to bring a fresh breeze into our stale atmosphere. You know what I mean?"

"Uh . . . kind of, but I'm not fond of your metaphor."

"Come on, how about we go to Yosemite for a few days? We all love it up there, and the mountain air would do us good."

"Honey, the lodging is so expensive, and even if we could get a campsite, we can't camp out because we sold all of our camping equipment," he explained.

"Oh, yeah, that's right. And staying in a hotel is out of the question. It's so expensive anymore having to get two rooms for our family. It would be nice if we could travel somewhere out of town and not have to pay for lodging, you know, somewhere scenic or interesting."

She sat down cross-legged on Alan's desk, staring at the ceiling, trying to come up with a nice trip for their family. She leaned back on her hands and her shoulder length hair softly cascaded down her upper back. Alan, who had been standing between the broken window and his workbench, looked in her direction. She was the absolute picture of loveliness. This was a scene he recognized as one he had gazed upon before. After a minute or so, he remembered where he first saw her framed like that. It was in Western Maryland on the summit of the mountain at the church retreat back in 1978. She was in the same exact position, basking in the warmth of the spring sunshine. He pulled up the memory as if it had happened yesterday.

"Man, Lord, I love this gal. She is all I have ever wanted. She's perfect, Dear Lord . . . at least she is to me anyway." He had slipped into his half-talking-half-praying thing.

Alan moved across the floor, his shoes making a scrunching sound on the broken glass. He stopped beside her and bent over to give her a kiss. "I love you, sweetheart. I'm so sorry for my outburst a few minutes ago. I'll do my best to make sure it never happens again, okay?"

Nodding her head slowly, she closed her eyes while puckering up her lips indicating she wanted another kiss. This time they lingered lovingly and deeply, recognizing certain kisses have definite meanings.

"Will you please forgive me, honey?" he whispered softly.

"Of course I do, my love," she sighed. "You never have to worry about that, but thank you for asking anyway."

"You're welcome. I'll talk to the kids as well. I don't want them thinking their dad is some kind of crazy, mad man or something."

"They don't think that, Alan. They love you and admire you. I know they think the world of their father. But I agree, it's always good to keep the channels clear. Although . . ."

"Although, what? Uh, oh, dare I ask?" bantered Alan.

"They may be much more forgiving, much more admiring, if their humble father arrived bearing an olive branch of peace when asking for their forgiveness." Her eyes were still closed, though she hadn't moved from the pose that she was sure delighted her husband.

"What olive branch? What are you talking about, you conniving woman, you?"

"Why, Alan Michael Browne, whatever are you referring to, sir?" She had now reverted to using a pitiful, fake Southern drawl that she believed Alan absolutely adored. She fluttered her eyelashes for emphasis.

"Oh, honestly, girl, you crack me up. What olive leaf? What do you mean?" Alan was, in fact, chuckling. No, he was more than chuckling; he was cracking up.

"Okay, Alan," she was back to her normal sweet tone. "Suppose you went in to talk with our completely devastated and vacation-deprived children, who, by the way, are probably still sobbing uncontrollably," she teased. "Then, after your most sincere and humble apology, you announce our family vacation. Now, don't you think that would go over well?" Her eyes were definitely open now, and she had swung around to plead her case with him face to face.

"Oh brother," he smirked, this time with a chuckle.

"What, darling husband?" she sniggled.

"Well, you know they would love it. But where can we go without paying for two rooms of lodging? I would guess that would be nearly two thousand dollars for one week, maybe more. Besides, I sincerely doubt they're crying. They're probably having a laugh knowing you followed me out to the garage and are giving me the verdict."

"You never know, our little angels might be . . ."

"Honey?!"

"Anyway, I was thinking . . ."

"Yes, my love?" interrupted Alan knowing she was determined to have her say one way or another.

"Well . . . how about Washington, DC?" she suggested while nodding her head.

"Whaaat?! Are you kidding me? DC is outrageously expensive!"

"We could stay at your parent's house," Annalisa argued. "I would guess they would feed us too. Well, maybe a meal or two anyway. Besides, your folks haven't seen the kids in what, almost two years? I think it's a great idea, Alan. What do you think?"

"Oh, I don't know, honey. We can't drive there. We'd have to fly, and that's incredibly expensive."

"Actually," admonished Annalisa confidently, "I read in the paper that a few of the airlines are in a price war or something. They're doing this ninety-nine dollar fare, uh, each way. That would only be a thousand dollars total, honey. That's a great deal. Let's do it, Alan. It would be so nice to see your folks, your brothers and sister, and all the cousins. Maybe we could have a big Browne family reunion in your parent's backyard, you know, like they used to do back when you guys were kids. Wouldn't that be great?"

"Yeah . . . it would. I really hate to spend the money at this point in our life. Although, I have to admit, it would be really great to visit with everyone. Hey, we could see Betsy too. Last time she wrote she mentioned she hadn't been feeling well. It would really be nice to see her?"

"She's a very special lady. That's for sure," agreed Annalisa.

"And who knows, I may even find a job there. I mean, I don't really want to move there or anything, but a job is a job. Maybe something would come up. I sure haven't found anything here," he sighed.

"Yes, that would be difficult, Alan. But God is on the throne, and He loves us. So I know we could be happy, even in Washington, DC." She allowed a grin to break across her face.

"Okay, then let's do some checking first. I'll call my parents and see how their schedules look. Then, I'll get ahold of Betsy to see if she would be up for a visit. Meanwhile, you contact the airlines. I would start first with United because we still have those frequent flyer miles cards. Report back here with your findings, and we'll compare notes before sitting down with the kiddos. If everything aligns, we'll go on a much needed vacation. How's that sound?"

Annalisa jumped up, threw her arms around his neck, and planted a huge kiss on his lips, which had quite a lingering effect. "Perfect." she smiled. "Just perfect!"

-eight-

Flying on the United Airlines wide body aircraft was a pleasure. Plenty of room and creature comforts made the lengthy flight enjoyable for every member of the Browne family. Before they knew it, they were on the ground at Dulles International Airport in Northern Virginia, looking for the baggage claim area.

Having just pulled their first suitcase off the luggage carousel, Alan heard someone behind him shout, "Welcome back, son!" He swung around to see his father, with arms wide open, walking toward him. As they hugged one another, Alan waved to his mother, who was already making the rounds, starting with their youngest, cute little Emily. She had continued hugging her way around the semi-circle ending with Annalisa when Alan saw two of their suitcases cruise by on the baggage conveyor. He tried to grab one, but before he could, his mother grabbed him.

"Come give your mother a hug, Alan," urged the elder Mrs. Browne. "It's been way too long, honey."

"But, Mom . . ." begged Alan pointing at their luggage, now bound for another lap on the suitcase merry-go-round. It was a vain effort as she now had a firm hold around her son's neck. He was somewhat glad himself to be back in the comfort of his loving mother's arms . . . even at his ripe old age of forty-one. She was correct, he decided, it had been way too long.

After finally retrieving all the various pieces of their baggage, each having completed more than one lap on the carousel, the entire Browne entourage headed out to the parking area. In an effort to avoid a scratch or ding on his new car, Alan's father had parked in a distant spot. After several minutes of walking in the hot, humid Virginia climate, all had worked up quite a sweat. When they finally arrived, Alan exclaimed in a loud voice, "Wow, when did you get this, Dad? What happened to the Browne family station wagon?"

"Well, son, it finally gave up the ghost or the transmission anyway. It was way too expensive to fix. So Mom and I went out last month and picked out this sporty number, a 1996 Toyota Camry."

Alan stood there half staring and half laughing at the brilliant silver metallic sedan. He was actually in somewhat of a state of shock as he had always known his parents to drive station wagons. In fact, he couldn't remember any family car they had owned that wasn't a station wagon of some size or variety. However, he understood with all of the kids grown, they really didn't need the extra space of a larger car.

"What a beautiful car, isn't it, Alan?" offered Annalisa with a smile.

"Uh, yeah, nice car, if we can all fit . . . a Toyota, eh, Dad?"

"Yeah, Alan. I remembered what good performance you got out of that old pickup truck of yours, so I thought I'd give them a try," explained his father.

"We love it. It's perfect for the two of us," added his mother.

"Yeah, I would hope, Mom. I mean, this is a really nice car."

"Well, everyone jump in," directed the family patriarch. "Alan, why don't you and Emily sit up front with me? I think we can all fit in if we squeeze a bit. I'll turn the air conditioner on."

There they were driving down the Dulles International Airport Access Highway on their way to Alan's parent's house. In addition to the three up front, Annalisa, Alan's mother, Julie, and Richard sat in the back seat along with five suitcases in a half closed, bungie-corded trunk. They were blistering down the road at less than forty miles an hour on a fifty-five mile an hour speed limit thoroughfare with the rear bumper no more than three inches above the roadway. They were quite the spectacle.

"Maybe we should have driven your LeSabre, dear?" Alan's father mentioned as he tried to find his wife in the rear view mirror.

"We'll drive it when we drop you kids at the airport to fly home," she laughed.

Everyone chuckled, but they were obviously relieved when they arrived at Alan's parent's home in Oakton thirty minutes later.

"Wow, you guys painted the house. When did you do that?" quipped Alan with a hint of an offended attitude. It gave the impression he thought his parents needed to ask his permission before making any improvements to his childhood home. "What else did you guys change?"

As they made their way to the guest bedrooms, Alan realized his parents had completed a lot of renovations since he had last visited. There were new carpets throughout, except in the kitchen and family room, which now displayed hardwood floors. All the rooms had been repainted and most had been redecorated, including Alan's old bedroom. He tossed their luggage upon his bed and plopped down beside it. Glancing around at what used to be familiar surroundings, he felt the strangest sensation. All traces of his influence were gone, removed, or painted over. It was as though, in this house, he had never existed.

"You okay, honey?" asked Annalisa, sitting down next to him with her arm draped over his shoulder.

"Strange," he sighed. "I just realized something. I lived in this room for several years, and there's not a shred of evidence that I was ever here. Honey, I don't want my life to be like that. I want it to count for something. For good, you know, to make a difference, if only for you, and our kiddos. I mean, I hope for more, but at least . . . for us."

She hugged him tight. "You are making a difference, my loving husband. It's hard to see sometimes, that's all."

"I hope so. I really hope so."

"Hey, Alan, why don't you give Betsy a call? You told her you would call when you got in. I know she's anxious to see you, and frankly, I'm looking forward to seeing her too."

"I'll give her a call in the morning. It's almost eight o'clock, and she's probably already getting ready for bed.

She's how old now? Seventy-five? Six?" he turned toward his sweet wife kissing her on the cheek. "I sure do love you. You truly are the love of my life." Then he gave her another kiss, although this time on the lips. She slid her arms around his shoulders as she kissed him back.

"I'm so glad we decided to do this, Alan. I feel better about our situation already."

"Yeah, I kind of do too," he yawned. "I will be listening closely to see if we get any direction out of this trip."

"You mean, for a job?"

"Well, yes, but also anything to give us a hint as to what we should do with the rest of our lives. A job is important, but it's not the only thing we should be considering here. I guess what I would like to say is, I really hope God brings some clarity on our current circumstances during our visit here."

"That would be nice," she acknowledged with a nod.

The next day was filled with activities and conversations as everyone was trying to catch up with one another. Alan's sister, Amy, and her family dropped by at lunch for a visit. She and her husband, Eric, had twin boys. They had tried for years to get pregnant but weren't successful. In a last ditch effort, they tried some new experimental drug. Nine months later, out popped twin boys. When their sons turned three years old, they felt two children were all they could handle and decided their family was complete. Although truth be told, Amy had always wanted a girl.

Later that afternoon, Alan, Annalisa, and their children borrowed his mother's car and drove around Oakton, including a stop at his old alma mater, Oakton High School, home of the Cougars. The children ran on the track competing in races like their father had for the school track team more than two decades earlier. Then, they ate dinner at Anita's Mexican Restaurant in the neighboring town of Vienna. Alan expressed to the family how Anita's had the best burritos on earth, and how it was a favorite eating spot for a couple of the local high schools after Friday night football games.

"Oh yeah, kids, I have many memories in this place. You know, I was thinking . . ." But before he could finish his sentence, he was interrupted by the waiter arriving with their burritos.

"Las placas son, muy caliente," warned the waiter.

"Yeah, be careful, kids. He said these plates are extremely hot. But as you are going to find out, it's some good eating. I think it's the green chili sauce they pour all over the burrito. But be careful, I got burned once." Alan chuckled and shook his head as he remembered a scene, years ago, which had taken place in this very restaurant.

"Kids," he started. "I was sitting by myself right over there by the big window. And over here," continued Alan pointing out a table across the room, "seated by herself, was a really cute gal."

"Dad!" barked Julie. "In case you hadn't noticed, Mom's sitting right beside you."

"This was years before I met your mother, honey. I think I was maybe a junior or senior in high school. Believe me, it was a long time ago, and your mother knows she has nothing to worry about, okay?"

"A long, long, long time ago," assured Annalisa with a smile and a wink in Julie's direction.

Julie nodded as she glanced at her mother.

"Anyway, to show you how hot these plates are, here, take a look at this scar?" Alan was pointing at a discolored mark on the underside of his right arm an inch or two above his wrist.

"I was dining at that table and my seat was the one up close to the window on my right. I had just cut a bitesize piece of my pork and bean burrito and scooped it up with my fork. I glanced around the room and noticed this attractive girl about my age smiling at me. So I did what all red-blooded American males would do, I smiled back. As we were continuing in this assessing-the-possibilities posture, I began to notice a searing pain on my right arm. I was immediately made aware that the extreme discomfort was caused by the sizzling heat of the plate upon which my burrito was served. No sooner had I awakened to this burning revelation, than I quickly thrust my arm upward off the scalding culprit and inadvertently launched the benign bite of burrito, which had been resting on my fork, as a missile of my self-imposed humiliation. This sauce covered, two inch square piece found it's temporary landing spot on the plate glass window about three feet above my head."

Annalisa and the kids had been giggling, but at this point they broke into a full-fledged howl.

"Yeah, yeah, I know it's funny, go ahead and laugh," joked their self-effacing father. "But it gets better. You see, while I was using the glass of ice water to cool down the burn on my arm, I glanced over at the cute gal, who was, to my further chagrin, finding my painful predicament rather humorous. As my attention was diverted toward her, I accidentally turned my arm to view my burn, pouring the contents of my glass into my lap. Startled by my chilly shower, I jumped up sending ice and burrito flying in all directions. I looked down to survey the damage—it appeared as though I had wet myself."

Now, Annalisa and the kids were practically falling out of their chairs. They were laughing so hard that some had tears running down their cheeks, and others were holding their stomachs, begging their father to stop. Mercilessly, he continued.

"So I took my napkin and tried to dry myself, but it was fruitless. The clearly conspicuous mark was embarrassingly evident, at least until it dried. Meanwhile, the slippery piece of saucy burrito had begun to make its way down the window leaving a two inch wide, slug-like trail in its wake. It looked really bad. So I took my damp cloth napkin and tried to wipe the window clean. The result of my feeble effort was a two foot wide, swirly smear. I felt terrible. I glanced back at my prospective acquaintance only to find that she was gone. Although, the rest of the patrons were watching with much delight as this humorous scene unfolded. I turned around just in time to see the cute gal outside. Stopping in front of the smeared window, she shook her head, pointed at my lap, and walked off snickering."

"Stop, Dad. Please, stop!" bellowed Richard.

"Yeah, Dad, I think I hurt myself laughing," roared Julie who was wiping tears from her eyes.

Emily sat there giggling uncontrollably with tears rolling down her cheeks. She was bellowing her deep belly guffaw, which always had the wonderful effect of making everyone else laugh even louder.

"True story," smiled Alan as he glanced around the table at his precious family, who were still holding their sides in joyous agony.

"Really, Alan?" laughed Annalisa.

"Yeah," he chuckled. "That was a real banner day for this would-be Don Juan. I didn't even get to finish my burrito." He then shoveled another bite of beans and rice into his mouth while he looked around at his family still struggling to compose themselves. "What's the matter? Eat up, you guys!"

After dinner, they piled back into Grandma Browne's Buick and drove down to Arlington to do a bit of drive-by-reminiscing, as Alan called it, before stopping at the Gifford's Ice Cream Parlor. Both Alan and Annalisa thought it important for the children to see some of the significant spots their parents had frequented during the formative period of their relationship. This way, when discussing something in the future, the kids would have a memory to hook the conversation to. Their first stop would be the church parking lot where they initially met.

Alan pulled the car a few feet into the lot and stopped. "Kids, you know what this is?"

"Your church?" guessed Richard.

"No, well . . . uh, kind of, but that's not why we paused here for a second. This is the exact spot where Mom and I first laid eyes on one another. She was a very pretty, petite runner from Walnut Creek, California, who had been introduced to me by her friend, Rebecca Jones. I had just thrown their luggage into the back of the church van when I turned around and saw her for the very first time." Alan reached across Emily, seated in the front seat between them, to hold Annalisa's hand.

"Seems like so long ago, honey," remarked Annalisa.

"Well, kind of, I mean, it's been about seventeen years or so," he smiled at her, looking over the top of the shorter Emily. "I love you now more than ever, honey."

"Me too, Alan," she agreed.

"Alright, you two," barked Julie impatiently. "How about the ice cream you promised us?"

"Well, I guess we don't have to worry about her and any would-be Don Juan!" laughed Annalisa.

"Yeah, thank the Lord for that." agreed Alan.

Turning the car around and before heading the family toward Gifford's, he made three quick stops, explaining to the children the significance of each spot.

The next morning the family slept in until nearly ten o'clock. Obviously, the jet lag along with the difference in time zones had finally caught up with them. They staggered, one by one, out to the kitchen table where they were greeted by the children's pleasant, albeit, overly cheerful Grandma Browne. She had blueberry pancakes, sausage patties, and milk waiting for them.

"What are y'all doing today?" she asked with her usual school teacher's high decibel volume.

"Mom, with all due respect, remember the Bible says, 'A cheerful greeting too early in the morning is considered a curse.'"[1] Alan was teasing, although his tone sounded serious.

"My dear son, I highly doubt anyone in the Bible would consider ten-thirty in the morning too early."

"Okay, Mom, but maybe a bit quieter, please?" he smiled.

"Sure, honey. So what are your plans?" she whispered with a smile, glancing in Annalisa's direction.

"We're meeting Betsy at her house at two o'clock," replied Alan with a wry grin. "I would imagine, depending on how she's feeling, we may eat dinner with her, if that's okay with you, Mom?"

"Oh, that's fine, honey. I needed to know if y'all wanted dinner here. Now remember, Saturday we're having everyone over for a Browne family gathering."

"That sounds so nice, Mom," affirmed Annalisa. "We're planning on being here. Looking forward to it, huh, Alan?"

"Yes, ma'am," Alan mumbled with his mouth full of blueberry pancakes.

"Oh, good," exclaimed his mother. "Well, y'all have a nice time at Betsy's then."

"Thanks, Mom," waved Alan as his mother left the kitchen. "And thanks so much for the pancakes too."

"Oh, you're welcome. I need to run to the market now; I'll see y'all later tonight."

Alan and Annalisa decided to bring the children along for their visit with Betsy. They left early because Alan wanted to drop by the bicycle shop where he had worked years ago. Upon entering the shop, he was greeted by the owners, Frank, Carol, and Bruce. Frank and Carol had married shortly after graduating from Georgetown, where they had met. Bruce was a number of years their junior and had spent most of his twenties in Europe on the road racing circuit. He wasn't good enough for the likes of the Tour de France teams but was very strong by American standards. They all looked very much the same as years earlier, maybe a bit older. After catching them up-to-date on most of what he had been doing the last few years, Alan inquired about the possibility of employment.

"We really don't have anything right now, Alan. Are you thinking of moving back to the area?" asked Frank with a surprised look.

"I'm not quite sure, Frank. Things are a bit dry in the Bay Area, and since we are here visiting, I thought to ask. Do you know if any other shops are hiring? I can manage multiple shops."

"I don't think so. I'm guessing everyone is kind of waiting to see how this election goes. Is it going to be another four years of Bill Clinton, or is Bob Dole going to be our new President?"

"Yeah, I think that's what some of the employers are doing in California as well."

"Why don't you start up another shop, Alan?" asked Carol.

"I can't. When I sold my shops, I signed a non-compete agreement, which prohibits me from opening a bicycle shop in California for seven years. I can't even work in one in the Bay Area for two years."

"Man, Alan, why on earth did you sign that agreement?" Bruce inquired.

"Because I was going to lose my shops anyway," lamented Alan.

"Oh, wow, I'm sorry to hear that, man," consoled Bruce.

"Yeah, it's been a really tough couple of years," answered Alan. "But I couldn't keep them anyway, so I was glad for the opportunity to sell them."

"Did you come out alright?" asked Frank with a nod of his head indicating he hoped Alan made some money on the sale.

"Well, okay, I guess, but not much to show for sixteen years of hard work. Really, I practically gave them away. Although, I must say, I'm grateful for what we do have." With this, he put his arm around Annalisa, who had been quietly listening while keeping an eye on their children. They were each trying out the new bikes on the showroom floor.

Glancing at her husband, Annalisa turned to their three bike-store-owner friends. "We really need to get going. It has been so nice seeing you, if only for a short visit. Alan, you told Betsy we would be there by two o'clock."

"You better hurry," advised Carol. "It's five of."

They hustled the kids into Grandma's old four door LeSabre, and as they pulled out of the bike shop parking lot, waved good-bye to Frank, Carol, and Bruce.

"They're good people, honey," expressed Alan. "If they knew of any openings, they would have told me. I'm really kind of shocked that in this area business isn't booming. Perhaps it's a temporary lull like Frank mentioned. Boy, I hope we find something soon."

"We will, Alan. God's got it all in control, and His timing is perfect," she further encouraged with a smile. "It's just a matter of timing . . . His timing."

Without taking his eyes off the road, Alan acknowledged her kind words with a nod. The drive from the bike shop to Betsy's house was no more than six to seven minutes. Alan started immediately counseling his children to remember their manners and to act politely, as well as respectfully around Betsy. Annalisa chimed in here and there with her own motherly tone to impress upon the children the importance of their father's instructions. They turned the final corner, and Betsy's home came into view.

"Now remember, you guys, your absolute best behavior, got it?" Alan was using his firm fatherly voice and was also displaying a stern, yet loving expression.

"Yes, sir," came the reply in unison.

Jumping out, Alan made his way around to the front of the car. He stopped to allow himself to take in the full view of Betsy's home. Nothing had changed in the almost three years since he had last visited. The white brick exterior was still beautiful. In contrast, the shutters and front door remained a deep crimson, except maybe a brighter shade than he had recalled. The screened porch was on the left side of the house and the detached white clapboard sided garage stood on the right. The matching white picket fence, which enclosed the entire yard, appeared just like he had remembered. In fact, he realized while he stood there taking in the idyllic scene, the only things that had changed were the trees and shrubbery, which had all grown somewhat larger.

"She has such a beautiful home, doesn't she, kids?" asked their mother as they started up the pea gravel driveway with the strip of bright green grass down the center.

"You hear that?" giggled Emily referring to the scrunching sound her sneakers made as she walked up the driveway.

"That's funny," whispered Alan to Annalisa, "that was something I too noticed the first time I ever visited her home. It was back in the late 1970s when her husband, Stanley, had recently suffered a stroke. I had come over to see how he was getting along. Wow, memories are peculiar things aren't they? Walking up this driveway, they are flooding into my thoughts. Look, there's the picnic table still sitting on the patio by the garage."

"What's special about that, honey?" she whispered back.

"That's where Betsy first told me all about The **rojocci** Fellowship. My head was literally spinning that night. I couldn't believe what she was telling me. It was absolutely incredible. It was like she could see inside my skull, into my thoughts, or something. I mean, today I recognize she was more experienced at discerning human nature than I was. But at the time, I was completely blown away."

Annalisa turned toward Alan and admonished, "Now, honey, you . . ."

At that moment, the screen door swung open and out stepped Betsy with arms wide open. "Welcome, welcome, my sweet, precious, little cherubs!"

nine

Well into her seventies, Betsy Taft was one of those rare friends who could pick up the conversation where it had left off, even if it had been several years previous. She also had the wonderful grandmotherly quality that made all feel so very welcome.

They entered through the wooden screened door, at the side of the house, directly into her tiny kitchen. Betsy urged them forward into the dining room where chocolate chip cookies and milk were waiting for the children.

"What do you say kids?" urged Annalisa.

"Thank you, Mrs. Taft," came the cheerful reply in unison.

"Now, children," she chided with a smile. "Please call me, Miss Betsy, okay? Please don't call me Mrs. Taft. That makes me feel older than I already am, and frankly, that's old enough." She chuckled as she patted Emily softly on the head.

"Here's a plate for you, Annalisa, dear."

"Oh, thank you, Betsy. You didn't have to go to all this trouble."

"Aww, it's no trouble at all, sweetie. I'm so happy to be serving you in my home. It's one of those simple joys of life, you know? Here's yours, Alan."

Alan glanced down at the plate of cookies and quickly recognized them as his favorite. "Oatmeal raisin?" he cheered. "How did you remember these are my favorite?"

"Oh, I may be old, but not that old," she countered with a gleam in her eye.

Alan gave her a big hug as he nodded in agreement, his mouth full of cookie.

"Come on in the parlor, dear, where we can talk," she suggested motioning with her free hand. "I want to hear how my sweet friends have been getting along."

During the next half hour or so, Alan, with Annalisa adding in some color commentary, replayed all the events over the last few years leading up to their current trip back to Virginia. He summarized the story of his unsuccessful search for employment in California and what wasn't looking too promising in the Washington, DC area either. He was attempting to stay positive and encouraged, reminding himself that the slippery trail of despondency never ends in a good place.

"Are you willing to go anywhere?" inquired Betsy.

"Yes, ma'am . . . uh, well, I think I am anyway," replied Alan tentatively. "Why?"

"Well, God will always make a way. Sometimes He tests us to determine our willingness to do whatever He may have planned. I was thinking about the area down along the Gulf of Mexico where you visited last October. You told me God, kind of, spoke to you there. I think you called it an awakening, right, dear?"

"Yes, ma'am, He definitely got my attention."

"Maybe He's calling you in that direction if nothing is opening up anywhere else. What do you think, sweetie?"

Alan glanced over at Annalisa, who wasn't looking enthusiastic about the suggestion. He turned to Betsy and replied, "Maybe. You never know, I guess."

"Something to pray about," offered Betsy. Then, she changed the subject. "Maybe the children would like to play outside? I'd guess it's starting to cool down now. We could sit at the picnic table. How does that sound?"

"Sounds perfect!" responded Annalisa with a smile.

"Wonderful! I'll bring a pitcher of iced tea."

"Let me give you a hand with that, Betsy," offered Annalisa as she helped Betsy to her feet. The two women then started for the kitchen.

"Come on, kids. Let's go out back," announced Alan while he held open the screen door. They all headed out into the warm July afternoon.

Following them out into the well shaded back yard, he strolled over to the picnic table. Choosing the exact spot where he had sat all those years ago, Alan gazed around the almost immaculate setting. His mind began to wander down through those nearly forgotten memories, now once again renewed. It was like his thoughts were walking along the shoreline of the vast sea of his memories. Each time a wave would lap across the sand, yet another scene came flooding into his thoughts. He turned to look across the table, and there in his mind he could picture a much younger Betsy wearing her flower print housedress, explaining to him the wonders of The **rojocci** Fellowship. It had been such an incredible time of discovery. He remembered continually feeling a unique sense of awe and anticipation. He hadn't felt something like that in almost a year—since he had returned from his trip to the Morgan's cottage along the Gulf Coast, near Pensacola.

"Maybe Betsy was right," he thought. "Perhaps we should consider that area. I mean, at least look into it. I wonder if I should give Joey a call in the next few days."

The wooden screened door slammed shut. Alan twisted around to see Betsy and Annalisa walking across the beautifully manicured green lawn, carrying a tray of glasses along with pitchers of iced tea and lemonade. He marveled at how comfortable they were with one another, almost like a mother and daughter. They were laughing and talking as they approached the table. He glanced back at the kids who were inquisitively studying Betsy's vegetable garden.

"Okay, if they're in there, Betsy?"

"Oh, sure, they're fine, Alan," assured Betsy.

After the cool drinks had been poured and the children were playing again, Alan turned to Betsy. He had been concerned for his dear friend ever since learning she hadn't been well. "How have you been feeling?"

"Oh, I'm fine. I mostly have good days . . . along with a few difficult ones. But each day I get a little closer to seeing our Lord and my Stanley," Betsy confided with a grin. "It certainly could be a lot worse. Like I said, most days I just feel like Betsy."

"I'm so glad to hear that. When you told me you had been ill for several months, I naturally thought the worse."

"Oh, now, Alan, you two sweeties have so much more to be concerned about than worrying about an old coot like me," she tittered as she motioned toward their three little ones playing among the azalea bushes.

"Well, that may be partly true, Betsy," concurred Annalisa as she gently put her arm around Betsy's somewhat frail shoulder. "However, we still love you very much and consider you our dear friend."

"That's so kind," she replied patting Annalisa's hand. "But there is so much more to life than worrying about me. Besides, the doctor told me that folks with my condition can sometimes last for years."

"What exactly is your condition?" asked Annalisa with a concerned look on her face.

"Oh, it's old age," smirked Betsy.

The three friends shared a quiet chuckle. Then, Alan changed the topic of their conversation. Ever since hearing from Joey about an apparent **rojocci** conference somewhere in Ohio, he had wanted to quiz Betsy about her knowledge of it.

"Hey, Betsy?" started Alan. "Are you aware of some sort of conference involving members of the **rojocci** fellowship?"

"Why, yes, Alan. Stanley and I attended that years ago. I believe it was down in the Shenandoah Valley, in Lexington . . . or was it Stanton? I'm sorry, dear. It was some time ago."

"No, no, this was a conference in Ohio back in the 1860s," explained Alan.

"Oh . . . well, no, Alan. We only got together with some friends back in the 1960s . . . but it wasn't in Ohio. It was in Virginia."

"Uh, Betsy, I'm sorry. What I meant to say was, have you heard of a conference in Ohio back in the last century . . . in 1866? The location was in a town named Pfeiffer Station. Have you heard of anything like that?" Alan had raised his voice a bit in volume and had slowed his speech to assure she heard him this time.

"Oh, I'm so sorry, Alan. I just got these new hearing aids last week, and I keep forgetting to turn them up. I usually don't need the volume higher because I'm inside the house. But sitting out here with all this background noise, I was having some difficulty making out what you were saying, especially at the end of sentences where you, like most folks, get a little quieter." She held her thumb and forefinger close together to indicate what she considered, a little.

Alan nodded and started to repeat himself again for Betsy's benefit. "Back in the 1800s in Pfeiffer Station, Ohio . . ."

"I heard you the second time, dear," smiled Betsy. "I turned up the volume on them. There's this tiny dial on the outside. It's real easy to adjust them."

"Wow, Betsy, I didn't even know you wore hearing aids," marveled Annalisa as she gazed at the side of Betsy's head. "I can't even see them."

"Oh, they're there, honey. You can trust me on that. But they are so tiny I was actually afraid I'd lose them. So one day at the pharmacy, I asked the girl behind the counter if she knew what other folks do with their helpers."

"Their what?" interrupted Alan.

"Helpers . . . I call them my helpers because they help me hear others."

Both Alan and Annalisa smiled, thinking it was a clever title for her hearing aids.

"Anyway," continued Betsy, "she suggested buying a roll of the 35mm film and saving the plastic case it is stored in. She said that if I don't have that type of camera, which I don't, I could give the film to a friend or maybe just throw it away."

"That's a very good idea," declared Annalisa. "Is it working well?"

"Yes, it's perfect. Do you all need any 35mm film? It's black and white though. That was the least expensive."

"Yes," nodded Annalisa. "That's the type of camera we are actually traveling with on this trip. We'd be happy to pay you for it?"

"Oh, no, dearie. You can have it; I was going to throw it out anyway."

"No, we'll pay you for it," affirmed Annalisa as she glanced across at Alan, who was becoming a bit impatient while this little film negotiation drifted onward. "I think Alan wanted to talk to you about something, Betsy."

"Oh, yes, Alan, about that conference in Ohio," echoed Betsy as she gazed up through the trees into the hazy Virginia sky. "Stanley and another man . . . I believe his name was Sherman. Yes, I remember his name was Sherman Wilkins. He, or was it Stanley, had discovered a document indicating there had been a conference shortly after the Civil War in a small tavern somewhere in Ohio. Although I can't remember the name of the town, it was definitely in Ohio. I do remember that."

Alan interrupted, "Pardon me, Betsy, I thought you had told me The rojocci Fellowship never had any meetings, conferences, or anything like that because it was more a set of principles, than any kind of actual organization."

"Oh, they never have any regular meetings, dearie. However, sometimes in cases of extreme conditions they may convene a meeting. Like the situation right after World War II. A few of the brethren decided to announce the need for a gathering. Remember, that's when they decided to change the spelling from rojocki to the current rojocci. It had to do with those folks who were building something they called kingdom halls. Since the 'k' stood for the word 'kingdom' in our acronym, they called a meeting to change the spelling to avoid any confusion. But that was a one-time meeting, Alan. There's no structure, no schedule or anything."

"How would they have gotten the word out to the others?" asked Annalisa. "I mean, there must have been thousands of them scattered all around the country. How would they have notified everyone of an upcoming meeting?"

"Oh, I imagine they would have used word of mouth just like they would today," figured Betsy. "How did you discover all the letters of the acronym, Alan? It's the same thing . . . God's leading."

"Okay, I can see that, Betsy," agreed Alan.

Betsy smiled.

"However," he continued, "word of mouth is a slow moving train. I mean, it's like a rookie novelist trying to sell his first book to the public . . . it's the trickle equation. You know, a mighty river starts with a drop of rain."

"Yes, I agree. But in our technologically advanced world, folks call you today to schedule a meeting next week or perhaps next month. In those days, if they decided a meeting was needed, they would select a date a year or more in advance, not the following week because few would know about it and few would be in attendance."

"Hmmm . . . there's something very interesting, Alan," added Annalisa. "Didn't you tell me the date of the meeting in Ohio was in August of 1866?"

"Yes, that's right, my love, why?"

"Well, if what Betsy is telling us is accurate, then something must have stirred up a number of those **rojoccians** about a year or so prior to that date. What could that have been?"

After pausing a few seconds, Annalisa spoke up again, "Wait . . . that would have been right after the conclusion of the Civil War. Perhaps something was going on throughout the country that had them concerned . . . I mean, other than repairing all the damage from the battles."

At that moment, Emily ran up to her mother and whispered something in her ear. Annalisa turned to her daughter, "It's alright, honey. I'll have Daddy talk to him. You go back and play, okay?"

Alan, who had been deep in thought, glanced across at Annalisa. "Trouble?"

Annalisa nodded. But not wanting to parade their dirty laundry in front of Betsy responded, "We can talk about it later."

Alan looked over toward their three children playing together. "Richard, you be nice to your sister if you want me to be nice to you when we get home, understand?"

The three adults seated at the picnic table heard a faint, "Yes, sir."

"Come here, son. Emily, you come too."

After a few quiet words from their father and a hug for each other, the two siblings headed back to the vegetable garden. "Love you guys!" Alan called out to them. "We won't be much longer, kids."

At this point, Annalisa gently grabbed Betsy's hand and gasped, "I figured out why they had the meeting. Alan, didn't you mention to me that Joey told you the meeting was called a Unity Convention or something?"

Nodding his head, Alan said nothing. It had taken him years, but he had learned when Annalisa was trying to explain something to him, he should remain quiet. Because if he didn't, it would either take her much longer to describe what she was thinking, or she would forget altogether and end up frustrated. And that wasn't good . . . for her or for him.

"Alright, so it took place about a year or so after the Civil War. The reason for the date was because something had occurred which concerned them. Alan, what did you just do for our kids, for Richard and Emily?"

"Uh, I don't know . . . threaten Richard so he wouldn't annoy Emily?"

"Well, yes, but more importantly, you helped them have unity. There was some 'damage' that had occurred in their relationship, and through a miniature conference there came some new level of unity."

"Why, of course, dear," agreed Betsy. "I vaguely remember Stanley telling me something along those lines. He and Sherman Wilkins had determined there must have been a mammoth division among the faith after the great conflict between the North and the South. In other words, the country had been horribly divided during the war. With devoted Christians on both sides, I would guess the church, as a whole, had experienced some tremendously difficult inner turmoil as well. I'm sure after four years of fighting there was some bad blood on both sides. Perhaps this meeting in Ohio had been called to try and find some sort of common ground, to bring some healing, some harmony, some sort of unity."

"Betsy?" asked Alan. "Do you have any of those letters that Sherman Wilkins sent to Stanley?"

"No, I'm sorry, dear. I got rid of most of those things years ago. Remember, my Stanley's been with Jesus almost twenty years now. The only mementos I kept are some photos of us together and his letters from when he was in the Korean War."

"Nothing more?" chided Alan with a smile. "Not even a little leather satchel in the bottom of a handmade wooden tool box?"

"Oh, no, dearie, I gave those things away long ago. Oh, Alan, you rascal," she laughed, "I gave those things to you! You are such a little stinker!"

While they all chuckled, Alan gazed off and allowed his mind to wander back to those days, many years ago. He had

R. J. Graves, Jr.

surely grown to love and appreciate this dear, saintly woman. Betsy was someone he had admired from the first day he'd met her, shortly after her husband, Stanley, had suffered a stroke. Stanley was a much older carpenter, who had worked with Alan on his first full time job. He'd told Alan of the "quiet road" and the somewhat mysterious **rojocci** Fellowship. After Stanley died, Alan had discovered a leather satchel in the bottom of Stanley's handmade wooden toolbox. This discovery had led Alan on the lifelong adventure of exploring and unearthing the marvelous world of insights and revelations that had changed him from within. And now, with this new clue, the possibility of another breakthrough whet his appetite for more.

"Betsy, I know a man named Joey Hinote. He and his wife, Pam, and their two daughters live in a petite village outside of Pensacola, Florida, called Hurst Hammock. Joey's a few years older than I am. He's taller with less hair, and what hair he does have is entirely grey. Well, uh . . . seriously, he's a good friend whose been a **rojoccian** for more than ten years." Alan paused for a second to assure Betsy was following his monologue.

"A few weeks back, Joey was cleaning out his parents' house, preparing it to become a rental, when he found a trunk in the attic. Inside this trunk, he discovered a letter indicating a Conference of Unity, which took place in a town in Ohio named Pfeiffer Station. The meeting occurred over a five day period in August of 1866. Now, it would seem reasonable to me that something must have been agreed upon, and a document or paper of some sort would have been created as a result of that historic conference. Have you any remembrance of hearing anything like that, Betsy?"

"No," she pondered. "Nothing reliable anyway, only rumors. I'm sorry, Alan."

"What do you mean 'rumors' Betsy?" probed Annalisa softly.

"Well, you know, dearie, something may have been mentioned over dinner one night or at a party somewhere but nothing significant. Nothing I would consider important enough to remember."

"Uh, could you give me an example?" requested Alan gently.

"Well, let me think," paused Betsy. "Nothing really stands out, dear, I'm sorry."

"Just a minute ago," urged Alan, "you mentioned something was talked about over dinner one night. What were you referring to?"

"Oh, I guess I was thinking about the time Stanley and I went out to dinner with this nice couple at a restaurant on Capitol Hill. I was trying to get to know the wife, so I wasn't really paying attention to the conversation Stanley and Sherman were having but . . ."

"Wait!" barked Alan. "Did you say the husband's name was Sherman?"

"Why, yes, dear," replied Betsy somewhat surprised at Alan's abrupt interruption.

"Was it the same Sherman that Stanley communicated with regarding the **rojocci** meeting in Ohio?"

"Yes, but that wasn't until a few years later. However, I do remember, as I was trying to concentrate on the conversation Roberta and I were having, overhearing the word **rojocci** at some point. It's not a word that goes unnoticed, but I didn't think it was anything important, not at the time, anyway."

"Really?" quipped Alan. "Nothing of any magnitude comes to mind?"

"No, not really, uh now wait a minute. Maybe . . . yes, yes, there's a little something that comes to mind, Alan. Yes, we were driving home from dinner, just Stanley and I, in our old Rambler station wagon."

Betsy paused as if she was trying to see something more clearly, something deep within her memory. "Yes, I remember now, we were on Key Bridge almost to Lee Highway. I asked Stanley what he and Mr. Wilkins had been discussing all evening and he responded that Sherman was convinced there must have been a big meeting in Ohio sometime soon after the close of the Civil War. Stanley told me that Sherman had received a letter from a woman in New England in response to his inquiry. She had inherited evidence of the meeting from her grandfather's estate back in the 1940s. At least, I think that's accurate. I'm sorry, Alan, my memory isn't what it used to be."

"That's okay, Betsy," consoled Annalisa. "Don't worry about it."

"Betsy," pried Alan. "Was there anything else?"

"Alan!" blurted Annalisa. "She already told you . . ."

"It's okay, dearie," comforted Betsy as she patted Annalisa's hand. "I love when I see a fire in Alan. I believe the Lord likes it too . . . to some degree," she smiled. "There should be more of us who are willing to seek out the mysteries of the Scriptures. In my humble opinion, that is exactly what The **rojocci** Fellowship was established to do—to develop a level of desire in each of us to continue searching the Scriptures and seeking His face always . . . and to never, ever give up."

Annalisa gave Betsy a long hug while the two of them gazed, with great fondness, across the table at Alan. Then, as she began to say something, she kissed Annalisa on the cheek.

"Alan, let me tell you something very important. You know, in every generation God has saved for Himself a remnant, a people after His own heart. Alan, Annalisa, I believe God has the two of you picked out for something very special. And listen, all you have to do is cooperate with Him. He has promised to do all the rest. I know your path, your direction may not seem clear right now, but He's got you in the palm of His hand, and to Him that path is perfectly straight. All you have to do is follow."

"I'm not sure what you're getting at, Betsy," bemoaned Alan. "We're trying to follow Him, to look to Him for answers. I mean, we're in a very serious situation right now, and if I don't find a job soon, we're . . ."

"Alan?" Betsy's tone sounded like admonishment, but her eyes were full of love. She waited to continue as she glanced back and forth from Alan to Annalisa and back to Alan.

"My sweet dears, I have been young, and now I am old, and I have never seen His people forsaken, or His children begging for bread.[1] He will provide. That's not your concern; that's His. It will come at exactly His precise timing, and when it does, be ready. Please hear my heart, my precious ones. His eyes are roving to and fro throughout the whole earth looking for those whose hearts are completely committed to Him."[2] Betsy paused for a moment as she brushed down her floral housedress.

"Yes, Betsy, what is it?" tugged Annalisa gently.

"Alan, Annalisa," she continued, "I've been sensing the need to say something to the two of you for years but never have. I think now is the proper time, so here goes," she confided with a firm tone.

"Yes?" urged Alan.

"Now, please, hear my heart on this," implored Betsy. "There are plenty of folks who study the physical body, its systems, problems, and diseases. They know how to train it to lift great weights, run long distances, jump high and far, or even swim enormous distances across open seas. There too, no doubt, are an almost equal number who make it their life's work to figure out all the deep recesses of the mind, its problems, and processes, as well as the emotions and how to deal with their forceful influences. They make it their life's calling to manifest all the mysteries of the hidden soul of man."

"But where, my dear cherished ones," posed Betsy, "can you find just one among a million, perhaps hundreds of millions, who is an expert in the spiritual realm? One who knows our great God and the Lord Jesus along with the ways and thoughts of the Holy Spirit? Where is there a guide, an interpreter, a lover of God, who first seeks His kingdom and His righteousness?[3] One who would be willing to help those who are seeking the face of the Lord and searching the Scriptures? That, my precious brother and sister, is a person more valuable than all the gold this world can hold. If there are two, and they are married, well . . . that's a cord that's not easily broken and can be used mightily by God."

Sitting stone-still across from Betsy, Alan listened to her every word as if God Himself was speaking directly through her. He sensed a most unique mixture of joy and conviction. His heart burned within him, yet he uttered no words. After several seconds more, which actually seemed like minutes, he glanced toward Annalisa and nodded slowly.

"Thank you so much for those kind and encouraging words, Betsy," breathed Annalisa with tears in her eyes. "You don't know how much they mean to us right now."

"Yes, thank you, Betsy. We love you so very much," agreed Alan.

"Oh, you're welcome. I felt I needed to say something, you know, to help. It's the only way I can assist any more, since I have this infirmity."

"Yes, ma'am, I could tell you sensed a need to say something, and thank you, Betsy. We really needed to hear those words because we are lacking direction at this point in our lives. We sure don't know where to turn next, you know, which way to go from here," confessed Alan as he slowly shook his head.

"Oh, I think we do now, honey," smiled Annalisa as she hugged Betsy again. The two women, who were seated across from him, were nodding their heads in unison.

"What? Where?" Alan asked with a look of astonishment on his face.

"The Gulf Coast of Florida, my sweet husband. I think you should give your friend Joey Hinote a call."

~ten~

After getting the children settled into their beds for the night, Alan and Annalisa hustled down to the family room, so they could discuss with his parents where they thought God might be leading them. They found his folks as Alan had always remembered. His mother was relaxing, reading a book on the sofa, while his father lounged on the recliner behind the newspaper or 'paper wall' aptly named long ago by his wife. Upon recognizing their presence in the room, the two elder members of the Browne family put aside the reading material to give their undivided attention to the middle-aged members.

The conversation was quite lively, although, as was typical, Alan's mother did most of the talking for both of his parents. His father usually spoke only if he had something he felt was important enough to say; a quality he had acquired, no doubt, after countless meetings in his career as an architect. The informal gathering lasted for nearly two hours when Alan's father broke a lull in the discussion and made what all considered to be a very pertinent suggestion. He had dropped the footrest down on his recliner and leaned forward. Over the years, the entire Browne family had learned that when he went through this ritual he was usually about to say something profound.

"Why not try an experiment?" he proposed. "Why not take a trip down there and see if it is at all feasible, if any opportunities open up. It may be something completely impractical or . . . it may be what you're supposed to do. Regardless, you'll never know unless you check it out."

"Hmmm . . . I don't know, Dad. It's a long trip from California. I'm thinking it would be very expensive."

"Then take the trip from here, son. You can use your mother's car. She doesn't return to teaching for another month or so." He then turned to his wife, "Okay, with you, dear?"

"Sure . . . well, I guess so. I'm not sure the children could handle such a long trip though. What do you think, Annalisa?"

Before Annalisa could answer her mother-in-law, Alan's father responded for her, "Look, honey, the grandkids could stay here with us. You're not working now, and I have a bit of vacation time I haven't used. Let's have them stay here and give this young couple a second honeymoon, uh . . . well, you know what I mean. What do you say, dear?"

"Oh, I think that would be wonderful," exclaimed Alan's mother as she clapped her hands together. "Just perfect!"

"Then it's all settled," concluded his father. "When are you two lovebirds leaving?"

Although the four of them were laughing, Alan's insecure emotions were beginning to flood his thoughts. To him, this whole situation was spinning out of control, moving too fast. He wasn't at all comfortable with driving a thousand miles away while leaving his little ones here. His mind was starting to run through all the terrible scenarios that could possibly arise.

"I don't think it will work," argued Alan. "Our airline tickets are for a return flight this coming Saturday, July 20th."

"Oh, you can change those for twenty-five or thirty dollars apiece. It's no big deal. I've had to do it many times when traveling for business," explained his father.

"Well, yeah, but multiply thirty dollars by five people, and that adds up to quite a bit of money . . . money we don't need to spend right now," complained Alan. He really wasn't as concerned about the money as he was about how quickly things were progressing before he had a chance to carefully consider any of the ramifications of this impromptu adventure.

"Alan, your mother and I will pay for the fees to change the flights," boomed his father as he jumped up from the recliner. "And look, we'll throw in an extra five hundred dollars toward your trip expenses. Okay, with you, mother?"

"Absolutely!"

"Mom, Dad, why are you doing this? We don't know if this is God's direction for our lives or not. I don't think you should spend that kind of money on a 'what if.'"

"Son," answered his father, "in business we spend money all the time on things we aren't sure will become profitable. It's called due diligence. I think in a very real way you two traveling to the Gulf Coast is what could be considered doing your due diligence." He patted Alan on the shoulder.

"Besides, it's been two years since we've had a chance to play with our grandbabies, and your mother and I want to spoil them rotten!"

Everyone but Alan started laughing. "Oh, now I see your ulterior motive," he accused good-naturedly.

"Oh, yeah, you two, we have an ulterior motive, and we can't fulfill it if you guys are here so get moving," his father expressed with the grin of a Cheshire cat.

The next day, which was Tuesday, was filled with planning their trip south. Alan had telephoned Joey to make arrangements, and Annalisa called the airline to schedule another return flight home for their family. The earliest flight back to California with five seats together wasn't until the morning of Wednesday the 31st. This made Alan rather restless because they would be away from home for over three weeks. However, after much convincing from Annalisa and his mother, along with the children chiming in, he relented. They were now booked on a return flight for San Francisco on July 31st.

Later that same afternoon, Alan changed the oil in his mother's old Buick sedan as well as checked all the belts, hoses, and tires. Everything, little by little, was falling into place for their visit to the Gulf Coast. Although, Alan still felt an uneasiness he couldn't quite identify.

Enjoying a plate of his mother's famous spaghetti at dinner that evening, Alan and Annalisa determined they would depart early Thursday morning. The children were actually very excited about spending a few days alone with their grandparents, especially after their Grandpa Browne promised to take them to nearby Great Falls National Park and to the ice cream store. They loved their Grandpa and were looking forward to all of the activities he and their Grandma had planned for them.

The trip south along Interstates 95 and 85 was pleasant as Alan and Annalisa spoke of all the events of the last two years. There were tears, to be sure, but mostly there was a shared feeling of amazement at all that God had done and was continuing to do in their lives. Alan marveled at the Lord's apparent spontaneity, clearly evidenced by the fact they were now on an unplanned escapade, in a borrowed car, traveling to a tiny, unknown burg of Hurst Hammock, Florida, to see a friend, who he had only met the previous October. The whole journey had uncertainty written all over it. Alan felt the same.

"Wow!" exclaimed Alan. "You sure could call this an adventure, couldn't you, honey?"

"Yes," she replied quietly as she rested her head on his shoulder. "An adventure with God."

A peaceful silence filled the interior of their car as they rolled southward crossing into South Carolina. He swung his arm around her, and she snuggled into his chest. He had always loved the way they fit together. Physically, yes, but more importantly their personalities and their hearts. He had decided, years ago, they were more than soul mates; they were, in every respect, a perfect fit. And he loved her with every ounce of his being. She was the love of his life. Annalisa was right, he determined as they neared Greenville, they were on a sort of expedition with God, another unknown yet grand expedition with Him. "Or, maybe," he inaudibly mused through the whine of the tires rolling over

R. J. Graves, Jr.

the pavement, "maybe all of life is supposed to be a marvelous journey to be enjoyed with God. He purposefully designed it this way. No wonder our Lord isn't fond of murmuring and complaining," Alan surmised.

"Perhaps His concept of this life is that it should be enjoyed. I have made it otherwise because of my insecurities and my fears. I'm not free to delight. I'm enslaved to dread," he softly pondered aloud. "Maybe my time here on earth is supposed to be savored as a lifelong safari of love and discovery with Him. It's not only this short foray to Pensacola that is an adventure; it's our whole life that is to be a grand adventure . . . a grand adventure with God!"

"What, honey?" yawned Annalisa as she lifted her head from Alan's chest. "Where are we?"

"Just coming into Greensville, South Carolina, sweetheart. We need some gas, so I thought to look for a restaurant too. I'm hungry, how about you?"

"Uh . . . yeah, I think so. Give me a minute to wake up."

"After dinner, I thought we could find a hotel."

"Alan, it isn't even four o'clock yet."

"Yeah, I know, but the next city on our way is Atlanta, and they have the Olympics going on right now. There won't be any place to stay within a hundred miles of there. Let's get a bite to eat, and we can figure it out, okay? How does the Olive Garden sound?" he asked, glancing over at her.

"Great. Hey, maybe we could stop in Atlanta and get the kids a souvenir from the Olympics?"

"Well, my love, now you're speaking my language. I found out the men's cycling road race is tomorrow outside of Atlanta in the suburbs. We could go see it. In fact, that new kid Lance Armstrong is racing. They're predicting he may win." Alan's voice had a hint of excitement in it when he realized that Annalisa might be open to a visit to the Olympic Games.

"I think that would be kind of fun as long as we can get the kids something, you know, a hat, or teddy bear, or something."

"Oh, baby, don't say maybe!" yelped Alan as they pulled into the restaurant parking lot. "I'm kind of hoping Frankie Andreu wins."

"Who's that?"

"Oh, he's another American cyclist competing in the road race. I met him once at a bicycle convention in Vegas. Great guy, really down to earth. I liked him, so I hope he wins. But if not, at least I hope someone from the USA wins. We haven't won a single medal since Alexi Grewal won gold in 1984 at the Los Angeles Olympics, remember that?"

"No, not really," she flatly replied as Alan opened the door to the Olive Garden for her.

"Sure, honey, we watched it at home. I really, really wanted Davis Phinney to win, but he ended up in fifth place. You don't remember?"

"No, sweetheart," she replied in a monotone with a wry grin.

"Oh, you're going to remember this race tomorrow. You can believe me on that one."

"Don't we need tickets, Alan?"

"No, we just walk up to the course and watch. It runs mostly through neighborhoods and then along a wide boulevard called Peachtree Road. I can't wait," Alan whispered excitedly as they sat down at their table.

"Alright," she chided gently. "Let's remember why we're on this trip, okay? Don't get sidetracked. You getting the Tour of Italy, honey?"

"No, no, it's called the Giro d'Italia. The Tour is in France, you know, Tour de France. This is the Olympics; it's entirely different. Although, for the first time ever, the Olympic Committee is allowing the professional racers into the competition."

"Alan," she blurted abruptly, "What are you ordering for dinner . . . the Tour of Italy?"

"Uh . . . yes, honey, I think I'll probably get that," he paused to let her decide. "I think you're really going to love this race and . . ."

"Alan."

By her tone, he determined it would be wise to let the whole race thing rest until sometime tomorrow. However, even though he didn't mention it again, he couldn't help but think about it, literally every minute, until they fell asleep late that night at the Hampton Inn Hotel.

Awaking early, they were on the road before eight o'clock. Once in the Atlanta area about three hours later, they immediately filled the gas tank. The parking was terrible at the start-finish area, so they parked a few blocks off the race course in a residential neighborhood. It was a perfect spot, no barricades to block their view, and very few people, except for the group in a nearby driveway cheering on the peloton of racers as they sped by. Alan noticed they had a television for viewing the race when it wasn't rolling by a few feet in front of them.

"Mind if we take a peek?" he asked politely.

"Sure, help yourself. It's a neighborhood television. At least, that's what we're calling it today. It isn't every day we get the top cyclists in the world racing right past our front door!" the man laughed. "Yeah, this is a proud day for this old Southern town."

Shortly thereafter, the man rolled out his grill along with a cooler full of sodas and adult beverages. "Help yourself, everybody. Hot dogs and hamburgers will be ready soon."

Alan offered to pay for a couple of cokes for Annalisa and himself, but the man refused. "No, thank you, friend. This is what we, down here, call good old fashioned Southern hospitality. It's my privilege to serve you. It's your job to enjoy," he smiled then offered Alan some potato salad.

While Alan walked back toward Annalisa those words were ringing in his ears. He mentioned to her what had been expressed by the kind man as they watched the pack of Olympic riders go by again. She turned to Alan and nodded her head.

"It's like Betsy told us, honey," she encouraged. "God has a job and we have a job." Then, she turned and cheered on the riders, especially the stragglers; she always felt sorry for them.

Contemplating what his dear wife had just conveyed to him so frankly, Alan sat down on the curb. She always seemed to work through something much quicker than he did. At times, he would be so bound up on the inside, while she would have such a freedom. He wanted, even longed, to have that kind of liberty in his heart; where he could enjoy life, whatever betide, regardless of the circumstances. He wanted; he needed that freedom within him.

During the last lap, as the peloton passed by their location, Alan noticed there were three riders out in front of the pack. He could make out a rider from Switzerland and one from Great Britain, but couldn't determine who the third one was. A few seconds later, chasing the three with all his might, was Alan's hopeful, the lone figure of the American, Frankie Andreu.

"Go get 'em, Frankie!" he shouted. "Catch 'em, man!"

They jogged back to the television to watch the finish of the race. Pascal Richard, the Swiss rider won gold, with a rider from Denmark, second, and the Brit, third. Frankie was first out of the medals in fourth place. The whole neighborhood group, huddled around the television, let out a sigh and then a cheer for their generous host. After handshakes and hugs, Annalisa and Alan were back on the road traveling to their next stop, Montgomery, Alabama, where they would stay the night at a Comfort Inn.

Waking up late, they decided they would enjoy a leisurely breakfast before continuing on toward the coast. They arrived in the Pensacola Bay Area early in the afternoon. Alan drove them directly to the beautiful white sand beaches and gorgeous turquoise water of the Gulf of Mexico. Although the effects of Opal were still evident, they walked hand in hand for nearly an hour along the shore, talking about all the "what if's" and "how comes" of their lives. Their eyes and ears were wide open to see and hear anything that had the faintest hint of God in it. They were trying their best to be in tune to His radio frequency. Strolling back to the old Buick, Alan opened the door for Annalisa as his phone rang.

"Oh, I'll get it later, honey. I'm so enjoying our time together. How about some seafood?"

"I would love that, Alan. But don't forget to take me by the Morgan's cottage. I really want to see where God met you . . . and where you weathered that storm," she reminded him.

"I'll take you by there on our way to Joey's, okay?"

"Sounds good. Now, where are you taking me for some yummy shrimp?"

"I thought we'd try a local favorite, Peg Leg Pete's."

The wait for a table and dinner had taken so long that by the time they reached the Morgan's cottage it was too dark to recognize any of its features. Alan promised he would take her there the following day. Then, off they went to find Joey's house. However, it was no simple task locating his house either. It seemed to Alan the little village of Hurst Hammock was not only difficult to locate but nearly impossible to spot in the dark. They finally came upon Beulah Road and continued down its long, winding, unlit way for several miles. Just as Alan was sure he must have missed it somehow, the town appeared. Joey was right. It was tiny.

Joey and Alan had a joyous reunion. Annalisa was introduced to Joey and his endearing wife, Pam. It was her first acquaintance with a truly Southern couple. Although she felt somewhat awkward initially, she soon fell in love with this delightful and sincere pair. After several minutes of pleasantries and sipping sweet tea, the gracious Hinotes showed their road weary friends to the guest room.

With the sun shining brilliantly through the window, Alan awoke Sunday morning to the delightful smells of coffee, bacon, and waffles. Joey and Pam had decided to skip church service in deference to their visitors. However, Alan and Annalisa both insisted they all attend, if only for the later morning gathering. On the way back home, they stopped for a lunch of barbeque pulled pork sandwiches with ranch beans, coleslaw, and yes, more sweet tea.

After a much enjoyed afternoon nap, Joey took Alan out to see his woodworkers shop in the backyard. "This is the place, Alan. This is where I refinish all the furniture and build kitchen cabinets."

"Nice, Joey, real nice," nodded Alan. "Man, you have some really fancy equipment here."

"Yeah, some of it was quite pricey, but it has more than made up what I paid for it. See that sander over there? It has pretty much tripled our production for those hotel refinishing projects I'm doing."

"Wow, really? Tripled?" Alan questioned with his eyes opened wide and eyebrows raised for emphasis.

"Yeah, and the word is out, my brother. I won two more hotel contracts. We'll see, but I should have the signed documents back tomorrow. It's been amazing. If only you could have seen me a few years back, I thought I was going to die."

"I'm so glad to hear you've got work. That's really incredible, man."

"Thanks, I'm so grateful," smiled Joey. "Hey, how long you guys staying for?"

"Oh, I don't know, a few days. If that's okay with you?"

"Yeah, stay for a month. We'd love to have y'all. In fact, I'm not sure if you would be interested, but I could put you to work for a few days. I mean, I could really use another experienced guy. I'd be willing to pay you real well or even do a piece work deal if you prefer. What do you say, Alan, want to make a few bucks for the trip back home?" quipped Joey as he patted Alan on the back.

"Well, Joey, that actually sounds kind of good. However, I promised Annalisa I would take her to see the cottage where I stayed during Hurricane Opal. So let me do that tomorrow and spend the day with her. Then, if she's okay with it, I'll work with you on Tuesday and Wednesday. How's that sound?"

"I think that works fine for me, my brother. I'll make sure we have all the tools ready for you. In fact, why don't you work right here in the shop? Then, you can be close by for Annalisa. I'll take the other guys over to the hotel to deliver our next rooms. I'll leave you a helper though. Work for you?"

"Sounds good to me," replied Alan as he stretched out his hand to shake Joey's.

"You know, Alan, I've been needing a second in command for some time now. Someone I trust, who could either run the shop or make the pickup and delivery runs with the crew back and forth to the hotels. We have to dismantle several pieces sometimes, and it requires a skilled guy. These guys are costing me money because they end up breaking things. I know you've been looking for a job, so if this works out over these few days do you think you might consider relocating here? I would pay you a decent wage, and you, Annalisa, and the kids could live in my parent's house until y'all get on your feet. We could work it out where maybe you would only pay the taxes and utilities or something; you know, keep the cobwebs down. I think it would only amount to maybe three or four hundred dollars a month, if that. And look brother, I'll pay you twenty-five an hour to start. What do you think, Alan?"

Alan slowly shook his head while gazing down at the floor.

"Wow, Joey, I can't believe this."

"Ah, I'm sorry, Alan. I didn't mean to offend you. I know you've been managing a business for several years, and I'm sure you're used to living in a nice home in California. You're way above this, man. I'm sorry, really."

"Joey," interjected Alan as he slapped him on the back still shaking his head from side to side in astonishment. "If you're ever handcuffed to an idea of how to solve your own problems, get the key and unlock those bonds quick."

"Huh? What does that mean?" inquired a curious Joey.

"It means, my dear friend, that the reason we're here is to determine if this is where God wants us to live. We've been listening closely to hear from Him. I'm not positive, but I think you just made His voice quite a bit clearer."

~eleven~

It was shortly after eleven o'clock that night when Alan's phone awoke him from a deep sleep. He and Annalisa had retired early, admitting to their gracious hosts they were still a bit travel weary. Once they had slipped into bed, Annalisa whispered to Alan that perhaps their exhaustion was due to all the Southern cooking they had enjoyed at the fish fry put on by the Hinote's church. Alan added that he was sure the gallons of sweet tea they had consumed the last two days had contributed as well. They both chuckled, but the accuracy of their diagnosis was evidenced by how quickly they dropped off to sleep.

"Hello," Alan answered in a hushed tone after fumbling around in the dark for the noisy device.

"Al?" the voice on the other end was loud and had a sense of impatience to it. "Al, why didn't you call me back? Didn't you get any of my messages? I've called you three times."

Still somewhat groggy, Alan recognized the urgent voice as that of their real estate agent in California, Todd Bickersum. He was known for his somewhat hyper, go-get-

'em attitude. In fact, that's why they had decided to use him to sell their home, but a call this late at night, well, this was a bit overboard.

"Toddly." Alan always called him Toddly when he was trying to let Todd know that his perky disposition was getting beyond the range of what most folks would call normal, "Do you have any idea what time it is, man?"

"Yeah, it's quarter after nine, why?"

"Oh . . . yeah, well, not here it ain't. It's after eleven . . . PM! Now, what's up? Sold the house or something?"

"Yes, I have, and it's a full price offer!" exclaimed an excitedly enthusiastic Todd.

"You what?" asked Alan loud enough that Annalisa rolled over and immediately started yanking on his arm.

"What's going on, Alan?" she asked as she tried to clear the fog from her head. "Did Todd sell our house?"

Alan turned around nodding his head in her direction although he was listening to Todd explain what had happened. He was smiling while Annalisa continued to urgently pull on his arm for more information.

"Okay, so let me get this straight, full price offer with only a couple of conditions, right?" repeated Alan to assure he had heard Todd correctly. "Oh, when do they want to close?"

"No later than August 30th. They have school-aged children," answered their agent.

Annalisa was still tugging on his arm. "Alan? Come on, what's going on?"

Alan held up one hand motioning for just a second more. "Alright, Todd, I'll call you in the morning with a phone number where you can fax the contract. Thanks again, great job, man."

Placing his phone on the night stand, Alan swung around to tell Annalisa they had a full price contract on their house in San Ramon. He told her all of the details Todd had expressed to him. Then, he lay down next to the sweet love of his life.

"Well, honey, looks like we're moving," sighed Alan.

"It seems when God is ready to pull up stakes, He doesn't waste any time watching the grass grow," yawned Annalisa.

"Yeah, I know, that's what concerns me," replied Alan. "I'm not so sure I'm ready, are you?"

"Doesn't matter, Alan," she replied with another yawn. "When the cloud moves, we move with it . . . or we stay behind. I think we both want to move whenever it moves and stay wherever it stays. Well, honey, it's moving . . . and so are we. Besides, I'm too tired to worry about it tonight. Goodnight, my love," she kissed Alan on the cheek and rolled over and drifted off.

After Todd's phone call, Alan's thoughts were churning, like a concrete truck on a construction site. The agitation effectively prevented him from falling asleep. Although Annalisa, as evidenced by her quiet snoring, had no problem at all. He had agreed with her in principle; they would always want to do what God directed, but this was way too fast. It was only in the last week or so they had decided to fly to Virginia for a visit with his parents and to do some sightseeing with the kids. It was to be a vacation away from the never ending pressure of their lives in California. Now, within a few days, they had decided to travel to Florida, been offered a job, and received a full price offer on their house. Plus, these events came fast on the heels of losing their son, leaving their church, and selling his bicycle shops. He resigned himself to the fact that they were moving. However, he wished he had more time to let his emotions catch up to the fast pace of reality.

The two of them spent the following day together carefully reviewing the sales offer on their home, visiting Joey's parent's house, and dropping by the Morgan's cottage. When they pulled into the gravel drive that led to the one bedroom bungalow, they noticed there were still several trees down, which had fallen during last October's hurricane. Parking their car by the shed in back, the two of them hopped out and walked toward the old structure where Alan had survived Hurricane Opal.

"Wow, Alan, this isn't at all what I had pictured. This place is really run down."

"Oh, it's not too bad on the inside . . . it's kind of rustic, uh, I mean, you could almost call it quaint."

"It looks like it could fall over in a stiff breeze," she chuckled. "And you stayed here in a hurricane?! Alan Michael Browne, if I had known, I would have demanded you leave."

"Well, I'm glad you didn't because I wouldn't have had that special rendezvous with God."

"True," she conceded. "On the other hand, I'm not sure you needed a storm for that."

Pulling the key out from its hiding place under the kitchen window sill, Alan unlocked the back door. He first poked his head in to be certain no one was there.

"Nice screened porch," remarked Annalisa.

"Come on in, honey." Alan put his hand on her back as he held the door open. "This is the kitchen, and that's the table where I studied every day. Over there is the living room with that awful drab green sofa. That's where I first heard His voice."

Nodding silently, Annalisa took it all in.

"Down the hall here is the bedroom and bathroom. It's not much, but it served its purpose very well. Of course, it was much gloomier with all the windows covered by the storm plywood. I mean, it was extremely dark in here."

The two of them peeked into the bedroom and glanced at the bathroom.

"Small bedroom," commented Annalisa as she made her way over to the sofa. "So this is the spot?"

"No, a bit to your left," smiled Alan. "There, right there."

Annalisa sat down softly as if she was expecting to feel something when she touched the sofa. "I don't sense anything," she whispered.

"Dear, it's not the spot that counts; it's the need, the heart . . . well, you know what I mean."

She glanced back at her loving husband. "I know, honey, it's just hopeful thinking, I guess," she whispered.

"Why do you keep whispering?"

"Because this is a memorable spot for you. A place you'll always remember. The cottage where you heard from God."

"Not really," mumbled Alan.

"What do you mean? Why not?"

"Because Bill told me he's tearing it down next year to make room for his retirement home. He's looking to move out of California by sometime in 1998 and wanted to have his home ready before he moves here."

"Oh, Alan, I'm so sorry. I didn't know. Actually, I wasn't referring to this physical house but more to the memory of your special meeting with the Lord while you were here."

"Yeah, I know, regardless, I . . . well, anyway, looks like we'll have to create new memories somewhere else."

"That's right, honey, and I hope I can be there too," she whispered as she put her arms around him.

"Me too, my love . . . me too."

The rest of their time with Joey and Pam literally flew by. Before they knew it, they were on the road headed back to the Washington, DC area. As they drove along the Interstate toward Atlanta, they decided it would be fun to stop at the Olympics one last time. Though it was getting late, the idea appealed to them both.

They found a parking spot about a mile from the Centennial Olympic Park. Annalisa shopped for souvenirs for the kids as well as a nice gift for Alan's parents. The area was a bee-hive of activity even though the hour was late. Shortly after midnight, Alan heard a band playing music at the park and convinced Annalisa to stay a bit longer. They met a delightful couple from Ontario, Canada, while listening to Jack Mack and the Heart Attack. A little before one o'clock in the morning, Annalisa finally convinced Alan it was time to leave. As they were pulling out of their parking spot, they heard an explosion.

"Sounds like fireworks," remarked Annalisa.

"Yeah," smiled Alan. "Kind of late at night for them though."

Within a few minutes, they were on the Interstate headed for Greenville, South Carolina, and their hotel. Alan noticed the absence of fireworks in his rearview mirror, so he decided to turn on the radio to see if they could learn what may have been the source of the loud noise. He flipped through a number of channels until he found the news. They were absolutely stunned to hear that a bomb had been detonated by a terrorist in Centennial Olympic Park a mere thirty minutes after they had left the concert. When she heard the news, Annalisa started weeping.

"Oh, Lord God, that could have been us!" exclaimed Alan.

"Yes, but what about that nice Canadian couple," sobbed Annalisa.

"No, honey, they left with us, remember? I'm concerned about everyone else. A lot of people were there listening to the band."

Alan was so full of adrenaline he drove right past Greenville and didn't stop for the night until Charlotte, North Carolina, nearly four hours from their stop in Atlanta. He found a Hampton Inn with a room available and awakened Annalisa only long enough to get her into bed. It was five-thirty.

Later that morning they were startled out of their slumber by a loud rap on the door followed by an announcement from the hallway that is was eleven o'clock and housekeeping needed to clean the room. Without much conversation, they made their way to the car and pulled through the drive up window of a neighboring Starbucks. They were both exhausted but, after last night's scare, felt the urgent need to get back to the children. Making good time, they stopped only in Richmond, Virginia, for fuel and food before arriving at Alan's parent's house, just as Alan's mother was serving dinner. It was a joyous reunion.

That evening, after the children were tucked in bed, Alan and Annalisa sat down with his parents to discuss all the events of the last several days. Alan did most of the talking with Annalisa adding in a few comments here and there. Finally, after nearly forty-five minutes and with many of Alan's rhetorical questions still unanswered, his father broke into the somewhat erratic monologue.

"Son, the goal in life isn't to be wealthy or attain a life of ease. It's to live in a way that enables you to care for others and keep a clear conscience. If moving down south will help you to attain that lifestyle, then so be it."

The room fell silent because all were grappling with what had just been spoken by the patriarch of the Browne family. After several seconds, Alan began to express his gratitude for his father's wisdom, but his father interrupted him.

"Look, you two, you're obviously exhausted. Why don't we discuss this tomorrow or even later, after you have a chance for it all to soak in? You're not leaving until Wednesday, so we'll have plenty of time to talk. Why don't you try and get some rest now, okay?" His father was smiling and nodding to confirm his suggestion was, in fact, a good idea.

The next day Alan double checked with their real estate agent to assure everything was still on track. Then, he telephoned Joey to let him know he would start work around the first week of September. There was one more thing Alan wanted to do before flying back to California to start "the great transition" as he entitled it. He wanted to see Betsy one last time. He made plans to visit her the day before they were to fly home. Annalisa, however, had to stay with the children since Richard and Emily weren't feeling well.

Making the familiar drive to Betsy's home, he parked in front of her house and walked up the gravel drive. He smiled as his shoes once again made the scrunchy sound under his feet.

"Oh, come in, dearie," called the sweet, somewhat raspy voice from within the kitchen. "Where are Annalisa and the children?"

"Oh, Richard and Emily weren't feeling well, so my sweet Annalisa agreed to stay and take care of them."

"Ah, bless their dear hearts. I'll be sure to pray for little Richard and Emily this evening."

"Thank you, Betsy. We're heading home tomorrow and sick kids on a plane would make for a miserable flight."

Moving into the parlor, they sat across from one another. Alan settled on the high back sofa and Betsy on her favorite overstuffed chair. They exchanged familiar topics, and Betsy asked about their trip south. Alan told her all about the Pensacola Bay Area, Joey, the job offer, Todd's phone call, and their close call at the Atlanta Olympics. He also expressed concern for her health.

"Oh, sweetie, it's nothing to be worried about. My body is just getting older. I'll live in it as long as it's habitable. When it isn't any longer, I'll go be with Jesus . . . and my Stanley."

"Well, did the doctor give you any hope that you'll get better soon?" Alan asked gently.

"No, I wouldn't say it was hope. It was more of an expectation than a hope. It could be months, it could be years. I sincerely hope it's not too long though," she confessed with a grin. "I'm ready to go home, Alan. This old body is so limiting and confining now. I'm looking forward to a joyful freedom from these earthly bonds."

"Really?" Alan's voice hit a higher octave.

"Oh yes, dearie. I'm pretty much free on the inside, you know, within me. However, I'm still so very hindered by this house I'm wearing, you understand?"

"Uh . . . I think, uh . . . maybe I know what you mean."

"Alan, this body isn't who I really am. It's only the house, the fleshy vessel I live in while here on earth. One day soon, thankfully, this house will deteriorate to a point where I can't live in it any longer. When that day comes, I'll get a new body, a spiritual body to live in . . . so to speak."

Alan had a perplexed look on his face, so Betsy continued trying to help her younger friend comprehend her meaning.

"Do you remember, dear, after Jesus rose from the grave in resurrection life?"

"Yes, ma'am."

"Well, why didn't Mary Magdalene recognize him?"[1] she posed. "In another case, the two disciples walking on the road to Emmaus, how come they didn't figure out who He was either?[2] Or how about in the last chapter in the Gospel of John; when Peter, John, and a few others went fishing, and Jesus told them to cast their net on the other side of the boat. Why didn't they recognize Him?"[3]

"I'm not sure, Betsy," replied Alan softly. "Maybe he had a different body or something."

"Well, I believe that's partially true anyway. We can read in the Book of First Corinthians that we die a physical body and we're raised a spiritual body[4] . . . or at least something close to that I believe."

"But how do you get to the place in your life, Betsy, when you are ready to go, you know, to die?"

"Oh, that," she smiled. "Well, number one, I've had a lot of practice, you know. I'm much older than you, so I'm much closer to being ready, and therefore I am at peace with it."

"What do you mean you've had more practice?"

"Dearie, it's a small matter of how you look at life, how you perceive trials, setbacks, and difficulties, you understand?"

Alan didn't say a word, but his head was slowly wagging involuntarily.

"Let's see," Betsy leaned back and smoothed out her checkered house dress and then scooched forward in her chair. "When you first become a Christian, you must die to whatever life you had before, to grasp the new life the Lord is calling you to, correct?"

"Yes, ma'am." Alan was acknowledging Betsy while remembering the CHP officer's advice.

"Then, in obedience to His word, you get baptized, right?"

Alan nodded in agreement.

"Baptism is a symbol of dying and rising again. You probably learned that in Sunday School."

"Youth group," added Alan. "I actually remember Pastor Fred teaching us that in youth group one Sunday evening years ago."

"Good," smiled Betsy. "All of our life as a Christian is just like that."

"Like what?" questioned Alan, raising his eyebrows.

"Hmmm . . . let me see. Yes, okay. Think about your first two major experiences as a new believer in Jesus Christ. The first is conversion, the second is baptism, correct?"

Alan nodded.

"Each one of those experiences with the Lord required something of you, right?"

Alan nodded again.

"Whether you knew it at the time or not, to some degree you were laying down your life, you know, letting go, surrendering, considering yourself dead. Before those experiences, you were living your life at a certain level of faith, of understanding. But then, you went down, so to speak. You died, to a certain degree, to what you wanted, to your will and decided to live a new level of life according to what He wants, what His will is for your life."

"Okay. But what does that have to do with me now or, more importantly, with you and your health."

"It's all the same, Alan. You never stop . . . well, dying, so to speak. Let me see if I can explain it a bit clearer, dear. Say you have been a believer for several years, and you're enjoying a certain amount of faith and discernment in your relationship with Him. However, one day you get some very sobering news, perhaps a financial issue, or a loved one is sick, or maybe has even died. Difficult days . . . it's like walking through the valley of the shadow of death. It may last a minute, an hour, a day, a week, or perhaps several years. But it will eventually pass, and you will rise up from the valley of death—but with a new level of faith, of love, of understanding in this wonderful, invisible relationship with Him. You are now walking on a higher plain than before you went down in the valley."

"Yes, I can see that, Betsy," agreed Alan. "But how would that work when you're standing at death's door?"

"If you have practiced it enough, it will come as natural as stepping through a gate. And because He has always met you in these 'practice rounds' here on earth, then you can be confident that He will be there to greet you when it's your final valley of the shadow of death . . . for on the other side of the valley is the final upsurge of resurrection life. So it shouldn't be a big deal, if I've been practicing all of my adult life for this final curtain call," she concluded.

"I think it may be a much bigger concern for someone who hasn't been practicing," he thoughtfully added, smiling back at her. Then, jumping to his feet, he crossed the parlor and gently placed his arms around Betsy.

"I love you, Betsy. You are such a dear friend and a sister who is closer than a brother," he chuckled, acknowledging he had misquoted the Scriptures. "Well, you know what I mean."

"Of course I do, dearie. And I love you and that wonderful little family of yours. Now don't worry about me. God's got me in the palm of His loving hand, and He'll bring me safely home one way or another."

"I know He will, Betsy, but I will miss you . . . terribly!"

"Oh, come on, dear. I'm not dead quite yet. Wipe those tears, Alan; I need you to do something for me," she smiled as she kissed him on the forehead.

"Anything for you, Betsy, just name it."

"It's The **rojocci** Fellowship, Alan. You're the next generation, and you need to carry on the principles and continue to search for the hidden mysteries in the Scriptures."

"Oh, I will, Betsy. Don't think for a minute that because I'm moving to Florida I'll stop digging and discovering. In fact, I think I'll have more time to devote to it. I'm hoping at some point to travel to Ohio to check out Pfeiffer Station and investigate the possibility of a meeting held in the 1800s. What did you say was the name of Stanley's friend, you know, the one you two had dinner with over on Capitol Hill? I think it was Sherman something . . ."

"Yes," she interrupted. "It was Sherman Wilkins, why?"

"Joey, my friend, in Florida, has a letter or two from his father stating something about this same **rojocci** meeting in Ohio. Maybe they all knew each other?!" exclaimed Alan enthusiastically.

"That sounds exciting, dear. But remember, your relationship with the Lord is most important and then these adventures, as you have time."

Standing up, the two old friends moved toward the kitchen like they sensed without acknowledging it that it was time for Alan to leave. There had been so many deep conversations between them over the years . . . and so many goodbyes. Alan never enjoyed farewells, but this one was particularly difficult because he wasn't sure he would ever see Betsy again.

Tears filled their eyes as they hugged at the back door. Even Betsy acknowledged there was the very distinct possibility they would not see each other again in this life. Alan kissed her head through her silvery curls and turned to leave. The tears were flowing down his cheeks.

"I love you, Betsy," he called, without looking behind, choking back his tears.

"I love you too, Alan," she sweetly responded. "And don't forget now, dear, he who loves his life will lose it, but he who seeks to lose his life, for His sake, will save it."[5]

"Thank you, Betsy, I'll remember. I'll write you as soon as we get settled in Florida, okay? Let's promise to stay in touch."

"We will. Thank you so much for visiting. God be with you in your travels, dear."

-twelve-

With the California sun beating hot upon their brows, the Browne family loaded up the rental truck with their remaining belongings. Wearily, they had organized many yards sales and more trips to the local thrift shop than Alan cared to remember. Fortunately, the closing on the sale of their beloved hacienda-style home had been moved up ten days, allowing them to leave earlier than planned for Florida. The uneventful road trip took them four long days to pass through Arizona, New Mexico, Texas, Louisiana, Mississippi, and Alabama. The home they had rented from Joey was a mere six miles from the Alabama-Florida Stateline, in a district of the city of Pensacola called Myrtle Grove.

It was a turn-of-the-century farmhouse with a steep gabled, standing seam roof and clapboard siding painted green. Although it was considerably faded by years of the Deep South's brilliant sunshine, it had a welcoming appearance. The expansive porch wrapped around three sides of the first floor. Despite being unkempt, the lawn was large and the shrubbery orderly, yet, like Alan's moving-day-hair, it was in need of a trim. Several enormous oaks stood throughout with tassels of Spanish Moss swaying in the gentle, balmy Florida breeze. As picturesque as a setting on a postcard, it was idyllic. However, as a home, it indicated much labor. Alan had failed to recognize this requirement when they had agreed to lease it.

"Man, things grow fast in the South," he proclaimed to Julie as they pulled the rental truck onto the asphalt driveway.

"Is this where we are going to live?!" she barked. "This is like something from back in the dark ages . . . or worse!"

Initially, Julie had been the one child in the family who had complained about the move. However, within a few days she had allowed herself to contemplate the excitement of new possibilities and had decided to give it a chance. It was a consideration which had lasted up until a minute ago when they made the final turn onto the property of their new home.

"Dad!? Seriously . . . is this where we're living?" she complained with an annoying whine that only another pre-teen could mimic.

"Yes, honey, this is where God has us for now. Maybe not where we'll be living in a few months, but we are here for the foreseeable future."

That future looked a bit ominous to Alan. He decided to attack it. Just like his father had advised, with an attitude of taking one step at a time. First, they set up their home, unpacking all the boxes, hanging drapes and pictures, and heading off to the grocery store to supply their new abode with all the essentials. Then, it was off to work a few days later. On Sunday, they attended Joey and Pam's church. It was all coming together little by little. And by that same sequence, Alan was feeling more and more at peace with their decisions. It had, most definitely, been a whirlwind for a few weeks. But here they were in Myrtle Grove, in a comfortable house, able to pay all their bills on time, and with none of the extreme pressures he had been enduring for the past several years.

The remainder of 1996 passed quickly by, so did the next year, and the following, until more than a few had come and gone, relegating those awful last days in California to the status of a distant memory. It wasn't that Alan and Annalisa couldn't recall those feelings, however, with the passage of time, the emotions attached to those events weren't nearly as strong. Time does aid in healing. Although, when one wants it to move fast, it seems to drag on endlessly. Later, when middle-age arrives, time moves too quickly, even though one wishes it moved slower. Alan and Annalisa were noticing this very fact as one year led to another.

"You know, honey, our kids really date us. Without them growing older each year, I'm not sure I would even realize I was approaching fifty. It's a scary thing really. I mean, we have a daughter in high school, and a son and daughter in junior high school. How can this be? I look at you and I still see this cute little sweetheart from Walnut Creek, California, riding in the back seat of the church van headed to the retreat," reflected Alan.

"You're not allowed to get glasses, old man. Your vision is just fine with me," assured Annalisa teasingly. "I like you seeing me as a twenty year old," she laughed while carrying the clothes basket to the laundry room.

"Thanks," Alan replied with a hint of sarcasm. "Look, I'm serious," he shouted from his recliner in the living room. "In less than two years, we'll have a daughter in college. I'm not old enough to have a daughter away at school."

"She's only finishing up her junior year. She hasn't left yet," Annalisa shouted from the laundry room.

He hollered back, "Where is she anyway?"

"I'm right here, dear, you don't have to shout." Annalisa replied in a monotone as she dumped the clothes basket full of clean laundry on the sofa, so she could fold them without having to yell across the house.

"No, I mean, Julie. Where is she?"

"She's at track practice. She should be home shortly. Why?"

"Oh, I don't know. I guess I'm missing her or something."

"Honey, you see her every day. Why would you say that?" she pondered aloud as she dropped another folded pair of jeans back in the empty basket.

"Well, I don't know . . . we've been here almost five years. I've been working for Joey all those years without a break, I haven't heard how Betsy is doing for weeks now, and my kids are all moving away," this last complaint he knew she would recognize as fictitious so he added a splash of Southern whine for emphasis.

"Oh, Alan, you crack me up," she smirked. "Sometimes, you handsome man you, I've got to wonder about all that goes on inside that old head of yours," she smiled, slowly wagging her head from side to side while she slid her arms around his neck.

"So you admit it, I'm old," he bantered, shifting in the recliner to accommodate her on his lap.

"Ha, hardly. But no matter how old you live to be, I will always love you with all my heart, okay?" she cajoled, then kissed him in the way she knew he liked to be kissed. "Now, carry this basket up to Richard's room for me."

"Oh, you wretched cutie you," he laughingly barked. "You're going to get yours!"

"I hope so," she replied in her sing-song voice, heading back to the kitchen.

Just then the front door swung open and Julie marched in fresh from track practice, stinky sweat clothes and all.

"What are you two shouting about, Dad?"

"Uh . . . nothing, honey, only taking the laundry upstairs to Richard's room, why?"

"Because I can hear you outside," she giggled.

"Really?"

"Oh, Dad, wait a minute. I've got something important to tell you."

"Yeah, what's that, sweetie?"

"Our track coach announced today that this will be his last season. He's retiring and moving to someplace called The Villages," she scrunched up her face to indicate she thought the name was weird.

"The what-ages?"

"The Villages; it's like a place where retired people go to live out the rest of their lives or something. Anyway, he said we won't have a coach for cross country starting in August or a track coach next spring either. So I got to thinking . . ."

"Yeah, what were you thinking, Julie?"

"Well . . . I think you should be our new coach!"

"Whaaat?!"

"Yeah, Dad, you'd be perfect. I mean, you were actually a fast runner and all, right? None of the other coaches even ran track. Our coach this year also coached tennis, and last year Coach Harris was the wrestling coach. You would be precisely what our team needs, Dad. A real track coach. What do you think?" her sweet face looked straight up into her father's with a most hopeful expression.

"Oh, I don't know. That was a long time ago."

"I think you should at least go talk to someone, Alan," contended Annalisa, holding a spatula she brought with her from the kitchen when she heard Julie's proposal.

"Please, Dad?!" begged Julie. "Please, please, please . . ."

"Oh, I don't . . ."

"Alan Michael Browne," chided Annalisa as she interrupted what was obviously going to be an excuse of some sort. "Are you not the same old man that was sitting right over there in that beat up recliner not five minutes ago whining about something?" Her arms were akimbo, spatula and all. "I think you may have the answer to your mid-life crisis."

"Now, Annalisa, wait just a minute . . . whaaat?! What mid-life crisis? I'm not having a mid-life anything . . . except for being ganged up on by two slick tigresses with the same last name, who happen to live in my house."

"Please, Dad? You really would be perfect."

"Oh, alright. I guess it can't hurt to talk to someone about the details of the job. I'll call your coach tomorrow and see what is required."

"Great! Here's his phone number. I told him you would call tonight," she gushed excitedly as she bounded up the stairs. "You're going to be fantastic, Dad!"

Alan glanced down at the phone number on the sheet of paper then looked up at Annalisa who, with fists still firmly planted upon her hips, was smiling back at him with eyes arched upward.

"I believe this will be the next level in your development," she predicted kissing him on the cheek. "I'll be fixing dinner if you want to talk, honey."

The conversation around the dinner table was all about Julie and the track team with Julie doing almost all of the talking. So much so, that Richard finally left half his plate of chicken enchiladas and headed upstairs to his room. Emily followed shortly thereafter. Alan wasn't really paying much attention to all the infinite details expressed by his enthusiastic daughter until she began describing a certain young man named Roger who, according to Julie's animated portrayal, was quite the runner. In fact, she seemed completely convinced that he would break world records and qualify for the Olympic team.

Now, Julie's father wasn't so much interested in a potentially good runner as he was in how his impressionable young daughter described this character. Her eyes lit up each time she said his name, "Roger this . . .", and, "Roger that . . ." her eyes were even arched upward, like both daughters of Annalisa Browne's genepool had the habit of doing. It indicated when something, or more importantly someone, really delighted them. For this, Alan was taking the most detailed mental notes.

"Uh, sweet daughter, how old is this runner named Roger?" he asked trying to disguise his real motive for the question.

"He and I are in the same grade. We have a couple of classes together. We sit at the same lab table in chemistry. He's really a nice guy, smart, and very competitive. I think he will one day be the first high school runner to break the four-minute mile," she chattered on with more than a hint of delight.

"That was done years ago, Julie, by a certain Jim Ryun," her father stated flatly. "Uh, actually, I think there have been several others since him, but he was the first." Alan glanced at Annalisa with a somewhat concerned look.

"What's his last name, sweetheart?" inquired her mother gently.

"Bellinger, Roger Bellinger."

"Where does he live, Julie?" Alan asked, trying not to seem too curious.

"I think down close to Warrington. It's just Roger and his mother. His father left them when Roger was five years old. He's never seen him since. It makes me sad, Dad, you know?"

"Uh . . . yeah, sure. What does his mother do?"

"He told me his mother had been a teller at a bank somewhere in Pensacola and then was promoted to head teller."

"Really? And she can support herself and her son on a teller's wages? Uh, pardon me, a head teller's wages?"

"Alan, honestly," commented Annalisa apologetically.

"Well, no, she's actually the Assistant Manager now. Besides, they only rent, like we do, Dad," replied Julie who was becoming slightly defensive.

"Julie, we are doing a rent-to-own deal with Joey. We are actually buying this house; we're not renting. But listen, that's beside the point and I'm sorry if I seemed judgmental. Sometimes I am, but I didn't mean to be, okay?" Alan reached out and held his daughter's hand.

Julie nodded her response.

"So how long have you known Roger?" asked her mother with a smile.

"I met him last year in history class. He's really cute and funny too," Julie giggled.

Annalisa, who had been gathering plates from the dinner table, motioned for Julie to follow her into the kitchen to continue their conversation.

"Alan, would you clear the rest of the dishes please?" she grinned in her husband's direction although her eyes were frowning.

Still seated at the head of the table, Alan was deep in thought while he strained to listen with one ear to the discussion in the kitchen. He marveled at how one's attraction to another appears to turn on or off as if by some invisible switch. One day his baby girl had no interest in boys. Less than twenty-fours later, she was practically in love with one.

"What a difference a day makes . . ." he sighed out loud as he picked up the final dishes and headed for the kitchen. He stood at the door listening to the feminine chatter for a few seconds before making his entrance.

"Look at her," he thought. "She's as tall as her mother now and with their matching auburn hair and deep brown eyes, they could be sisters, even twins. Man, I remember how I felt when I met Annalisa at about Julie's age. Uh oh, maybe . . ."

Now standing fully in the kitchen, Alan pushed the door closed with his elbow and blurted out, "I decided I will apply for that track coach position after all."

"Oh, that's awesome, Dad!" chirped Julie as she hugged her father.

Alan glanced at Annalisa, who was standing at the sink smiling at him. He knew it was the right decision, but her smile was certainly confirmation.

That night while they were readying themselves for bed Alan opened the closet door, and the knob fell off, again.

"Alan, I wish you would fix that thing," complained Annalisa.

"Well, I wish Joey's father had fixed everything in this house before he moved out, but he didn't. And you know what they say about a carpenter and his house," he haggled. "Especially if I happen to be the carpenter who owns the . . ."

"Oh, Alan, I totally forgot!" exclaimed Annalisa as she shuffled through the clothes lying on the cedar chest at the foot of their bed. "I can't believe I forgot this. With all the excitement about Julie and her friend Roger, and the possibility of you coaching, I guess I got distracted or something. Now, where are my jeans?"

"Which jeans?"

"You know, the ones I had on today. Didn't I take them off and put them here?" Even though she asked Alan, she was actually questioning herself.

"I don't know, honey. I thought you had on your sweatpants when you came upstairs tonight."

"Oh, no!" she yelped, and dashing out of the room she called, "Be right back."

Pulling back the comforter, Alan adjusted the pillows so he could prop himself up in bed. "This should be a comfortable place while she makes her presentation of whatever she can't seem to find," he mumbled to himself.

He could hear Annalisa downstairs in the laundry room moving things around and opening and shutting first, the washer then, the dryer. After several minutes, he heard footsteps coming up the stairs, and she appeared back in their bedroom with a sigh.

"Found it," she grinned with a modest amount of self-satisfaction. "I was afraid I had lost it forever in the washing machine. That would have been terrible." As she closed their door, she held up, what appeared to Alan to be, an envelope that had seen better days. It was ragged, crumpled, and more than a little grungy.

"What have you got there, my love?" he asked in a deadpan tone trying not to reveal his curiosity.

"You're not going to believe this, Alan," she proposed. "I was up in the garage attic today cleaning out some of those old boxes and things that were left by Joey and his parents, you know, the ones way in the back. I've been trying to do a little each week this last month or so. I pulled all those boxes out of the back corner. Afterwards, I hauled them down those rickety pull-down steps and out onto the driveway. When I climbed back up in the attic, I noticed a tiny white paper sticking up between the floor boards. I walked over to take a closer look, and when I stepped on the board next to the paper it slipped further through the crack and disappeared." Annalisa, who had been standing at the foot of their bed, held up her hand with the envelope and slid it through her fingers demonstrating how the situation in the garage attic had taken place.

"I grabbed my flashlight and dropped to my knees, shining the light into the crack. I could see the paper, just below the surface, but couldn't discern what it was. I thought about how to snatch it out with something and quickly came up with an idea," she smiled at Alan. "You're going to love this part, honey."

"Why? What did you do, tear apart the attic, and now you need a carpenter, uh, me to put it back together?" he remarked with a tone of sarcasm and a smirk that would usually land him in the proverbial doghouse, but Annalisa was so excited she hardly noticed his comment.

"I climbed down the attic steps, ran over to the house, jogged up the stairs to our bathroom, and dug through my makeup drawer until I found my eyebrow plucker," she declared with a sense of pride for her problem solving ability.

"Eyebrow plucker?" he smirked. "What on earth, honey?"

"Yeah, it's like tiny tweezers and worked perfectly. So after retracing my steps back to the attic, I reached down inside those floor boards, gripped the paper, and pulled out this!" She held up the envelope proudly like one holds up a prized catch after a deep sea fishing trip.

"What is it?"

"It's an envelope with a postmark from back in 1961, and it's addressed to Joey's father. But the most important aspect of the envelope is the return address," she beamed as Alan quickly jumped out of bed.

"It's from a man named Boswell Storder, who lived in Worthington, Missouri. The envelope was already opened, so I pulled out the letter and read it. And guess what?" her eyes widened as she handed Alan the letter.

"What?"

"In the letter he mentions Sherman Wilkins. That's the guy Betsy said she and Stanley had dinner with years ago on Capitol Hill, remember? And guess who else?"

"Who?" asked Alan while he unfolded the letter to read it.

Then, just as his eyes fell upon the name, both he and Annalisa pronounced in unison, "Stanley Taft!"

"Oh, this is absolutely incredible!" blurted Alan as he threw an arm around Annalisa's shoulder while he continued to read the letter.

"Yeah, I know. This guy, Boswell, also mentions the woman in New England that inherited those papers from her father, and there is also someone who he calls P.D. in Bend, Oregon. I mean, this is so unbelievable, isn't it, honey?!"

"Yes, it certainly is un-be-stinking-lievable!" he bellowed. "This is an amazing find."

"And look at the bottom of the letter, Alan."

"I'm getting there. Hang on a second."

Alan's mouth dropped wide open as his eyes read the words at the bottom of the page. He slowly sat down on the side of the bed and read the entire letter again. Annalisa sat next to him with her arm tucked through his. He lowered the paper to his lap after he had read it through the second time. His mind was running at a thousand miles an hour. He replayed all the events from over the years that had been mysterious at the time, but now were beginning to make some sense and have some newfound clarity. He glanced across the letter one more time to assure himself what he had read was actually in the letter.

"I wonder if P.D. are the initials for the Police Department in Bend, Oregon?" he questioned out loud as he caught a glimpse of Annalisa's wide eyes.

"I never thought of that."

He smiled at Annalisa. "Wow, what do you make of all this?"

"I would say more evidence than you can shake a stick at. What do you think, Alan?"

"Well, frankly, I'm a bit dumbfounded, as well as rather ashamed that I haven't been pursuing my hunches, those nudgings, which were obviously from God. I'm becoming increasingly more convinced there must be something that He would like to reveal to His people in these days. And He's looking for someone, like us, crazy enough to go on some wild adventure with Him." Alan was slowly wagging his head in what was bordering on disbelief.

"I don't think He thinks it's crazy, Alan. To Him it's another faith adventure He has presented to us. If we're interested, He is allowing us to participate with Him. I believe this to be an honor, certainly not an accident. We were meant to find that letter!"

"You know something, my love? You are absolutely correct. He did this on purpose. There is something very important He wants to disclose to our generation in a particular way. I think there have been too many clues and unusual circumstances to think they're merely coincidence. No, there's definitely something here, and we need to search it out like a treasure hidden in a field," he pronounced with more confidence than Annalisa had heard from him in years.

Alan continued, "Yes, somehow, some way, we need to get to Pfeiffer Station, Ohio. Something major happened at that tiny crossroads back in the summer of 1866 that must have some significance for us today in 2001. For some reason, The **rojocci** Fellowship felt a need to gather and meet for a very rare conference in a very inconspicuous location."

"Why do you think they chose that town?" she quizzed intently.

"I'm not at all sure, my love. There must be something unique about it though."

"Well, remember it was a stop on the Underground Railroad. Maybe that's a clue. What do you think?"

"Yeah, it's probably telling us something important, something meaningful. Or . . . it may be a central location with a building to accommodate all in the meeting. It may have no real significance at all, but somehow I believe it does."

"Yeah, I do too. The Underground Railroad was a big deal, especially in those days. I mean, around the Civil War era and all. Yeah, there's something to that, Alan."

"I think you're right, but the thing I'm stirred up about is the second to last paragraph in the letter. I knew there had to be some sort of documentation generated from a conference of such magnitude. I mean, they met for five whole days after not meeting together for an entire century. There has to be something in writing." He glanced again at the letter as Annalisa peered around his side.

"Oh, you mean . . ."

"Yeah," interrupted Alan. "What on earth do you think is in a document which they would honor with a title such as 'The **rojocki** Manifesto'?"

-thirteen-

Although he wasn't often quiet, Joey was peculiarly silent when Alan arrived early to work on Monday. Things had been going so smoothly the last couple of years for Joey and his business. But now, with a problem looming on the very near horizon, he wasn't quite sure how to broach the subject with his close friend and second in command. However, he was sure Alan would recognize the symptoms, so he decided to discuss the topic at lunch. Shortly past noon, they sat down together at a local barbeque restaurant. After ordering Joey spoke up.

"Alan, old buddy, we're winding up this last contract on the hotel furniture refinishing projects. We should have it totally completed by end of next month. I do have those three house contracts for all the kitchen and bath cabinets, but after that . . . well, I'm not sure what to tell you." Joey sounded very apologetic.

"Joey, don't worry about it, man. You have been so generous with me and my family. You don't owe me anything. If and when you need to let me go, its fine. God will provide something else for me. In fact, I applied for the high school track coach position I told you about. It looks like I've got the job, so I was going to have to figure out some unique working hours anyway. It's only for August through November along with February through May. The position doesn't pay much, but I think it will be rewarding. So maybe I'll open my own woodworking shop, and when you need help, I'll contract work from you. Maybe I'll get some other jobs on my own as well," Alan smiled trying to appear hopeful.

"Yeah, that could work out, Alan."

"You think so? I mean, I would have to purchase some tools and all, but not too many just yet. I'm pretty sure I could handle almost all of the work with what I have in my shop in the garage."

"Alan, I'll sell you some of mine, real cheap. I won't be using them with a lighter workload, so you might as well put them to productive use. In fact, I'll give them to you, brother," he proffered and thrust his hand across the table to seal the deal.

"Wow, Joey, you're an amazing friend. I've never known anyone remotely like you, man. I feel guilty for accepting your generous offer. However, I've known you long enough to recognize if I didn't accept, I'd find the tools in my driveway early one morning anyway," smiled Alan acknowledging the true character of this Southern gentleman sitting across from him.

"That's right!" chuckled Joey in agreement. "I learned long ago, since God has been so kind with me, He expects me to be kind with others too, especially His own."

"Thanks, I really appreciate it," Alan smiled again. Then his expression turned serious. "Hey, there's something I need to talk to you about, okay?"

"Yeah, sure, what's up?"

"Well, I know we're buying the house from you and all, but there was something we found, uh . . . Annalisa found in the garage attic the other day that I think you should know about."

"Yeah, what is it?"

"It's a letter addressed to your father from back in 1961."

"Oh, no, if he did something wrong . . . uh, you know, if I have a brother or something I don't know about, please don't tell me, okay? You guys keep the letter or maybe burn it or something."

"No, no, no, it's nothing like that, Joey," laughed Alan.

Joey sighed, "Well, that's a relief." Then with a shrug of his shoulders and a partial grimace on his face, he timidly asked, "What is it?"

"No, man, you're too funny. It's regarding The **rojocki** Fellowship conference in Ohio back in the 1800s. Remember that?" questioned Alan with a grin. He pulled the envelope from his back pocket and slid it across the table barely missing Joey's tall glass of sweet tea. "Here's the letter. Sorry it was already opened, Joey."

"Nah, don't worry about it. I'm so glad its good news. My Dad's been gone for almost four years now, so there's nothing I could do about it anyway. Just the same, I'm relieved."

Opening the envelope carefully, Joey unfolded the letter, and silently read it. When he finished, he lowered it slowly to the table while gazing across the restaurant with his mouth hanging open.

"Wow, The **rojocki** Manifesto! This is huge, Alan. You were right. They did put together some document at the conference." Joey leaned back in his seat and peered out the window. The two would-be-explorers were both lost in thought. Each of them pondering how to obtain this newly discovered artifact. "We've got to go up there, Alan . . . the sooner the better. We need to figure out how to get to Pfeiffer Station and this tavern mentioned here, like el pronto."

"Betsy mentioned it too, Joey. So did the woman from New England; she wrote about it in her correspondence. Man, I don't even know if that tavern still exists. Or if it does, how we could gain entrance . . . or even if there's a trace of evidence the papers are still on the premises. More than likely, they were lost or destroyed long ago."

"Yeah, I didn't think about that," reflected Joey.

Just then their barbequed pulled pork sandwiches accompanied with french fries arrived. The two halted their conversation long enough to devour their lunches before washing it all down with tall glasses of sweet tea. Alan's mind was busily trying to work out a way to get to the tavern as Joey read his father's letter again.

"You go, Alan. You're much better at this exploration stuff than I am. You and Annalisa make a run up there. Pam and I will watch your kiddos."

"They're in school. We can't go now," complained Alan.

"Then go next month or how about going this summer?"

"I would love to travel to Ohio and do some digging, but we really don't have the money right now. It's not that we can't pay our bills; we can. It's the extra expense of hotels, gas, and all that stuff that would set us back a bit. So you guys go, Joey. You could always call me from Ohio if you hit a snag."

"Look, let me talk it over with Pam tonight, and I'll get back with you tomorrow. One way or another, one of us has got to get up there . . . and soon."

That evening the ideas were really percolating in both the Browne and Hinote households. Alan and Annalisa both decided that each one of them should be on the exploration team. He deemed himself as having the most at stake, and she thought, as the discoverer of the latest vital piece of this puzzle, she should be chosen to go too. However, both acknowledged the virtual impossibility because of finances along with needing someone to care for their three children. What they didn't expect was that Joey and Pam had reached the same conclusion, and were prepared to help Alan and Annalisa.

The next morning at work, Joey explained to Alan the plan he and Pam had developed the evening before. Alan and Annalisa would drive to Ohio sometime this summer. Joey and Pam would help by caring for Julie, Richard, and Emily in their home for up to one week and would contribute two hundred dollars toward Alan and Annalisa's travel expenses. With this last offer Alan's mouth dropped wide open.

"Are you kidding me? I can't let you do that, Joey! We can wait until we have the money and then plan a trip."

"Alan, it's not like we're giving y'all some money. We look at it as investing in a mission trip . . . well, kind of anyway. We would do the same for someone at church who was going to a remote spot in South America, Africa, or someplace. This time we're doing it for someone who happens to be going to some remote location in Ohio, that's all," explained Joey. "We want to participate, and this is the way we decided we could."

"Wow, when you put it that way, then it's like you're making an investment in a venture. It's like we're partners. Only you're staying here to hold down the fort, and we're going to climb the mountain, so to speak."

"Yeah, that's exactly it. We don't consider it like we're giving you money. We're giving the expedition funds, so the exploration team can be successful."

"Alright, I buy that, Joey," agreed Alan with a smile. "I'll sit down with Annalisa and start planning our "Grand **rojocki** Expedition!"

That evening as Alan and Annalisa were scheduling their trip, Alan received a phone call from the Principal at Julie's high school informing him that he had been selected to be their Track Coach for the spring and also the Cross Country Coach starting in August, a mere two months away. This news, although exciting, somewhat squelched their plans for a visit to Ohio.

"I have to start formal practices on Monday, July 29th. That really only gives us a window of the last two weeks in June until about mid-July," he calculated as he sat down on the sofa close to Annalisa.

"Let's go sooner, rather than later," she bartered. "How about the second week of June, so we get back before Fourth of July weekend? Then you won't feel hurried in preparing for coaching. How's that sound?"

"I like it, honey. Let's plan to leave on Saturday the 15th. I'll drop by the AAA store and pick up a map for the area, so we'll know where we can find a hotel and restaurants."

The next few weeks flew by as the two explorers organized everything needed for a successful trip to Pfeiffer Station. Amazingly, all their plans had come together as if some higher power was carefully ordering everything, helping them with all the various details.

Before long, they were on the Interstate headed for somewhere just south of Louisville, Kentucky, and their overnight stop. At least, they thought they were. However, while they were driving through Nashville, Alan noticed the engine light indicating the motor was overheating. He pulled over at the closest exit and found a service station. The news was not good; they needed a new water pump.

The mechanic gave a price Alan thought was twice what it would normally cost and nearly half the funds they had available for the trip. Alan became even more discouraged when he was told the repair wouldn't be completed until the following afternoon, at the earliest. This meant they would have to find a hotel and spend the night. His emotions were beginning to push their weight around, goading his insecurities with more than a gentle shove. It was getting dark, they were without a car in a section of the city which appeared rather seedy, and now they would have to walk almost two miles, with luggage, to what was, no doubt, going to be a very sketchy accommodation for the night. He was becoming convinced that maybe this whole trip was a bad idea.

"Honey, it's only for one night. God will watch over us. Don't let this current situation dissuade you from what we're trying to do, okay?" Annalisa sat on the side of the double bed, which barely fit in the room they had rented for the night.

"I wish I had a 44 Magnum. This place gives me the creeps."

"Honestly, Alan, sometimes I really . . ."

"Well, at least the door has a deadbolt lock," stated Alan sarcastically.

"Alan, the mechanic told us we would be out of here tomorrow afternoon."

"At the earliest," interrupted Alan with a hint of disgust in his tone.

"It's a minor detour, that's all," continued Annalisa trying to ignore his attitude. "We'll be back on the road and headed for Ohio before you know it," her voice sounded cheerful although she was somewhat concerned about their predicament as well.

"I know, my love. But it seemed like everything came together so smoothly and then this. Now, I don't know what to think. Should we head back home tomorrow?"

"Absolutely not! This is only temporary. Maybe it's just a test sent from God to see if you're going to have a negative attitude," she half-smiled as if she was half-joking. She was not.

"Really? Well, how am I doing? Man, it's hot in here. Does that air-conditioner work?

Side stepping around the bed, Alan made his way to the single window with the air-conditioner. "It sure is stuffy in here. My cheeseburger was nasty and those fries were more grease than they were potato. Man, that guy we passed on the street was . . ."

"Alan Michael Browne, stop it!" Annalisa was using a voice that she usually reserved for disciplining the children, but now her husband was needing a bit of juvenile admonishment.

"Stop what?" he barked.

"Alan, listen to yourself. You're acting exactly like the Israelites did after they left Egypt with Moses. They complained and murmured against God. You're doing the same thing."

"So I'm the Israelites?! What's that make you, a female Moses?" he jabbed.

"Quit sissifying!"

"Now, wait a second . . ."

"No, Alan, you listen to me. Where's your faith? You're whining about circumstances we have no control over. This is precisely the same thing as the Israelites complaining against God. They blamed Moses, but God declared they were blaming Him. Look, if He rules and controls everything, and I know you know that's true, and if He loves us, then all of this is for our best. It may not appear that way, but it is. And bellyaching about it isn't going to do us any good, nor will it help our attitudes. So please, for my sake, stop it!"

The room fell silent except for the clanging of the fan inside the old air-conditioner. Alan sat on one side of the bed with his knees pressed against the wall, and Annalisa sat on the other side using her foot to hold the door to the bathroom closed. Neither faced one another as they listened to the sounds of the city night, deep in thought. After nearly twenty minutes, Alan broke the invisible tension in the room.

"Wow . . ."

"Alan, any sentence that doesn't have some resemblance of an apology in it would be just as well left unsaid." Alan noted her voice still had a tinge of anger.

"Honey, I was going to say," he replied softly. "Wow, thank you for shaking me out of my despondent funk. I sure don't want to come across as ungrateful . . . especially not toward God. I mean, I remember what happened to those Israelites for the next forty years as a result of their complaining."

"Really? Are you being sincere?" she asked as she swung around on the bed, which allowed the bathroom door to swing open again.

"Yes, my love, and I'm very, very, sorry for my lousy attitude and for being a discouragement to you. Thank you for helping me to see that." He turned partially around to look at her face to face. "I'm so sorry, sweetheart. I'll do my best not to act that way again, okay?"

She moved across the bed, slid her arms around him, and kissed him on the cheek. "Thank you, Alan. That means so much to me." She held him close and kissed him on the lips.

She whispered in his ear softly, "You know, this doesn't have to be a bad thing."

"What do you mean, my love," he quizzed.

"Perhaps you should turn out the lights, honey."

The following morning, they found a local restaurant open for breakfast. By the time they made their way back to the service station, it was shortly after eleven-thirty. To their surprised delight, the car was repaired and ready to go. Alan paid the mechanic, thanking him for his extra effort on their behalf. Then, they were back on the road once again, heading north.

"I saw what you did back there, sweetheart," she smiled, reaching across their minivan to hold his hand.

"What?"

"You gave that mechanic a twenty dollar tip. I'm really proud of you, dear. That's the man I married; the one who goes the extra mile, especially when it isn't the easy thing to do. And, Alan . . .?"

"Yes, my love?"

"I believe God is proud of you too." She leaned across and smooched him on the lips.

"Honey, stop. You're going to make me crash the car," he frowned. Although, they both knew he really enjoyed her frisky impetuousness.

"I know," she teased resting back in her seat. "You hate it when I kiss you."

"Yeah, what a bummer to have a wife who wants to kiss," he teased. Then reaching across he held her hand softly as they both had a good chuckle.

"I wonder why our Father in Heaven had us go through that little detour yesterday?" posed Alan as he changed lanes to pass a semi-truck.

"Perhaps He knew you had an area of your heart not surrendered to Him yet. Or maybe it was something else entirely. Whatever it was, He had a purpose in it. That's for sure."

"Hmmm . . ." pondered Alan, glancing in his rearview mirror as they passed the *Welcome to Kentucky* sign. "Or maybe it's something to do with Ohio. It's possible He needed to delay us a day or two. I don't know, just thoughts."

Arriving in Kenton, Ohio, late the following afternoon, they checked into a room at a nice hotel. From the map, they could tell Pfeiffer Station was only a few miles to the east. The next morning they were up early, had some breakfast, and headed for their destination. It was a quarter of nine when they pulled over in front of a historic marker indicating some details regarding the Underground Railroad.

"That must be the old Tavern," asserted Annalisa pointing at a brick house with a shallow angle metal roof behind the marker.

"Yeah, I think so too," agreed Alan. "But like I thought, I'm afraid it's a residence now. That's not good."

"What do you mean, honey?"

"Well, a couple of things. First, they may not want a couple of strangers traipsing around their property and certainly not inside their home. Second, it most assuredly means that over the course of a century plus thirty-some years the house has no doubt been cleaned out. Perhaps several times, and maybe even remodeled a time or two. This isn't a good sign."

"Oh, no, what should we do?"

"Let's go knock on the door. I mean, we came this far. I'm not going to leave without at least trying to get a look inside."

The two walked hand in hand across the bright green lawn, damp with morning dew. Alan knocked on the front door. No answer. He knocked again, this time longer and louder. When they determined no one was going to answer the front door, they walked around to the side of the home. No cars in the driveway. Annalisa peeked in one of the windows while Alan admired the beautiful landscaping.

"Have you ever seen something so brilliantly green?" he gushed.

"It's blue," she retorted.

"No, it's definitely green," he mocked.

"Well, I say it's blue-green at the most."

"No my love, that grass is . . ." He laughed as he swung around to explain to her the obvious mistake in her color assessment of the lawn when he discovered her face pressed against the glass of the front window.

"What on earth are you doing?" he barked. "Stop that. You want to get us thrown in jail?"

"It's the dining room, Alan. Looks like there's nobody home and that wall color is a pretty shade of turquoise. I don't see any **rojocki** clues though," she smirked.

"Well, there won't be any sitting out on the dining room table. They're probably hidden in the basement, the attic, or somewhere. We need to get inside, but I'm not going to risk being accused of burglary or something. Let's try back a little later. Maybe, at that point, the owners will be home."

"It's a beautiful home," confided Annalisa as they walked back to their car. "Are you sure this is the place? Doesn't look like a meeting hall."

"That was over a century ago. I'm sure it has changed since then. It does look old enough though. Let's drive around the town a bit. Maybe we can find someone who knows the owners," he suggested as he opened the door for her.

"Good idea, honey. Certainly someone should know something in this tiny village."

Annalisa was correct. Pfeiffer Station was a petite burg of no more than a cross road with a railroad track running alongside. The town was quiet and peaceful. There was no one to be seen anywhere except an elderly man, who was driving away from his home in an old Ford pickup truck. As they turned a corner, they almost drove into an Amish buggy pulled by a single black horse.

"Whoa, did you see that?" yelped Alan after he had swerved to avoid hitting the buggy.

"Yeah, I've never seen any Amish in person before."

"Since the owners of the tavern aren't home, let's take a drive in the country and see what we can find. Maybe we'll see some more Amish folks. We'll head back here in a couple of hours, around lunch time, and see if they're home then, okay?"

"Sounds perfect," agreed Annalisa with a smile.

The two adventurers marveled at the buggies clip-clopping along the narrow country roads, which were dotted with the evidence of recent and frequent horse travel. In fact, the Amish folks were the only people they saw in their exploring that morning. They made their way back to Pfeiffer Station and parked in front of the tavern at twelve-thirty. This time, because the building still appeared devoid of inhabitants, only Alan walked to the front door. After knocking several times, he put his hands to the glass in the door and peered inside. It was a beautiful home, but there was absolutely no sign of anything remotely resembling a clue that a **rojocki** conference had convened here many decades ago.

"Well, my love, I don't know what to tell you," he postulated. "Except, this I do know, there is no one in that house. Who knows, they may even be on vacation. Perhaps they leave each summer for Canada, living up there in the cool climate while it's hot down here. I'm not sure what to think. We are kind of striking out. What do you say we head back to the hotel and try again later this afternoon?"

"Sounds like a plan . . . with one variation, please."

"What's that, sweetheart?"

"I've been watching a steady stream of folks going in and out of that General Store across the street. They all come out with what looks like lunch plates. Some are even sitting on the front porch eating, see what . . ."

Catching a glimpse of what Annalisa was referring to, Alan interrupted. "Hmmm . . . man, that sounds good to me. I'm hungry. How about you?"

"I'm starvin' marvin," she concurred.

Sitting at one of the picnic tables on the front porch of the Pfeiffer Station General Store, they devoured one of the best home cooked lunches they had ever tasted. It was Tuesday, and evidently, Tuesday was Chicken and Dumplings day. This, coupled with mashed potatoes, gravy, and some green beans, really hit the spot. Alan even went back for seconds, and Annalisa had some Amish berry pie she pronounced, "Was good enough to die for."

"Oh, I think I hurt myself," complained Alan with delight. "That was so incredibly good."

"Yeah, I'm stuffed. I couldn't eat another bite . . . unless they placed that pie in front of me again. Oh, my, that's delicious pie," she declared with her fake Southern drawl. Then repeating the phrase over and over, she moved into a sort of seated, happy dance.

"I think I'll vegetate here until the tavern owners across the street show up. What do you say, you pie eating cutie you?"

"Good idea, Alan. I don't think I could walk all the way to our car anyway," she laughed, recognizing it to be parked a mere twenty yards away.

"Ha, it's only across the street, Miss Plumpkin."

Just then, the owner of the General Store came out to greet them asking if they enjoyed their meals. She offered them more lemonade and cleared off the paper plates and plastic utensils. A few minutes later, she emerged with more of the sweetened cool beverage.

"Kind of hot today," offered Alan.

"Yeah, about typical for around here," she stated in a friendly tone. "It's muggy in the mornings, but always a breeze in the afternoons. You folks aren't from Ohio, are you?"

"What makes you say that, ma'am?" replied Alan.

"Well, for one thing, you use the word 'ma'am'. I rarely hear that around here, at least not from my recollection anyway. Plus, I noticed the tag on your car, and that don't look like no fancy rental car," she cackled.

Laughing along with her, Alan and Annalisa introduced themselves. The store owner had a kind face with quiet blue eyes. Alan guessed she was raised in the area as she appeared to come from sturdy stock. Her somewhat wild grey hair was partially hidden under an old visor, giving her that old west, gambling-hall-card-dealer look, rather than a general store owner demeanor. Although she wore a tank top, blue jeans, and sneakers, there was no mistaking she had a savvy, entrepreneur persona. Alan told her how they had traveled all the way from Pensacola, Florida, to have a chance to look inside the old tavern. He alluded to the fact that there might have been some historical documents buried away in there somewhere.

The amiable store owner inquired as to what kind of papers. "Something to do with the Underground Railroad?" she smiled.

"No, not directly, anyway," replied Alan. "We're looking for some papers regarding a conference held here back in the Summer of 1866, shortly after the Civil War."

"Really?!" she asked. "Are you talking about The **rojocki** Conference?"

"Yes, ma'am, that's precisely what I'm talking about. Do you know anything about it?"

"Well, I can assure you they didn't meet at the old tavern. This I know for a fact."

"What? Why do you say that?" asked Annalisa, her voice hitting a higher octave.

"When the group arrived from the South, they refused to meet there because they discovered the tavern had actually played a significant role in the Underground Railroad. I guess old wounds heal slowly. However, after several hours of bickering, one of the attendees, a man from Iowa, made the suggestion to meet across the street at the General Store."

"What? You mean . . ." begged Alan.

"Yep, they met right here in this store, which is now my store. They gathered upstairs for nearly five days to come up with a plan to help heal our country . . . and to heal the Christian fellowship in all the churches nationwide." At this point, she leaned forward and lowered her voice to a whisper. "It's rumored there was some loud fussing at each other until the last day when something very miraculous happened."

"What happened?" asked Alan and Annalisa in unison.

"Well, I don't remember all the details. But there's a file drawer full of those original writings upstairs in the meeting room."

At this last revelation, both Alan and Annalisa practically fell out of their seats. This was the very thing they were hoping to find when they set out on their journey to Pfeiffer Station. Now, here it was at their fingertips, and with a guide disguised as a store owner.

"Ma'am, would you kindly allow us to look over some of those documents for a few minutes." Alan was using his most sincere voice. "We're looking for something called The rojocki Manifesto. We think it may be in those papers you have upstairs."

"No." She placed the lemonade pitcher on the table top. "Not today, anyway. I have to leave for Wapakoneta in a few minutes; it's where I pick up some of my supplies for the store. But if you want to come by tomorrow morning, I'd be happy to let you have a look-see."

-fourteen-

Hardly sleeping a wink the entire night, Alan finally dozed off shortly before dawn. Annalisa woke him at seven-thirty and handed him a hot cup of coffee. The couple cleaned up and had a quick bite to eat downstairs at the hotel's breakfast buffet before heading to the General Store a little after eight o'clock. In his haste, Alan spilled nearly half his cup of coffee in his lap as he was driving out of the hotel parking lot. This warm awakening prompted an immediate U-turn for a clean pair of jeans for him as well as a few snickers from her.

When they arrived at the General Store, it was apparent it was already open for business. Alan and Annalisa strode across the wooded planks of the porch floor, pulled open the screened door, and stepped inside. Tantalizing fragrances from the early preparation of the day's lunch special along with the aroma of hot coffee wafted throughout the rustic interior. Hanging from long rods, two antique paddle fans turned slowly. The walls were a dark beaded wood siding with some type of decorative metal panels covering the ceiling. It was a sparsely lit interior yet, with the morning sunlight beaming through the windows, the items presented for sale were well illuminated and easily viewed. Alan noticed the wooden flooring continued inside, giving him the feeling he had been transported back to the 1800s. The overall sensation was quite pleasing and made him smile.

Annalisa's eyes roamed back and forth between the three aisles. Each contained densely packed shelves overflowing with everything from jams and jellies to hand operated can openers and mixers. There even was a candy counter with a wide variety of homemade goodies, more than either of them had ever seen. However, she lingered the longest in the baked goods section.

"Those are all homemade cakes and pies, made right here in Hardin County by our Amish community," explained the friendly voice from behind the old cash register.

Looking up to see the kind-faced owner they had met the day before smiling back at her, Annalisa declared, "Oh, they all look too good to eat. I'm afraid I'd gain twenty pounds if we stayed here much longer. That berry pie yesterday was absolutely to die for."

Alan, who had been staring at the dairy case full of Amish cheeses and yogurts, moved over to where Annalisa and the owner were talking. He discovered the store had been left in somewhat of a state of disrepair until this current owner bought and remodeled it. She explained how she loved the whole romantic idea of an old general store and had kept her eye on this one for several years.

"When it came up for sale one day, I jumped on it," she boasted. "I'm so glad I did. I just love this lifestyle," she paused while waving her hands in the air indicating what held her affections. "Well, I'm sure you folks are anxious to get upstairs and do some research."

"Yes, ma'am," exclaimed Alan and Annalisa together.

The owner led them up a dark, very narrow set of stairs so closed in it felt claustrophobic. At the top, was a landing. To the left stood a single dingy door, which she unlocked, and after opening it they all continued inside. Again, the décor followed what they had experienced on the first floor, but instead of the white display shelves with products for sale, there were grey metal shelves full of cardboard boxes. The room appeared to be about fourteen or fifteen feet wide and twenty feet long. It was difficult to estimate the size because many of the boxes were stacked quite high. However, in the middle of the room under several boxes rested an old, very dark mammoth table. Above it, in the center of the ceiling, hung a single paddle fan with two lights switched by a dangling pull chain. Unfortunately, when the owner yanked on the chain, only one light came on.

"Sorry about the lack of light in here," she confessed. "This other light has been broken for years. However, we can open these two windows and that should help. No air-conditioning though. I couldn't afford to have it installed up here when we got it downstairs a few years back. There's usually a nice breeze in the afternoons, so it shouldn't be too bad by then. Kind of makes you feel like they must have felt back in the 1800s, eh?" she postulated with a grin.

Having walked Alan and Annalisa all the way around the table to the far side of the room, the store owner led them to the corner diagonally opposite the only door. She moved a few smaller boxes and pulled back a single leather swivel chair that had been under, what appeared to be, a desk. Alan helped her move several more boxes. After removing the final one, there it was . . . the tomb awaiting discovery. It appeared ancient and nearly black, yet readily discernable as an oak roll top desk. Upon inspection, the trio agreed its better days were at least a century ago. The owner pulled a rag from her back pocket and tried to remove the decade worth of dust, which lay only in spaces where boxes had not been placed. When her dusting efforts were revealed to be inadequate, she blew off the rest with several large huffs and puffs.

"There," she smiled with a sense of satisfaction. "That's what you've been searching for; you're at the end of your quest."

Pulling on the handle to the roll, the owner was having difficulty obtaining her goal of opening the top. Alan immediately jumped in and with one mighty yank the top rolled up and disappeared within the hutch, instantly exposing the contents which had been hidden inside.

"Wow!" gasped Annalisa. "There's even a quill and ink-well."

"Yes, I left everything precisely like I had found it way back when I bought the place," she pronounced with a firm tone. "And you will do the same, won't you?"

Alan immediately responded, "Oh, yes, ma'am, absolutely, we certainty will."

"Okay, then. You folks have fun, and let me know if you need anything. I'll be right down stairs. I'm going to close the door. I think the fewer folks who know about this room the better."

"Thank you, ma'am, we promise we'll be sensitive as well."

She nodded her head as she shut the door. "Oh, and by the way, there's file drawers on either side. I think that's where you'll find what you're looking for, and you are not to remove anything from this room, understand?"

"Yes, ma'am," replied Alan quickly to avoid giving her any reason to kick them out when they were so near to the mother lode of their exploration.

Alan motioned for Annalisa to sit down on the desk chair. The two explorers gazed at the old desk, stone still like gold diggers finding evidence of their long and difficult excavation. He reached out his hand taking ahold of hers, knelt down there beside her, and prayed. He thanked their Father in Heaven for all the years, the circumstances, the clues, the searching, as well as for Stanley, Betsy, A-Dub, Joey, and Pam. Finally, he thanked God for his precious wife and dear life partner, Annalisa. All these, and so much more, had led them to this place, this room, at this point in history, to discover what had lain hidden within this desk for all these many years.

After the "Amen," Alan asked Annalisa to open the drawer on the far side of the desk. While she was trying to work it open, Alan jerked one of the two wooden windows up, releasing the stale air in the room to move outside.

"Sure is stuffy up here," he complained as he moved toward the other one, pulling and then pushing it open as well. With the second window open, a breath of fresh air blew through, stirring up the dust that had been accumulating for who knows how long. The particles swirled in the air giving definition to the rays of bright morning sunshine, which filtered in through the back window.

"Alan," called Annalisa from behind the wall of boxes hiding the desk. "I think I found something here."

"What is it, honey?" he replied as he quickly walked back over to where she was seated.

"Well, I'm not sure. There aren't any files in this drawer, but there are several books. Now, in this other drawer there are quite a few files, but they seem to be from a more recent era, looks like around the 1930s to 1960s. There's nothing regarding The **rojocki** Fellowship though and certainly nothing about a conference back in 1866."

"Here, let me take a look. You check out all those little drawers and cubbies in the hutch, okay?"

With several minutes of unsuccessful digging, the two prospectors had come up empty-handed. The files had only revealed business documents and records from years past. Although they were a very interesting read, it was not at all what Alan and Annalisa had traveled all the way from Florida to discover. Disheartened, but unwilling to give up, Annalisa slumped back in the swivel chair, and Alan, after testing them first, sat down on a couple of stacked boxes.

"This is somewhat puzzling, my love," he confided while stroking her soft hair with the palm of his hand.

"It's got to be here someplace, Alan. We have too many clues from too many people over too many years for it not to be here somewhere."

"I agree, honey, but where?"

The room fell silent as they were deep in thought wondering if maybe they had missed something, somewhere, at some point in time. Alan's eyes glanced around the room, stopping on anything that might provide a clue. Still seated, he pivoted on his stack of boxes taking in the rest of the room until his eyes fell upon Annalisa, who was staring back at him. Neither spoke a word so as not to interrupt the other's thoughts. Alan gazed at the desk, noticing the ink-well and the quill. Then his eyes widened. Glancing back at Annalisa, he motioned for her to change seats with him.

"Get up, a second, please, honey."

"Why?" she questioned as she moved across to the stack of boxes Alan had used as his perch to view the room. "What is it, Alan? What are you thinking?"

"You said this other drawer was filled with books," he asserted while he removed a hand full of four volumes from their wooden coffin. He then pointed to the quill and ink-well as he fingered through the first book.

"They wrote by hand back in the 1800s. The quill and ink-well is what they used to pen the documents," he smiled as he swung around to look at her face to face. "What did they write upon?"

"Paper, I guess," she shrugged.

"Books, my love, they wrote in books, and here is a file drawer full of old books. It's in here . . . in this drawer somewhere."

"Wow, Alan, how did you think of that?"

He pointed at the quill and ink-well, though never looked up from his search within the musty stacks of books silently waiting to be discovered. He continued downward through several large and small volumes, until lying on the bottom of the wooden drawer, under what seemed to be more than a dozen hardbound tomes of various historic significance, was an album, the size of which nearly covered the entire floor of the drawer. Alan quickly glanced at Annalisa and then reached down to grasp the dark red binding. It was rather thick, an inch or more, and had three embossed letters on the front: "T r F". If they had been in gold, silver, or another color, it had long since disappeared.

Alan handed the volume to Annalisa while holding up one finger, indicating he wanted her to wait so they could open it together. He quickly loaded the other books back into their resting place, thereby clearing a spot for them to view the object he had unearthed. Neither said a word. Taking it from her hand, he placed the musty, old hardcover record on the desk in front of him. He then moved her stack of boxes, so she could be seated right next to him.

"Ready?" he whispered reverently.

Nodding her head slowly, Annalisa never took her eyes off the book.

"Nah, let's come back tomorrow, honey," he teased, moving like he was putting the book back in the drawer.

"Alan Michael Browne, are you crazy?!" she barked as she playfully slapped him on the shoulder.

The two of them laughed until he reached over and kissed her softly, acknowledging the importance of the moment. She smiled and gave him a hug as well.

"Thank you, my sweetheart, for all your help," he expressed lovingly.

"We make a great team, honey. Always have and always will," she furthered.

"Well, here we go," he announced quietly while he opened the cover.

The old binding cracked and creaked as Alan opened it wide, gingerly resting the front cover upon the desk. They gazed at the first page, which had been handwritten over a century ago. There, indicated at the top, was the conference name, location, and dates. Below this was listed the name, county, and state of each of the attendees. Alan counted twenty-three in all. Two of the total number had the words "freed slave" under their names. One of those names was Elijah Whitaker, Allegany County, Maryland.

"Annalisa, look at this!" exclaimed Alan as he pointed at the name. "I think this may be A-Dub's ancestor, who must have been here for this conference. I wonder if A-Dub knew that?"

"I saw it too. That's amazing!"

"I'm sure he was a relative of A-Dub. I mean, what are the chances?" he nodded with delight.

"I sure did enjoy old A-Dub. What a godly man," she professed.

"Yeah, I doubt he's still alive, but I'll never forget him. In fact, he predicted we'd get married, remember?"

"Hmmm . . ." she pondered. "Hey, look at this."

Before turning the page, Annalisa noted that there was practically the same amount of attendees from Northern as from Southern states. A fact they pondered, considering how close the date of the conference was to the end of the Civil War. They both acknowledged there must have been some emotionally charged discussions during the course of those five days. There were eighteen men and three women crammed in this room, in the August heat, with no air-conditioning or even fans, trying to find some harmony, some ideals, some common ground they could agree upon.

"It's amazing to me that it didn't end in bloodshed," stated Alan as he slowly wagged his head.

"Yeah, honey, I'm sure at least some of them had to work through some bitterness. I wonder how they did it?" she asked softly.

"Let's find out," suggested Alan as he turned the dry, crackly paper.

The next page revealed the purpose for the meeting with the facing page indicating the beginning of the conference minutes, a log of some sort. Alan and Annalisa spent the following four hours reading the numerous pages of that log. Although it appeared all attendees, at one point in time or another, had spoken up, the majority of the recordings gave evidence to seven main figures: two of whom were from Massachusetts, one from Vermont, three Virginians, an Iowan, and one particularly wordy gentleman from South Carolina.

The five day discussion had revolved almost entirely around establishing a written statement delineating the purpose for the unprecedented meeting, and more importantly, generating a document that would call everyone within the Fellowship, both North and South, to once again dwell in unity. Alan pointed out to Annalisa how they had opened and closed each and every session with lengthy prayer. In fact, several had prayed each time, according to the journal. And when, on occasion, the discussion had become heated, someone invariably led out in prayer and soon all would follow. Evidently, at one impassioned session, the whole group prayed for nearly the remainder of the day, led by Chance Worthy, a freed slave. Prayer always precipitated an apology from all offending parties.

"What an amazing example these people were, Alan."

"I know, I was thinking the very same thoughts. We modern day believers could use a heaping dose of that," he smiled. Then added, "Me included."

As they turned the last page of the recorded minutes of the conference, they finally found the object of their journey to Pfeiffer Station. Their eyes opened wide as they took it all in. Annalisa placed her arm on his shoulder and Alan, in turn, kissed her on the cheek acknowledging their remarkable discovery. They read it together with only the occasional grunt from Alan breaking the stillness in the room. It was a quiet reverence they had not planned. They were in awe of what they were reading—an ancient document signifying a unified declaration after an intensely embattled few days. Little did those twenty-three members know, all those years ago, what they would be preserving for future generations, for those who endeavored to live like a believer in the Lord Jesus Christ.

When Alan finished reading it, he fell back in the swivel chair and exhaled a deep sigh.

"That's absolutely amazing."

"It sure is," breathed Annalisa. "We need to write it down word for word."

Alan motioned for Annalisa to hand him the legal pad of paper they brought to record notes of their findings. He turned to a clean sheet and began drawing an outline around the perimeter, similar to the page he was copying. Starting at the top and center of the page, he, like the scribes of antiquity before him, began to copy, with delicate care and attention, the following:

<u>The rojocki Fellowship</u>
Pfeiffer Station, Ohio
August 17-21, 1866

Whereas the purpose for this unprecedented gathering is clearly stated within the pages of this, our journal and minutes, we have endeavored, in an effort to quicken and speed along the unity of the faith in the bond of love, to place upon the corporate mind and conscience, a set of tenets, both based within the Holy Scriptures and confirmed by the Holy Ghost;

Whereas has been noted within these pages an alarming resentment, albeit bitterness between the brethren, separated by no more than an invisible line etched within each mind of political views that have pressed upon the very moral and ethical fabric of each congregation indicated by only the titles of North and South;

Whereas it is incumbent upon the heart of each and every believer to do his utmost to maintain the unity of the faith, we do hereby present, in the spirit of the Apostles counseling the new Gentile believers in Antioch as recorded in the Book of the Acts of the Apostles, this first and only document we most humbly entitle:

The rojocki Manifesto
II Chronicles 7:14

1. **Love is the calling.** Matthew 22:35-40
2. **Pray first and unceasingly.** 1 Thessalonians 5:17
3. **Check first your heart when searching the Holy Scriptures.** Proverbs 4:23
4. **Thankfulness is the evidence of trust.**
   Hebrews 13:15
5. **Generosity toward others, frugality with self.**
   2 Corinthians 9:6, 7
6. **Judge yourself, allow God to judge others.**
   Matthew 7:1-5
7. **Freedom is an offspring of the truth.**
   John 8:31, 32

We, the undersigned, do hereby maintain, if the above tenets be followed within the Fellowship and Body of Christ as a whole, then a seedbed of healing will be planted amongst us. And with the Lord's providential cultivation, water, and care, a forest of mighty oaks, fit for the shade and shelter of many generations of His congregation to come, will began to grow and heal our terrible divide. To all, peace.

Once Alan had finished copying the priceless document, he asked Annalisa to photograph all the pages within the book for future reference. He carefully held each page open flat and she clicked the photo with their camera. While they were finishing up, they heard footsteps coming up the stairs toward them. There was a fumbling at the door knob, and soon it swung open hitting the wall behind with a thump.

247

"I thought you both may be getting a bit hungry. It's almost three o'clock," declared the store owner. An enticing aroma filled the room as she walked over to Alan and Annalisa, arms loaded with heaping plates of the daily lunch special.

"How's spaghetti and homemade meatballs sound?"

"Oh, my," yelped Annalisa. "Let me help you with that."

"Thank you, thank you, thank you," gushed Alan. "I didn't realize I was so hungry. But now that I've gotten a whiff of your spaghetti, I'm starving."

"Oh, it's just what we had left over. I hope you'll enjoy it, with my compliments."

"Oh, no you don't, we want . . ."

"I won't hear of it, so put your money away. Besides, I'm so happy today. My sweet little granddaughter was so dangerously ill over the weekend that we had to stay overnight in the hospital on Sunday. We even had to close the store Monday. Thankfully, I got a phone call a few minutes ago. My precious grandbaby is going to be just fine."

"Oh, that's wonderful news!" exclaimed Annalisa with a smile between bites of the meatballs and spaghetti sauce.

Alan dropped his plastic fork on his plate. "You weren't open this past Monday?"

"Nope, first time in years, except for snow days, of course, why?"

"Oh, nothing," he grinned, winking at Annalisa. "We had planned on being here first thing Monday morning, but we had . . . shall we call it, a divine detour for a day in Nashville."

"Our car broke down," confessed Annalisa candidly.

"Yeah," expressed Alan, "and I'm thinking, if it hadn't needed a new water pump, we may never have met you ma'am or found what we traveled so far to find. We'd still be thinking these documents were in the tavern across the street."

"Well, God most certainly works in mysterious ways," chuckled the owner shaking her head.

The following morning Alan and Annalisa were up extra early and on the road, anxious to get home. They decided the night before, as they were talking to Joey and Pam on the telephone, that they would drive straight through if at all possible. If they limited their stops and shared the driving, they calculated they would arrive home sometime around midnight. Regardless, they would be home two whole days ahead of schedule, and that would be good for everyone, or so they thought.

-fifteen-

Well after midnight, the road weary couple finally arrived home. Alan pulled the car up to the side door near the front of the garage. He had noticed a strange car parked out front by the entrance. Julie must have visitors he thought although no lights were on inside. Annalisa groggily commented that maybe their daughter was having a slumber party with a few girlfriends. They soon discovered while their daughter did have a visitor, he wasn't of a feminine variety. Alan swiftly flipped on the lights to find his sweet baby girl, of seventeen years, reclining back on the living room sofa with a young man. When light filled the room, both leapt to their feet. The two looked rather disheveled and more than a little guilty while trying quickly to straighten their attire.

"What on earth, Julie?!" roared her distressed father. "Do you have any idea what time it is? What are you doing in here with all the lights out . . . and with a boy?"

"Uh, sir . . . I can explain," interjected the young man.

"For now, buster, it would be better for you to shut up, understand?" Alan's tone sounded both authoritative and angry, but at this point it was more to show the younger male who exactly was the alpha in this house, his house, than to express his shock and disappointment.

"Dad, I'm sorry, but we weren't doing anything wrong."

"Yet!" barked her father.

"Sir, I assure you, I would never do anything to hurt your daughter."

"Son, I told you to be quiet," Alan firmly advised, pointing a finger at the guilty fellow.

"Look," retorted the younger man. "With all due respect, sir, I'm not you're son, so just back off."

Alan lunged toward the boy with such fierce indignation that Annalisa grabbed his arm begging him to back down. The young fellow bounded for the front door.

"Roger, wait," yelped Julie. "My dad's not going to hit you. He's only upset, that's all. Please, we can work this out. If you care for me, please don't leave." Her soft voice melted her father's enraged heart while calming Roger's as well.

Placing herself between the two offenders and her husband, Annalisa stretched out her hand.

"Hi, Roger, I'm Mrs. Browne. Nice to meet you. Although, I wish it had been under different circumstances."

Roger shook her hand. "Me too, ma'am, I'm very sorry about this whole situation, uh . . . I mean, misunderstanding."

"Well, I hope you realize where we, as Julie's parents, are coming from. Having arrived home in the middle of the night we found an unknown car in our driveway and a stranger, uh, on the sofa with our daughter. It was quite upsetting."

"I'm very sorry ma'am," apologized Roger again, his Southern drawl giving some credence to his sincerity.

"This is my husband, Julie's father, Mr. Browne," motioned Annalisa to the man standing behind her.

Alan and Roger reluctantly shook hands. Roger chuckled softly.

"What's so funny?" rebuffed Alan.

"I just realized you're my new Track and Cross Country Coach, and I'm probably going to suffer like a dog the first week of practice next month."

"Only the first week?" mocked Alan, who's tone was heavily laced with sarcasm.

"Okay, Roger," interrupted Annalisa. "It's almost one o'clock in the morning. You should go home now. We'll have a talk with Julie in the morning. Then, she'll call you to let you know what we have decided."

"Decided, ma'am?"

"Yes, Roger, we have rules in this house and Julie knows full well she's committed a serious infraction in a major way. There will be consequences of one sort or another."

Annalisa moved Roger to the front door and opened it. "But for now, it's very late, and we all need our rest. So you have to go on home."

"Will Julie and I still be allowed to see each other, ma'am?"

"I wouldn't worry about it tonight," she winked as she closed the door behind him. "Good night, Roger."

"Young lady, you are in such big . . ."

"Alan, it's so late. Let's deal with this in the morning, when we're all rested and can discuss it rationally," reasoned Annalisa as she slid her arm around his waist.

"Julie, phone," she extended her hand for her daughter to surrender her mobile phone to her. "Good night, sweetheart," her mother smiled with a half frown. "We'll talk about this in the morning."

"Good night, Mom and Dad. I really am sorry, but we weren't doing anything."

"Julie . . . bed," commanded her mother firmly.

The morning sky was hazy, and so was Alan's head as he stumbled down to the kitchen for his mind-clearing cup of coffee. Annalisa and Julie were silently sitting at the kitchen table. It was apparent to Alan that he must have interrupted a mother-daughter conference and started for the living room with his caffeinated cup of reveille. He could see Richard out the front window kicking and then running after the soccer ball. This scene had replayed time and time again, ever since his son had received the ball for his birthday over a year ago. After several sips of the hot beverage, which had the effect of awakening his senses, Alan couldn't help but hear whispers coming from the kitchen. Within a few minutes, footsteps approached the living room.

"Honey, Julie has something she would like to say."

"Where's Emily?" Alan asked abruptly.

"While you were still asleep, dear, I ran over to the Hinote's to pick up Richard and Emily. Richard was ready, but Emily asked if she could stay until after lunch because they were having grilled hot dogs and hamburgers. In fact, I

R. J. Graves, Jr.

need to leave shortly, but before I run to get Emma, Julie has something . . ."

"Wait a minute, what time is it?"

"Uh, it's eleven-thirty, dear. You slept right through the morning."

"Well, I drove almost the whole way and besides . . . I had a bit of a hard time falling asleep last night. I wonder why that could be?" he questioned with an unhealthy, heaping dose of his unique brand of sarcasm. "Yeah, I wonder. Now, let me think . . ."

"Mom!" moaned Julie. "This isn't going to work."

"Alan, come on. Hear Julie out, okay? This is important, honey."

"Uh . . . well . . . okay. What would you like to say, sweetheart?" he smiled letting her know, whatever it was she may have done, she was still his precious daughter, and he still loved her.

"Daddy, I'm really sorry about last night. I want you to know I won't do it again. But I didn't do anything wrong. And it wasn't Roger's fault."

"Oh, really?!" the contempt had crept back into his tone. "Then whose fault was it . . . your mother's?!"

"No, it was my fault. I asked Roger to come over," she confessed softly with her eyes lowered, gazing at the floor. "You see, I asked him to come over because I was scared. I came home from Ebby's house about ten o'clock last night. When I drove up to our house, I saw this creepy guy out at the street. As I shut the front door, I noticed he was looking right at me. It really scared me, Dad."

"Why didn't you call us, Julie?" pressed her father, who was trying to believe the best about his daughter.

"Because you were in Ohio and couldn't really do anything to help. I thought it would just worry you and for something that might turn out to be nothing. So I called Roger. I was pretty sure he liked me, and I've seen the way he watches out for his mother, so I thought he would defend me too."

"Well . . ." sighed Alan.

"He got here in less than ten minutes, made sure everything was locked up, and then we sat down on the sofa and started talking. He's really a nice guy Dad. He called his mother to assure her all was okay with me and asked her if he could stay a bit longer."

"Look, Julie . . ."

"Let her finish please, dear," Annalisa coaxed softly then glanced at Julie while nodding her head.

"Anyway," continued Julie, "I think it was getting close to midnight. We were both getting so tired. I kind of rested over against him, and we must have fallen asleep."

"You expect me to believe that last part, Julie?" snapped her father, although his voice held no anger. "You guys weren't making out, or something even worse?"

"Well . . . he did, uh, kiss me."

"And you kissed him back," blurted Annalisa with arms folded across her chest, glaring at her husband, "Alan, honestly! You hadn't kissed a girl by the time you were seventeen?"

"I have a different standard for our daughter than my parents had for me. I'm not saying it was better or worse, just different. Besides . . . it hasn't been so long ago that I have forgotten what a boy thinks about. Let's be honest here. I'm not the one on trial, okay?"

"I'm on trial? Really, Dad?"

"It's a figure of speech, honey . . . and I was talking to your mother, not you."

"Julie," added Annalisa. "I think I know what your father is trying to say here. Sweetheart, you're not on trial. However, you have violated a pretty serious rule, so there will be consequences."

Alan nodded his head in acknowledgement.

"Alan," continued his wife. "I feel you didn't hear our daughter. What she was trying to tell you was that she very well could have gone up to her room with a boy. She could have done things that we wouldn't want her to do. But the fact is, she didn't. We found her on the sofa, downstairs, granted with a boy's arm around her . . . but fully clothed. And frankly, I believe her story. I think it happened exactly like she explained."

Still seated with coffee cup in hand, Alan turned toward his daughter and slowly nodded his head. "I believe you too, Julie. But please understand your father's protective instinct, okay? Look at the circumstances. It's the middle of the night, no lights are on, and a strange boy is in the house alone with you. It's easy to see how I could imagine the worse."

At this point, he stood up and encompassed his daughter with his arms and promptly waved Annalisa over to join them as well. He whispered in his daughter's ear, "I love you so much, my sweet Julie. I'm sorry I got angry. Will you please forgive me, honey."

Julie, whose face was nestled in her father's chest, nodded her head but made no sound except the soft weeping of a daughter who was, once again, assured of her father's acceptance.

"Now, my love," he asked her mother with a smile. "What is this child's punishment?"

"She will be grounded for one month, starting today."

"Whaaat?!" blurted her father. "That's too long. How about two weeks for this juvenile troublemaker," he teased.

"No, sir. We already discussed it, and it will be four weeks. She'll be off restriction just in time for the dance."

"Dance? What dance?" he prodded Julie.

"Last night Roger asked me to the dance," she glanced up at her father, still nestled in his loving arms.

"Oh, he did, did he?" laughed Alan with a bit of disguised disgust. "Let me get my calendar."

"What for, dear?" questioned Annalisa with a puzzled look.

"I want to see how long before cross country practice starts . . . that fellow is in dire need of some character building, uh . . . I mean, endurance training, and I'm just the coach to make sure he develops it!"

That afternoon, when Alan and Annalisa went to pick up Emily at the Hinote's, they shared with Joey and Pam all they had discovered in Ohio. Joey seemed more excited than even Alan had been upon finding the book in the bottom of the old desk. Finishing up their informal presentation at the dining room table, the room became silent as each contemplated the significance of their discovery. After several minutes, Joey spoke up.

"What do we do with this now?"

"Well, I've been thinking about that too, Joey. And . . . I'm not sure. It appears to me, we should send it out, maybe in booklet form along with the story of how we discovered it," suggested Alan, glancing around at the others.

"I think that's a great idea," agreed Pam.

"One problem though," retorted Alan. "Suppose one or more of the tenets of the Manifesto aren't scripturally accurate. We can't send out something without the Scriptures as a basis for its validity."

"Good point. What do you think we should do, Alan?" asked Joey.

"We need to have at least two or three witnesses[1], just like it states in the Bible," pronounced Annalisa. "That's how a thing is established."

"Yes, yes, that's perfect, honey," smiled Alan as he patted her on the leg. "Let's do this; each one take a copy of the Manifesto, and this week try to find any verses in the Bible that would validate the seven tenets individually. We'll get together next weekend and see what we've come up with. If it's not enough to give it legitimacy, we can work on it further."

"And if we have our two or three witnesses?" asked Joey.

"Then, we can send it out to folks we think would be interested. How's that sound to everyone?"

"Perfect, except for one problem," balked Pam. "That's the weekend we're going to my parent's sixtieth wedding anniversary party. We have to go, honey. You know that, right?"

"Yes, of course, sweetheart, I wouldn't miss it for the world," assured Joey.

"That's okay, Pam, it gives us a little more time to come up with verses," comforted Alan.

"So two weeks from tomorrow we'll meet to determine if this **rojocki** Manifesto is scripturally valid or if those folks back in 1866 were a bit off, agreed?" proposed Annalisa.

"Agreed," they all exclaimed together.

The following day Alan began using his discretionary time to search the Scriptures for anything that would validate one or more of the Manifesto tenets. He also scheduled his first preseason meeting as the new Cross Country Coach for Julie's high school. It was a hot Thursday morning, six weeks before the fall semester would begin. The potential team met on the bleachers beside the track. There were eleven boys and eight girls in attendance, including Julie and Roger, who sat together. They hadn't seen one another since the "Midnight Incident" in the Browne's living room.

"Welcome to high school Cross Country, my name is Coach Browne. Yes, for those of you who didn't already know, I'm Julie Browne's father. But that's not entirely why I took the job. I accepted this responsibility because I believe, if you will listen to me and do what I tell you to do, together we can make this the best cross country team this school has ever known. I say this, not from theory read in training manuals but from actual proof. Yes, I have evidence, if you work hard, you can be a State Champion Cross Country team. However, you have to be committed, dedicated to suffering, and willing to turn away from the easy shortcuts because there's only one way to win . . . hard work! So before we get into the details of what we're going to be doing this season, are there any questions?"

After a few seconds passed, a hand went up in the back row. It was Roger.

"Yes, Roger."

"Will we be practicing every day and weekends too?" he asked smiling at Julie.

"Yes, good question; we will meet in this spot each weekday promptly at three o'clock in the afternoon. We will also practice Saturday mornings at seven. Sunday's are a rest day."

When Alan mentioned Saturday morning practice sessions there was an audible groan from several of the would-be runners. One such individual raised his hand with the next question.

"Uh, Coach Browne, why do we have to practice on Saturdays and why so early in the morning?" His facial expression revealed his intent. Alan also detected a hint of a whine in the question and responded appropriately.

"Good question. Number one, we practice on Saturday mornings because I'm the coach and I say we practice on Saturday mornings. This is not a democracy, folks. This is a dictatorship. I'm not a rapacious, ruthless ruler, but I do expect you to put forth your very best effort."

"Uh, excuse me, Coach Browne?" asked a runner in the front row.

"Yes?"

"What's number two?"

"Number one, two, three, or one hundred and twenty-seven will always have the same answer, 'Because I'm the coach and I say so.' Any further questions on the subject?"

"Uh, no sir."

"Listen, anything worth your time and effort, especially the effort you will be putting forth running, is worth doing well. Get the most out of every sustained mile, every excruciating pain, and every anguished thought. If you commit to giving it your best, and I know you will, then you're going to love running," he exhorted them with fire in his eyes. "And you'll not only be physically fit, but equally as important, you'll be mentally tough."

Pausing to allow his words to sink in deep, Alan glared at Roger who was staring back at him.

"When I ran cross country and track, I won races. I achieved success because I learned how to love suffering. I didn't just tolerate it. I acquired an appetite for it. I enjoyed it, and yes, I loved it. Why? Because I knew if I endured the temporary difficulty, I would see the result, and the result was winning. By the way, in case you didn't know, winning is much more fun than losing. If you haven't discovered that yet, you will this season."

The team sat as silent as new recruits on the first day of Boot Camp after just meeting their Drill Instructor. Alan's eyes darted around the intimidated faces which, were contemplating their new coach. He wondered what was going through those young minds. He wasn't sure what to think until his eyes fell upon Julie's face. She was smiling back at him with a pride he had rarely seen in his precious daughter.

Returning her smile, Alan concluded his pep talk to the team. "So we have a little over two weeks before the first official practice. I want you to be running at a slow to moderate pace, several miles a day. Try to get in three to four miles in the morning and another three to four in the evening. Remember, run easy for now. We're looking for base miles here that we can build upon for the rest of the season. We want to start slow and easy but finish fast and strong, okay?"

Alan waved the team, both girls and boys, down to the start/finish line on the track. After aligning them all across the finish line, he exhorted them. "Look down. What do you see?"

"A whole bunch of running shoes," commented one of the girls.

"What else?"

"A finish line," asserted Roger.

"That's right!" confirmed Alan. "Always, always, always, keep your heart, your mind, your eye on the finish line. This is good advice for life too," counseled their coach. "You can endure all kinds of suffering, difficulties, inconveniences, and pain if you will only keep your thoughts on the finish line. Never forget it . . . however, if you do forget, I'll be right here to remind you. You got it?!" he barked while staring at Roger.

Alan glanced across at the solemn high school faces nodding back at him but remaining silent. They had never had a coach speak to them like Alan. He communicated with authority, not principled guesses he had read in a book like their previous coaches. He talked like he knew from personal experience exactly what they needed to be champions. Smiling back at them, he nodded his assurance, his guarantee, that he would be there to help in their times of distress.

"Okay, everyone, one warm up lap, and then we will have a time trial. This is very important in your early season development. It sets a baseline, a benchmark, from which we can work individually to set goals and measure your angle of progress along the way. But first, let's get in that warm-up lap. Off you go."

"Only one?" asked Julie. "That's not much of a warm-up, Dad."

"What? No, not a lap on the track, this is cross country. I meant, one lap around the entire school grounds. There's a faint path right behind the bleachers, follow it clock-wise around the school until you arrive back here. I measured it last week. It's nearly one and a half miles. Now, let's go!"

When the whole group arrived back, Coach Browne lined them up on the start/finish line once again. Walking among the sweaty runners, he scratched out a chart on his clipboard paper with columns for each name, date, time trial time, and heartrate.

"Okay, good. Now, we are going to run a one mile time trial on the track. Remember, you're being timed, so run as fast as you think you can run. When you finish, immediately take your heartrate. For those few of you without watches, find me. I brought a couple of extra ones. I want to know how many beats per minute as soon as you cross the finish line. Then, two minutes later, count it again. Finally, at ten minutes after you have finished the time trial do a final heartrate count, okay? Any questions?"

"How do we count our pulse?" asked a freshman boy.

"Good question," encouraged their coach. "Take two fingers and slide them along the side of your neck until you feel something thumping. That's your pulse. Count how many thumps in six seconds. Multiply by ten, that's your heartrate. Got it?"

The team was completely silent except for their somewhat labored breathing. Many were shifting back and forth from one foot to the other shaking loose the leg in opposition. Alan could discern, even though this was only a time trial, the high level of nervousness among the individual runners. This was good he acknowledged to himself. A healthy competition amongst the members of the team would foster steady progress.

"Okay, just two commands," instructed their coach. "'Runners ready', which means you should move to the line, staying behind it, followed by 'Go', okay? I'll be calling out your lap times with each interval across the start/finish line. Anybody have any questions?"

The group of runners, who would become his cross country team, corporately shook their heads. To Alan they appeared more like an anxious line of race horses waiting for the start bell signifying the beginning of the race, than a group of untrained high school joggers hoping to do their best to impress the new coach. The thought made him smile.

"Runners ready!" He held his hand high above his head, then slashing it downward, he boomed, "Go!"

-sixteen-

Julie was right. Roger could run like the wind. When he passed Alan at the end of the first lap of this mile long time trial, there were three other boys and one girl running in the same pack ahead of all the other members of the cross country team. The girl was his daughter, Julie, and the time was sixty-seven seconds. By the half-mile mark, there was a total of two boys and one girl. They had completed the half-mile in two minutes-seventeen seconds. If they continued running at this pace, they would accomplish just over a four minute-thirty second mile. Their coach shouted his encouragement.

"Go, go, go! Keep it up, only two laps left! Come on you guys, push through! Next one is the bell lap!"

By the time the little pack had reached the bell lap, Roger was running all by himself and moving at a speed that caused his coach to marvel.

"Three twenty-one!" bellowed Alan as Roger started into the last lap. "Go, man, Go!"

Continuing to call out lap times for all the team members as they passed by, Alan's eyes were on Roger, who appeared to pick up speed with every silky smooth stride of those runners legs of his. When he entered the final straight to the finish line, Alan hollered his encouragement to finish strong. With fifty meters left to go, Alan glanced at the stopwatch and was amazed with what he saw.

Crossing the finish line, Roger's coach called out, "Four nineteen!" He had run the second half of the race much faster than the first half. A sure sign, to his delighted coach, that he had a thoroughbred miler who, if properly trained, could go much faster.

Roger plopped to the infield on his back with arms and legs splayed out like a beached starfish on a hot summer day.

"Get up, man!" admonished his coach in a loud voice. "Don't ever do that! Walk, or better yet, jog around a bit. But first, heartrate, Roger, I need your heartrate."

Just then, the second runner crossed the finish line, "Four thirty-one." Then a few seconds later two more runners completed the mile, "Four thirty-seven, four thirty-nine. Great job guys don't forget your heartrate," reminded their coach.

Next, Alan's eyes fell on his precious daughter Julie sprinting up the final straight in fifth place overall. She was faster than half the boys and ahead of all the girls by nearly a lap.

"Come on, Julie," Her father started to yell, but Roger had beat him to it.

"Yes, come on, Julie!" agreed her proud father-turned-coach.

"Four forty-two, sweetheart!" beamed her father, realizing he probably should reserve the use of the term of endearment for home and not at practice. "Great job, uh . . . Julie!"

Later that evening at dinner, Alan confided in Annalisa.

"We have the makings of a really good boys' squad, but our girls' team is incredibly weak. At the time trial, we had five boys all recording times under five minutes. And of course, Roger, well, I think I could find him another twenty seconds."

"Another twenty seconds?" questioned Annalisa.

"Yeah, that would put him under the four minute mile. I think he could do it."

"Wow, Alan, really?" she exclaimed, holding her mouth wide open in disbelief.

"Yeah, he's strong but holds back too much for the finish and needs to work his arms more. We'll get him there though, if he's willing to go the distance."

"How about, Julie?" she probed. "Is she any good?"

"Oh, honey, I was so proud of her. She's got guts; she pulls it up from way down within her. She's incredibly strong and her stride is really smooth. She's her mother," he smiled.

"She's her father," challenged Annalisa with a chuckle.

"She's both," answered Alan. "Look, not to change the subject, but we need to get working on those Scripture verses for the Manifesto."

"I thought you were paying bills this evening," expressed Annalisa with a bit of concern.

"Well, we don't really have enough in the account to pay them all, so I thought to see if maybe something would come in next week. I'm almost done with the kitchen job for the Mitchell's, you know."

"I could try selling crafts down at the flea market, Alan. I know I could make a little money that way, anyhow."

"Oh, I don't know. I thought about taking on a part-time job or something, at least until my woodworking business takes off."

"Where would you get a job that would pay you enough?"

"I'm not sure. However, about a month ago, Jimmy Anderson mentioned he was looking for help down at his moving and storage company. Maybe he would be willing to pay me by the job then I could make more money."

"Alan, that's hard work," she protested. "You'd be exhausted every day. I doubt you would have the energy to coach or do any of the woodworking projects."

"What projects?" he answered in a monotone. "The business is dry right now."

"Well, surely something will come in soon. You're bound to get something any day now."

"Oh, honey, how I long to be free," he moaned, shaking his head. "Free from paying bills, free from having to struggle with money every month, free from these fears that creep into my thinking, free from anxious thoughts, and free from these insecurities that have plagued me all my life. Oh, I am so tired of this fight. I just want to be free."

"I know you do, Alan. But our God hasn't seen fit to do that for us yet. He may one day, and it may be sooner than we think. In the meantime, He'll take care of us. He always has and He always will. None of this surprises Him. He's already got the solutions on the way. They just haven't arrived yet."

"Well, I wish they would get here sooner, rather than later," he complained.

"They will, Alan. His timing is perfect."

A couple of weeks later, Alan was moving household furniture for Jimmy in the mornings, doing some woodworking in the afternoons, driving to the high school where he would coach the cross country team until well after six o'clock, then hustling home afterwards for a quick dinner and more time spent working in his shop. The schedule was exhausting, but it enabled him to keep the bills up to date, for now.

That weekend Alan and Annalisa met with Joey and Pam to comb through and organize all the Scripture verses each one had found for The **rojocki** Manifesto tenets. Joey pulled out their exhaustive concordance and a Bible. It was obvious to all that each had done their homework because now they had too many verses. This left the somewhat daunting task of determining which verses were the most appropriate for each individual tenet. Finally, after nearly four hours of deliberation, and with the time getting toward eleven p.m., Alan suggested they continue the following Saturday evening. Before leaving, Pam, who was somewhat of a computer whiz, volunteered to work up something presentable for that weekend with all the Scriptures they had agreed upon.

However, their next meeting had to be rescheduled because Alan had to work at the moving company all day Saturday. He didn't arrive home that evening until after seven-thirty and was thoroughly exhausted. The long days were catching up with his middle-aged body. He was still very athletic, still wiry, at least to some degree, but older. His age was prohibiting him from recovering as quickly from the draining efforts like the one he had endured today. Barely mustering enough strength to finish his dinner, he fell face first onto the living room sofa. And that's where he remained, until he woke up at three-fifteen in the morning. Slowly and gingerly sitting up, he realized how achy his body felt. Moaning, he slouched back against the arm of the sofa.

Once he became aware that he was in the living room, he gradually remembered how he had gotten there. He quickly shook his head to get rid of the putrid fragrance of dried sweat that had wafted into his nostrils. His mind wandered, as everyone's does in the wee hours of the night, to his circumstances and how difficult his life seemed at this point in time. He admitted to himself that these were not the worst of times he had seen, but they weren't the best either.

"I thought by moving here things were supposed to get better?" he whispered to himself, although acknowledging the invisible One in the room.

"Father, help," he prayed softly. "When I was younger, I could do these things; I can't any more. My body cannot continue to work like this. I get up at the crack of dawn, move furniture until noon, come home for a couple of hours to try to make some extra money working with wood, and then I'm off to coach those kids until dinner time. I won't even mention how almost every evening and weekend I'm back out in the garage with woodworking projects. Uh, I know I just mentioned it . . . sorry. Regardless, will you please open the windows of Heaven and pour out a blessing?[1] Would you kindly, Dear Lord? I really need your help."

A thought popped quickly into his mind, "I have blessed you with my everlasting love.[2] Beware of the leaven of the Pharisees."[3]

"I know, Father, I am grateful for You and for all You've done in my life and in the life of my family. But, Lord, I am so tired of the fight. I am so weary. Will you please bless me a little bit more? You say you own the cattle on a thousand hills.[4] Could you kindly sell a few and send the money my way? I promise I will be eternally grateful. Lord, we're not in those desperate straits like we were in California, but it's a constant, continual concern. It never leaves me. It's relentless. I feel like I'm a slave to it. Please set me free. Please, God. I can't do this any longer. Please, dear Father, set me free."

The room was silent. Alan glanced around trying to see in the pitch black darkness. Little by little, he sensed gratefulness building up inside him. It was like a new found confidence that everything would, somehow, be okay. It was more than confidence. It was faith. He recognized it as a gift of faith, which he quickly acknowledged as an answer to his prayer. He was hoping it wasn't the only answer, but it was an answer nonetheless, and he was happy to receive it.

"There is something already on its way from Heaven," he proclaimed out loud as he started for the stairs with a few moans and groans involuntarily escaping his lips. Making his way to the bathroom, he closed the door, got undressed, and took a much needed shower. The hot moisture was a healing balm to his painfully overworked muscles. After getting dressed in his pajama pants and tee-shirt, he very quietly slipped under the sheets and rolled over for some more rest.

"Oh, you up already, honey?" questioned a sleepy Annalisa from the other side of the bed. "How about turning on the coffee machine? I need to be up soon too. Thanks, sweetie."

Glancing at the alarm clock, Alan noticed it was five-thirty in the morning.

"Sure, honey, no problem," he sighed as the moans continued with each movement of his achingly tender carcass.

"Thanks, I'll be down in a few minutes. I just need a little more rest."

That whole day, in fact, that whole week, Alan felt like he could never quite catch up. His energy level was undeniably low; he couldn't seem to replace what he spent each day. Feeling incredibly weary, he ate more to try to regain some level of vitality. This solution only worked for an hour or two and then left him more drained than before. It was a vicious cycle, and he was losing with every circuit he completed. Two Saturdays later, it finally came to a head, at least in his mind it did.

"Honey, I need to quit this moving job. It's killing me. I thought I could handle it, but I can't. I'm a physical wreck. My back always hurts, my muscles are always stiff and sore, and I woke up the other night with leg cramps. I about flew out of bed. It was terrible. Plus, I couldn't get back to sleep for hours. By every afternoon, I am so absolutely exhausted I can barely function the rest of the day. Hey, I even cancelled a practice last week."

"I'm sure God will provide for us, Alan. I think you should do what you need to do, honey."

"I hope He does, my sweetheart."

"Oh, He will. Don't worry about that."

"Well, we're already living at the poverty level. We can't go much lower, I guess. But if I quit this job, we will. I just can't do it any more though. I'm worried I may have a heart-attack or something."

"It's alright, Alan. God will provide, you watch. It's already on the way from Heaven," she declared with a smile. "Now, go get cleaned up for dinner."

"There's confirmation that God heard my prayer," he agreed while washing up at the bathroom sink. "Something is most assuredly coming."

That week, even with the lack of close attention from their coach, the cross country team won the boy's race and placed third in the girl's race. Roger and Julie both won gold medals for first place and were becoming more openly affectionate with one another. This caused her father no small amount of consternation. But for now, he held his tongue. At the end of September, the boy's team was still undefeated, and the girl's team was in second place in their district. The end of the month also saw a marked enlargement of the time Julie and Roger spent with each other. By Thanksgiving, both Julie and Roger were Cross Country State Champions. The entire team had also been awarded runner-up to the State Champions, a high school from Jacksonville.

Julie and Roger appeared to be using their new found notoriety as an excuse to spend more and more time alone together. Julie missed several dinners at home with her family in favor of dinners with Roger and his mother. Weekends found them alone on very long distance runs because, as Julie would defend, there was nobody else who could keep up with them. Their pride was becoming an issue with many on the team, along with a few at home, none more than her father. Alan perceived trouble was on the horizon for the young couple. He had lived enough of life to know "Pride comes before a fall."[5]

Spring was right around the corner and the outdoor track season with it. Somehow, Alan and Annalisa had made it through the winter months paying their bills on time. There were no extra funds though, which made for many a restless night. Alan was happy to get back to full time coaching and the meager compensation that came with it. Unlike cross country, there was a bonus attached to the job if the track team won the State Championships. Money the Browne family could put to good use. Alan's woodworking business didn't have much in the way of incoming projects and with his resignation from the moving and storage company things on the home front remained quite snug, financially speaking.

By the first of February 2003, Alan, Annalisa, Joey, and Pam had finalized all the Scripture verses for The **rojocki** Manifesto. After several revisions, it was ready to mail out for all who might be interested. Regardless of the mailing list, which included only seventeen names, the four explorers had a wonderful sense of accomplishment, and a belief that they had done something useful and needed for the Fellowship and the Body of Christ as a whole. They included the seven tenets, a copy of the original Manifesto, the extra Scripture verses they had found helpful, along with a cover letter of explanation.

The Seven Tenets of The rojocci Manifesto
August 21, 1866 / Revised February 7, 2003

1. **Love is the calling.** Matthew 22:35-40; 1 Corinthians 13:13; 1 John 3:24; Colossians 3:14; 1 Peter 4:8
2. **Pray first and unceasingly.** Luke 18:1-8; Colossians 4:2; 1 Thessalonians 5:17; Ephesians 6:18
3. **Check first your heart when searching the Holy Scriptures.** Hebrews 4:12; Proverbs 4:23; 2 Thessalonians 2:7-13
4. **Thankfulness is the evidence of trust.** Colossians 3:16-17; 1 Thessalonians 5:18; Hebrews 13:15
5. **Generosity toward others, frugality with self.** 2 Corinthians 9:6-7;   1 Thessalonians 4:9-12; Proverbs 19:17
6. **Judge yourself, allow God to judge others.** Matthew 7:1-5; Romans 14:4;   1 Corinthians 4:5
7. **Freedom is an offspring of the truth.** John 8:31-32; Galatians 5:1; 13-14; John 14:6

After the mailings went out, Alan and Annalisa had Joey and Pam over for a cook-out. It was one of those absolutely beautiful early spring evenings where the setting sun is still warm, but the air is cool and crisp. The two couples sat on the side porch, facing the garage and the grill, so Alan could keep an eye on the pork loin he was roasting. The aromatherapy that wafted from the seasoned meat, being grilled to perfection, was just what Alan needed to help him forget his monetary ailments. Somehow, the fragrance mysteriously transported him back to happier, carefree times when he was a teenager playing in his parent's backyard with his brothers and sister, as their father barbequed dinner on the grill.

Chitchatting about all they had accomplished in the last few weeks, the four of them were enjoying a much needed healthy dose of satisfaction, feeling they had completed something really worthwhile. They smiled at one another in acknowledgment that not one could have done it without the help of the others. Alan glanced at Annalisa, who was leaning back in her chair with her face to the setting sun enjoying its warmth. This picture of her was a sight he loved and never grew tired of viewing.

Suddenly, he was shaken out of his daydreaming stupor to the sound of a car approaching up their driveway. Alan immediately recognized Julie and Roger returning from a long run at the beach.

"Well, aren't you two the decorated couple?!" Joey announced with a sense of pride that he knew them. "State Champions both. Well done!" he proclaimed. "What've y'all been up to?"

"Oh, we ran a ten miler on Perdido Key beach, no biggie," declared Julie with equal amounts of ego and pretense.

Joey glanced at Alan who was rolling his eyes.

"Running in the sand is an awesome workout," she continued, "but it really makes my calf muscles tight, so Roger volunteered to massage the knots out."

"Really?!" insinuated Alan sarcastically as he gazed over at Annalisa.

"Julie, you guys do that out here on the porch and put a beach towel underneath you," commanded Annalisa without opening her eyes.

"Mom?! Whaaat?!" complained Julie thinking she was being treated unfairly and with suspicion.

"Either out here or not at all, understand?" Annalisa's tone was firm as she pointed in her daughter's direction, eyes still closed.

"Mom, it's getting chilly out here," she negotiated with a hint of a whine.

"Out here or nowhere, you choose." This time her mother turned her head from the warm rays of the sun and with eyes wide open intensely glared directly at her daughter.

"Oh, alright," acquiesced the younger Browne.

Julie and Roger walked around to the front door and went inside. Alan sat up in his chair and leaned toward Annalisa, who had returned to her sun basking. He looked at Joey and Pam.

"Sorry about that, you guys. She's getting quite independent and all this notoriety about her and Roger being State Champions together has given her a rather enlarged ego. I've wanted to give her a stern talking to many times, but I'm concerned she'll rebel even more. Besides, she'll be eighteen in a couple of months and off to college in the fall."

"Where's she hoping to attend?" asked Pam.

"Well, that's a tricky one. I think both are trying to get scholarships to the same school, so they can continue to be together," replied Alan. "I mean, to some degree I empathize with their situation; long distance relationships are no fun."

"Yeah, but," added Annalisa, "Roger has gotten offers from Florida State, Tennessee, and Texas-El Paso."

"UTEP?" asked Joey. "Why would he want to go way out there?"

"It's a big track school," replied Alan frankly.

"But here's the problem," whispered Annalisa while peering around the corner of the porch to see if Julie and Roger were coming out of the house yet. "Julie hasn't been accepted to Florida State, and she didn't apply to Tennessee or UTEP. The only other chance they have is where they've both applied, the University of Florida and Clemson."

"Wow, those are expensive schools," commented Pam.

"Yeah, Julie has to pretty much get a full ride. We don't have that kind of money," confessed Alan. "Right now, we couldn't pay for one semester, much less, four years."

"So what do you think they'll do?" inquired Pam.

"Not sure, but we're praying," acknowledged Annalisa.

"Praying about what?" probed Julie as she poked her head around the corner.

"Uh . . . money stuff, honey," answered Alan relying upon his quick wit. He was being honest. It was going to take a lot of money for Julie to attend college.

"Hmmm . . . well, there's someone on the phone for you, Dad."

"Thanks, Julie. Do you know who it is?"

"Uh, it's a woman. I think she said her name is Mrs. Henderson."

"Mrs. Henderson?" inquired Alan curiously as he got up and headed for the kitchen. "I wonder who that could be?"

"I don't know," responded Julie while glancing at her mother. "She said she lives in Arlington, Virginia."

~seventeen~

Rushing down the expansive airport corridor, Alan desperately needed to catch his connecting flight, or he would end up sleeping on the floor in the cavernous terminal. His backpack was slung over one shoulder, and the soccer duffle bag, he had borrowed from Richard, was hung over the other. With each stride of his now middle-aged physique, his last minute, make-do luggage banged against his legs, hindering him from extracting the most from his effort to propel himself forward.

Finally, after several minutes in his aerobic threshold, he reached the gate for his next flight. The waiting area was vacant. He quickly glanced at the monitor to determine if he was actually in the correct location. If he was, he had missed his connecting flight. If not, there was still hope. Hustling over to the window, he scanned the tarmac, no plane. Again he checked the enormous screen and caught sight of a flashing announcement indicating his flight had been moved to another gate, thankfully in the same terminal. He swung around and fired up the stride-thump-stride propulsion system that lumbered him along to the newly corrected gate.

Falling back into a seat at the waiting area, Alan noticed his departing flight had been delayed an hour and therefore decided to close his tear weary, bloodshot eyes for a few minutes. What seemed like a couple of seconds later, he was awakened to an empty room by the friendly feminine voice of the ticket-counter agent, who quickly advised him his flight was about to depart. Jumping up and stumbling over his makeshift luggage, he ran for the gate. To his vertiginous relief, he was still able to board his flight to Washington, D.C. It had been a long day and it wasn't over yet.

Parking his rental car in front of Betsy's house, he jumped out and jogged around to the side door of her kitchen. Under the garage light, he noticed two vehicles parked in the driveway: a faded blue 1970s VW bug and a much larger, black sedan. Alan glanced at his watch as he knocked softly on the wooden screened door. It was very late, nearing midnight. A petite elderly woman, with curly silver hair, opened the kitchen door. She was wearing rimless rectangular glasses and a full length brown coat. Before she could greet Alan, he anxiously blurted out.

"Is Betsy okay? I mean, is she still . . ." he wagged his head, fumbling for a different way to ask his most pressing concern. "Hi, I'm Alan Browne."

"Yes, yes, Mr. Browne, please come in. I'm Mrs. Henderson from across the street." She motioned to him as she closed the door. "We're all in here."

"Thank you, ma'am, I know where the room is," he mumbled as he walked past her to the same room where Stanley had died years ago.

The door to the dimly lit room where Betsy lay in her bed was open. Alan could hear the refrains of hymns playing softly from within her room. He peered around the corner, walked quickly to her side, and gently, yet firmly grasped her hand. Alan was so grieved to see her in a coma that he hardly noticed the other two people in the room. One, judging by her attire, was obviously a nurse of some sort, and the other wore a rag wool cardigan with a light grey tie that had been loosened at the collar of his pale blue shirt. He quietly introduced himself as Betsy's pastor, Melvin Patterson. Mel, as he asked to be called, was a giant of a man, who must have had to stoop to gain entry into Betsy's room. Alan guessed him to be in his forties with extremely strong hands and face. His eyes and speech, however, exuded a softness Alan had rarely observed.

Mel motioned toward the stocky woman in the nurse's attire, "This is Gertie Johannsen. She's been seeing to Betsy's needs these last few days. She was just telling me she believes Betsy is very near death, Alan. I thought, if you're willing, we could help her into Heaven and into the arms of Jesus," he quietly confided with one hand on Alan's shoulder.

"Uh, sure, absolutely . . . uh, what do you need me to do?" Alan questioned eagerly.

"Sing," replied the massive man with the gentle voice. "She's struggling with letting go. Most everyone does until they see Jesus. By singing worshipful songs, we can help her let go of this life and embrace the next. Are you willing to help a sister in need?"

"Yes, sir," complied Alan.

He and Mel moved across the room to where Gertie and Mrs. Henderson were standing by the small CD player. Mel turned off the music and softly began the song "Seek Ye First". He then led the foursome in a familiar hymn, followed by four more songs. While singing "Turn Your Eyes Upon Jesus", the most astonishing thing happened. Betsy, who had been lying completely still, abruptly leaned forward, opened her eyes, and gazing into the far corner of the room reached up with both arms. A joyful smile began radiating across her face as her eyes brightened. Mrs. Henderson gasped, but the other three continued to sing. As suddenly as she had leaned forward, Betsy collapsed back to her semi prone position. She had passed away.

Quickly checking Betsy's vitals, Gertie gave a slight nod of her head to confirm what they already knew. Alan and Mrs. Henderson wept softly while Mel spread his huge wing span around the two of them. Although sad, it was the most utterly astounding, peaceful, and even joyful death that Alan had ever witnessed or even heard of. He was a bit apprehensive and after composing himself asked Mel some questions as they moved to the living room, allowing the nurse to prepare for the coroner's arrival.

"What exactly happened in there, Mel?"

"The bodily death of a saint, Alan. We helped a dear sister, who was struggling with letting go of this life."

"Yes, I think I understand," replied Alan softly. "But why did Betsy sit up like that?"

"As her physical body was nearing the point where it was no longer habitable, her spirit, still full of vitality, was eager to return home to the One who had endowed her with

283

eternal life. But that's sometimes a difficult transition for even the strongest of believers, like Betsy. However, when she saw Jesus, she willingly let go of this temporary life, so she could be reunited with the One she so loved. Her spirit left for a joyous reunion, and her weakened body, devoid of that spirit, lay dead."

"I didn't see Jesus," remarked Alan, perplexed at Mel's answer.

"No, but you could, no doubt, sense His presence."

"Well, yeah, I did, but I didn't see Him."

"That's because, unlike Betsy, we are still full of this life, so we don't have eyes to see the spiritual, only the natural, for the most part anyway. But there comes a day for each and every one of us," smiled Mel as he patted Alan on the shoulder.

At the funeral three days later, Alan marveled how, even in her passing, Betsy spoke to him of all the depth and wisdom of God. She truly was the most saintly person he had ever known, and as tears once again filled his eyes, he realized he sorely missed her.

After the graveside service was dismissed by Mel, Alan followed him to his faded blue VW bug. He thanked him for his kindness, especially for allowing him to be a participant in helping Betsy. The two men hugged, slapping one another on the back. Then, Mel poured his giant frame into the vehicle more likely to accommodate Lilliputians than himself. Alan chuckled while he watched the, undoubtedly, often practiced contortionist exercise.

As Alan turned in the direction of his rental car, he was approached by a tiny figure of a man. He stood no more than five feet-two and barely weighed one hundred and twenty pounds, soaking wet. He was wearing a long, black trench coat with a plaid, wool scarf fully wrapped around his head and neck. His freckled face was beet red due to the biting February wind. His grey eyes peered up at Alan through small round spectacles as his heavily gloved hand stretched toward Alan.

"Mr. Alan Browne?" the frail man inquired.

"Pardon?" gestured Alan.

"Are you Mr. Alan Michael Browne of Pensacola, Florida?"

"Yes, sir," replied Alan as he grasped the minute gloved hand. "And who might you be, please?"

"I'm Wilber W. Wilifred, Stanley and Betsy Taft's attorney and executor of Betsy's will. Would you have a few minutes to meet me at my office within the next few days, Mr. Browne?"

"Well, no sir. I'm sorry, I need to get back home as soon as possible. My flight leaves early in the morning. Why? What's this about?"

"Mr. Browne, you have been named an heir in Betsy's will."

"What? I'm not part of her family. Are you sure?" asked Alan with a furrowed brow.

"Yes. As you may or may not know, Stanley and Betsy never had any offspring. Her only other relative was her brother, Bernard Himmel, of Falls Church. He was married although he died too without having children."

"Uh . . . Mister . . . what did you say your name is?" asked a very curious Alan. "I apologize, sir, for not remembering, but a lot has been going on these last few days."

"Wilifred, Wilber W. Wilifred, but please call me Will. Okay, if I address you as Al?"

"Uh, please call me Alan," he smiled down at Will. "Who are the other heirs then? I mean, if it is okay to tell me."

"Sure, sure, Mrs. Henderson will receive Betsy's car and some kitchen appliances, including a set of dishes. The church where she and Stanley attended will acquire everything else."

"Then what do you need me for? What else is there to inherit?" quizzed Alan trying hard not to sound sarcastic to this somewhat annoying little fellow with the nasally voice.

"Well, you, uh . . . inherit the property, of course."

"What property?"

"The house, the garage, you know, the property."

Alan's jaw dropped wide open. "Me? Are you sure?"

"Yes, I made out the will myself several years ago after her brother died. Alan, Betsy wanted you to have the house as a blessing from her, for being such a blessing to her. She also wanted me to convey to you that it is yours to do with as you please . . . and in light of that, I want you to know I would be very interested in purchasing the property from you at fair market value. I won't cheat you. I just really love the house and it's convenient to my office, the subway, and mother's house."

"Well, uh . . . I don't know what to say. I would have to get an appraisal done before I could agree to something like that."

"I already have three per Betsy's request a couple of months ago when she realized the end was near."

"How much is it worth?" asked Alan quietly glancing around to assure no one was eavesdropping on this private conversation.

"I believe it would easily fetch three hundred and seventy-five to four hundred."

"Thousand?" yelped Alan, his eyes wide open to match his gaping mouth.

"Yes, thousand," confirmed the attorney. "I am willing to offer you a contract today in the amount of four hundred thousand, and I will pay all the closing costs. You see, my office also does title work."

"I'm not sure what to say," Alan smiled sheepishly. "What about realtor fees?"

"There are no realtors involved in this offer. You will be paid in cash, check, or I can wire funds directly into your bank account, your choice, Alan."

"Okay, look, uh . . . Will, right? Uh . . . let me call you in the morning. I never expected, uh . . . I'm not really prepared to, you know, uh . . . Do you have a card? I have to talk this over with my wife before making a decision to sell a house that she doesn't even know we own," explained Alan.

"I understand," acknowledged Will. "I will be at this number tomorrow morning. Give me a call when you've made a decision. We can close on this within ten business days."

"I need to get back home. I can't stay here another ten days. I mean, I can move my flight a day or two, but I can't postpone it for that long."

"That's okay, Alan. We can fax all the documents back and forth. I will wire the funds to your bank account the same day we go to the closing table."

After delaying his flight a day, Alan was anxious to get back home to Annalisa and the children. Because of this, his flights seemed to take longer than usual. He sat by an elderly lady on the first flight and practically talked her ear off with all that was currently going on in his life. On the connecting flight, he picked up his story where he had left off on the first flight. Sitting next to a younger gal who held a somewhat fussy baby in her arms, Alan rambled on seemingly oblivious to her predicament. However, he did continually retrieve the toys and pacifier the irate little lad kept throwing on the floor.

Annalisa, Richard, and sweet Emily were a very welcome sight to Alan. After catching a glimpse of them, he hurried down the final passageway and into their loving embrace. He had only been away from his precious treasures for six days, but so much had happened it seemed more like six months. Alan and Annalisa strolled arm in arm while Emily, who donned his backpack, struggled to stay in front of them, and Richard, who slung the duffle bag over his shoulder, lagged behind.

"Where's Julie?" inquired Alan with a look that revealed he already knew the answer to his inquiry.

"I'm sure you could guess," remarked Annalisa.

"Roger?"

"Yep," she grimaced. "I'm really getting concerned."

"Yeah, well, me too, honey. I have been for quite a few weeks now," confessed Alan. "I think they spend way too much time together. Any word from the other schools yet?"

"No, nothing."

"Is she getting worried?" asked Alan.

"I think so. While you were gone, she and Roger appeared to be much clingier than I've seen before. That's what makes me worry. I believe something's going on," she confided quietly to keep the other children from hearing her concern.

"Yeah, I know. I think so too."

"Well, let's try to enjoy our good news and not let it be an issue tonight, okay, Alan?"

"Of course, sweetheart," he agreed as he kissed her forehead. "Let's keep praying."

"How about that Betsy. What a wonderful, precious woman," she smiled with tears welling up in her eyes.

"Other than you, my lovely bride, she is the most magnificent woman I have ever known and the most cherished of friends. I will dearly miss her for the rest of my life," he sighed as he wiped at the tears filling his eyes.

"There aren't many like her," agreed Annalisa as she hopped in their car.

"What a blessing in life, and what a blessing in death. She was absolutely amazing. I want to live my life like that," he proclaimed just before closing her door.

Sitting down behind the steering wheel, Alan reached across to hold Annalisa's hand. "We've seen a lot of life together so far, my love. It looks like our God is helping us.

We need to keep praying though. It would be wonderful to have peace on all fronts, wouldn't it?"

"He hears our prayers and is answering," she professed confidently with a smile, giving his hand a firm squeeze.

Three weeks later, on a chilly Saturday morning, Alan was working on an elaborate two piece furniture project in his shop. A local woman had contracted with him to build two rocking chairs for her fiftieth wedding anniversary. It was both calming and relaxing to smooth out the joints and angles of the beautiful cherry wood. With money in his bank account from the sale of Betsy's house, he was really enjoying woodworking again. He had the roll-up door open to his garage letting in the clean fresh air while he was sanding. For Alan, it was as near an idyllic setting as he had enjoyed since moving to Florida several years previous. There was something soothingly peaceful about working with wood.

He noticed Roger pull into the driveway and waved to him when he got out of his car. To Alan's surprise, he walked toward the shop like he wanted to speak with his track coach. Alan turned off the sander and removed his ear and eye protection. He stretched out his hand to greet his star miler and potential record holder.

"How's it going today, Roger?" he asked.

"Uh, pretty good, I guess, sir," he replied, feigning a grin.

"What's up?"

"Oh, I don't know, Coach Browne. Even though all seems to be going well with school and track and all, I feel so empty sometimes."

"Is it Julie?" her father asked hoping for a particular response.

"Oh, no, she's perfect. I really care for her, sir."

"I know you do, Roger," answered her father with a hint of concern as to where this conversation was headed.

"I don't know, I think maybe because my father left my mother when I was so young . . . well, maybe that's why I feel empty. You know, lonely or something . . . I mean, on the inside, uh, in my heart. Do you know what I mean, Coach?"

Alan smiled and putting his arm around Roger's shoulder remarked, "I know exactly what you mean." Alan motioned for Roger to sit down on the stool beside his desk while Alan dropped down into his chair. "I have known those precise feelings myself. Since my youngest remembrances I have felt that emptiness. You know why?"

"No, sir."

"It's because there is a hole, a vacancy in there," Alan nodded, pointing at Roger's chest. "Yes, Roger, you are perfectly normal. Everyone, until it is filled, has that same sense of hollowness deep within them. You see, mankind was created by God in His own image.[1] Do you know what I mean by that, Roger?"

"No, sir . . . not really, anyway."

"Well, in the Scriptures, the Bible, God tells us that He is a Spirit, and those who worship Him must do so in spirit and in truth.[2] In another place in the New Testament, which is the title for the part of the Bible that contains what happened during and after Jesus Christ walked on earth, we find that all of us are created with a body, a soul, and a spirit.[3] Now, what part of us do you think was created in God's likeness?"

"Uh, the spirit part?" responded Roger with more of a question than an answer.

"Yeah, that's right, Roger. The body is what you easily recognize to be a person, and the soul is kind of like the personality of that person. When you combine the two, the body and the soul, the Bible calls that our flesh. In many chapters, God tells us that our flesh part of our life is at war with our spirit part of our life.[4] Why do you think that could be?"

"Hmmm . . . because our spirit part is like God and it lives forever?"

"Yes, it does, but what happens to our flesh part?" asked Alan with a hidden excitement because this conversation was heading in a very interesting direction.

"Well, that dies, right, Coach?"

"Yes, it does, Roger. So the two parts have totally opposite outcomes and therefore completely opposed means and goals in this lifetime. The flesh part is grasping for every last ounce of life, of enjoyment for itself, because it knows it has a limited number of years. It fears death. Our spirit part, on the other hand, lives forever, either as redeemed in Heaven, or as condemned to Hell," explained Alan with a serious expression on his face.

"Why do I sometimes feel so empty inside then?"

"Now, here's the problem, and why you sometimes feel so empty."

"Yes, Coach?"

"Have you ever heard of Adam and Eve?"

"Yes, sir, in the Sunday school class I used to attend, back when I was younger."

"Do you know what they did and why it was a huge deal?"

"Yeah, they, uh, you know . . . had relations or something and God hated them for it," replied Roger with more confidence in this answer than all the rest he had given thus far.

"What? No, they didn't, uh . . . I mean, uh, yes, of course they had relations, because they had a couple of sons, Cain and Abel. But that's not why they got in trouble. It had nothing to do with physical relations. They disobeyed God and did something He told them specifically not to do. They ate the fruit of the tree of the knowledge of good and evil, which was exactly what God had warned them against.[5] They were guilty of a sin. And the consequence of sin is death.[6] Therefore, the spirit part of them died, and just as bad, the flesh part of them grew stronger."

"That's interesting, Coach."

"Why do you say that, Roger?"

"I think that's why someone would have that empty feeling inside."

"Why?" questioned Alan with a smile.

"Because the place inside of them where their spirit is supposed to be alive and well is actually vacant and dead. You know, like it's missing or something."

"That's right. And anyone who has ever sinned, meaning they disobeyed anything that God has said, has that same empty spot too. Have you ever done anything that you knew God said not to?"

"Well, uh . . . yes, sir, I guess I have."

"Then you, like all the rest of us on earth, have sinned and fallen short of His glory.[7] The Bible tells us that there is none righteous, no not even one.[8] Even though your sins are like a scarlet blotch upon you, He can make them whiter than snow."[9]

"Really, how can He do that?" asked Roger with tears welling up in his eyes.

"Well, while we were still sinners, Jesus Christ died for us, the righteous One for the unrighteous ones like me, like you.[10] In another place in the Bible He tells us that without the shedding of blood, there is no forgiveness of our sins.[11] However, this blood must be without sin in itself, or it isn't good enough to buy forgiveness for us all.[12] It would be just like everyone's blood, tainted with sin."

"Hey, Coach," interrupted Roger. "Why do folks say Jesus had blood that was pure?"

"Because He never sinned. He was more than a man; He was God before He was man. He existed with God and was Himself God.[13] But He didn't think that equality with God was something He would selfishly grasp. Rather, He willingly let go, humbled Himself, and became a man, born of a virgin. He suffered, bled, and died a horrible death, even the death on a cross.[14] Afterwards, God raised Him up, and in doing so, proclaimed to all mankind everywhere and for all generations that Jesus is indeed the Messiah.[15] All who believe in Him will not perish but have eternal life forever with Him.[16] Roger, would you like to have your sins forgiven once and for all time, and to know for a certainty that you will live with Him forever in Heaven?"

"Uh, yes, sir, of course I would, but what can I do?" asked Roger with tears running down his cheeks.

"All you have to do is ask Him, in faith, believing He will come in and live in your heart. His love, His Spirit will fill your empty hole, your dead spirit, and make it alive again. He will live within you, His Spirit in your spirit, making you whole once again.[17] He stands at the door and knocks. To whoever opens the door of his heart to Him, He promises to come in and live inside his spirit.[18] Do you hear Him knocking, Roger?"

"Yes, I think so, but I don't know what to do, Coach," sniffled Roger.

"All you have to do is ask Him. Do you want to ask Him, Roger?

"Yes, I do."

"Come on, let's kneel down here together and pray."

The two, as close as father and son, knelt down in the sawdust of Alan's makeshift woodworker's shop and prayed a simple prayer of faith for Roger to receive the Lord Jesus within his heart.

"Just follow and repeat after me, Roger," Alan guided quietly. "Dear Heavenly Father, I know I have sinned against You. I confess to You that I am a sinner in need of your forgiveness. Please forgive me and save me and become my Lord forever. Thank you for the blood of your dear Son, Jesus, which forgives all my sins, and for sending your Holy Spirit to live within me. I thank you for saving me in Jesus' name, Amen." Roger repeated every word and after the 'Amen' threw his arms around Alan, hugging and thanking him profusely.

"I really feel like I'm, uh . . . saved, Coach! I really feel like that emptiness has gone away! This is absolutely amazing. I feel like I am a new person, like I've been . . ."

"Born again?!" smiled Alan.

"Yeah, I finally know what that means. I actually have experienced it, and no one has to explain it to me. I've been born again, Coach!"

"Yes, you have, and the angels in Heaven are rejoicing[19] with you and so am I, Roger!"

At that point, the two joyful believers, who were standing in the garage, heard the kitchen screen door slam shut. They both turned to see Julie striding across the driveway toward them. Roger ran out to meet her halfway.

"You're not going to believe this," shouted Roger as he laughed and cried all at the same time.

The young couple embraced while jumping up and down. Then they both thanked Alan before getting in Roger's car and driving away. Alan plopped back down in his desk chair with such an overwhelming sense of peace, joy, and satisfaction that he literally burst out loud with a joyous shout of praise for all that the Lord was doing in his life.

"I think this must be what being free on the inside feels like. I am at peace at last. I have a wonderful wife, my health, money in the bank, my bills paid, I love coaching, and now my daughter is actually dating a Christian. Now, that's what I call freedom within me, total liberty from cares and concerns. Thank you, Dear Lord."

Jumping up from his chair, Alan ran to the house looking for Annalisa. He found her in the kitchen. The screened door slammed shut behind him as he threw his arms around his sweet life partner, announcing his great news concerning Roger. Then he had an idea.

"Honey, I know we already tithed the portion of the money we got from Betsy's house, but what if we gave an extra amount anonymously to help some folks out? You know, someone who may be having a rough time or is financially strapped. What do you think?"

Annalisa laughed as she planted a kiss on her joyous husband's lips. "I was going to ask you that very question today at lunch. God has helped us, and I really want to help others. You know, like being His arm, or hand, or something extended into another's life. I would love to be used by Him that way."

"Me too, my love. But nobody can know about this, okay? It has to be in secret, so God gets the glory and thanks, not us. This will always remain between the three of us only, okay?"

"The three of us?" questioned Annalisa, scrunching up her face.

Glancing upward, Alan gave indication of Who the third Person was in the "us".

"Gotcha," smiled Annalisa with a nod, then whispered, "Don't let the left hand know what the right hand is doing."[20]

"Now, my sweet, generous wife, how much should we give?"

"I was thinking around ten percent."

"Me too, honey."

"That's a lot of money, Alan."

"Yeah, but God has been generous with us, so we need to be generous with others."

Annalisa agreed, "Generosity toward others, frugality with self."

"Precisely, my sweet **rojoccian** sister. Who do we know that could really use a helping hand, you know, financially? That's what the Bible tells us to do. To help with material things those who have helped us along our way spiritually.[21] So who comes to mind, my love?"

-eighteen-

Since his prayer to become a Christian, Roger was a frequent visitor in the Browne's home especially Alan's woodworker's shop. He and Alan had grown to be fast friends and even more than friends, they regarded one another as family. Alan would, on occasion, call Roger "son" and believed Roger regarded him as the father he never knew. This was a far cry from when they first met and rather pleasing to Alan. He was enjoying not only the closeness of another son, but also the pride a father has in a son who is nearing an incredible accomplishment: the four minute mile record. Spending hours together, they talked of woodworking, running, and spiritual matters, sometimes to Julie's consternation. She felt she and Roger weren't getting much time alone.

As of April, neither of the athletes had heard from the two remaining schools of choice, the University of Florida and Clemson University. Sometimes the tension between them could be sensed if someone happened to walk into the room where they were sitting. Roger confided in Alan, and Julie in her mother. Many times Alan and Annalisa would later compare notes from their talks. Evidently, Julie and Roger were doing the same.

On the last day of April 2003, Alan got a phone call that instigated a major change in his life and that of Annalisa's as well. It was a Wednesday. Alan was in his shop, and Annalisa was in the kitchen when she answered the phone that afternoon. It was a beautiful, mild spring day, and Alan could hear her through the open kitchen window. He could discern that whoever was on the other end of the call was someone she knew but hadn't spoken to in a long time. After a few minutes of cheerful conversation, she called out the window.

"Alan, phone call for you; it's Teddy Wilbeam."

"Who?" asked Alan as he started to jog toward the kitchen.

"Reverend Teddy Wilbeam, you remember, the pastor from Wiggins, Mississippi. He came and spoke at our church in San Ramon years ago."

"Oh, yeah, right. We sent him a copy of The **rojocki** Manifesto. I'm guessing he wants to discuss it a bit."

The phone conversation lasted over thirty minutes ending with Alan gently hanging the phone on its base, his mouth gaping wide open. His thoughts were running through his mind like cars on a big city freeway, one after another, as well as several at a time. The flow was only interrupted when Annalisa walked back into the kitchen where Alan was seated at the table.

"What did he want?" she chirped.

"Uh . . . are you sitting down?" he smiled sheepishly.

"No, should I be?"

"Well, he wants me to speak at his church two weeks from this Sunday."

"Alan, that's our anniversary weekend. We are supposed to be going to Destin."

"Yeah, I know, honey."

"Well, what did you tell him?" she pried.

"I told him I needed to talk with you before I could give him an answer."

"Where's Wiggins anyway?" questioned Annalisa, looking for a possible solution to their new dilemma.

"It's a bit north of Gulfport, which is on the, uh . . . Gulf," he smirked, "of Mexico."

"Funny," she remarked snidely with a grin. "Isn't that close to Biloxi?"

"Yeah, it neighbors it, why?"

"Well, I hear there are some really nice hotels in Biloxi, and since I read about it a few years back, I've always wanted to take the boat trip out to Shipp Island."

"Shipp Island?"

"Yes, it's part of the Gulf Islands National Park," she quipped. "You know, in the Gulf of Mexico."

"Funny," he chided with a chuckle. "Well then, what do you say to an anniversary-slash-speaking-engagement trip?"

"Works for me, as long as we get to go out to Shipp Island," she bargained.

"Oh, I think we can arrange that, honey."

"Why does he want you to speak at his church?"

"He remembered a couple of my lessons back in our church in San Ramon. He mentioned he enjoyed the way I made the Scriptures practical," shrugged Alan. "Plus, he wanted his congregation to hear about The **rojocki** Fellowship, by way of an analogy."

"Why did you shrug, honey? You have a unique way of presenting spiritual things and making them very practical. You've told me many times over the years, 'If it isn't practical, what good is it in this life,' remember? Besides, you love to teach using metaphors and analogies."

"True. Well, anyway, he said when he received our letter about the Manifesto and discovered we had moved so close, he thought it would present a good opportunity to get reacquainted."

"That's nice, Alan."

"Yeah, kind of," he hesitated.

"What's wrong?"

"He asked regarding what happened at our church, you know with the pastor and all."

"Ooooh . . ."

"Yeah, ooooh, is right. I really don't want to discuss it. I feel like we've worked through all those issues years ago and have long since moved on. Regardless, if it's okay with you, I do think I would like to accept his offer to speak in two weeks."

"Sounds good to me, as long as we get to visit Shipp Island. Uh, do you know where that is, honey? You know, out in the Gulf . . ." she mocked with a giggle, throwing a dish towel at him.

After track practice the next day, Alan telephoned Teddy Wilbeam and accepted his offer to come speak. Two weeks later, he was standing at the pulpit in the moderate sized church building addressing a growing congregation of approximately one hundred and fifty people. He taught on all things **rojocki** and **rojocci**, including its fascinating history, how he got involved in the fellowship, and why the spelling of the acronym was changed shortly after World War II. He skillfully tied it all together as an allegory to the Christian life and in particular, a life lived in the Holy Spirit.

Following a delightful lunch with Teddy and his wife Margaret, Alan and Annalisa headed off on their two night anniversary trip to Biloxi. When they arrived home, there were three messages on their telephone's answering machine. The first was a call from Teddy requesting Alan to return his call as soon as possible. The second was from a pastor in Monticello, Arkansas, inquiring if Alan would consider speaking to his congregation. Lastly, someone identifying herself only as Mary, calling on behalf of her church. She didn't mention what she wanted or where the church was located. She did leave a number to call though.

Apparently the word was getting out that Alan had an encouraging message that churches might want to hear. Annalisa, who had listened to the answering machine, called to Alan from the kitchen just as he reached the top of the stairs with their luggage. Her voice sounded concerned, if not a bit panicked.

"Alan," she shouted. "Come here quick! You're not going to believe this."

"What's wrong? Something broke? What's leaking?" he asked, a bit winded from the efforts of carrying their suitcases upstairs and then running back down to the kitchen.

"Nothing's wrong." she rebuffed with a wry grin. "Listen to this."

The small, harmless, unemotional mechanical device resting on the kitchen countertop revealed the recorded messages it had stored within it, stirring up in Alan a rising concern mixed in an elixir of swelling insecurities and guarded excitement.

"Uh, oh," he chuckled, trying to hide his nervous enthusiasm.

"Yeah, uh, oh, is right, Alan. What if this is only the beginning? What if more churches want you to speak? What are we going to do? How are we going to handle this? I mean, you could be traveling every weekend. That wouldn't be good for us, for our family, or for you."

"Don't get carried away just yet," he consoled as he swung his arm around her shoulder. "Yeah, I know this could possibly signal a life change, but it may be something that only lasts a few weeks. Whatever it is, don't get upset. God has this all in His control. He knew this was coming our way. It didn't surprise Him, so He's got a plan . . . I hope, I hope, I hope."

"I know He's got a plan. But I'm concerned it may include you traveling away from us for long periods of time. The kids need their father, and I need my husband. You got that, mister big-time, fancy-pants speaker?!" she gibed playfully.

The next day, the entire family along with several members of the track team, who had qualified for the Florida State High School Track and Field Championships, were off to Gainesville and the University of Florida Track Stadium. Julie's mile final was set for late Friday morning with Roger running his mile final at ten after five that evening. There weren't many people in the bleachers when Julie stepped onto the track for her race.

With the pop of the starter's gun, Julie and the pack of female milers were off, charging around the first curve of the track. In her excited, overzealous state of mind, Julie ran her first lap of the four lap race a full eight seconds faster than normal. She had, in fact, outpaced all her competitors by mid-way through the second lap, although her time was slower than her fastest recorded for the halfway point in the race. By the start of the final lap, it was obvious to her father-coach that she was hurting like he had rarely seen. She was struggling to even maintain her form. He shouted encouragement from the infield, running a smaller loop on the grass within the track that was half the distance she had to cover. As she finally made it to the beginning of the finishing straightaway, he called out her time, willing her forward. She crossed the finish line exhausted from her over enthusiastic, miscalculated effort. Her time was less than two seconds from the National High School record. Julie had won the gold medal but missed the all-time best performance for a high school girl. Both elation and disappointment were painted upon her anguished face.

Running to his wheezing daughter, Alan threw a dry towel over her shoulders telling her how proud he was of her, his daughter the champion. She smiled radiantly through tears of great joy. "That was incredible, Julie! Congratulations, honey, you are the Florida State Champion!"

Soon Roger was holding his girlfriend, giving his own version of accolades for the feminine paladin. It truly was an amazing run by Julie. Not only was she undefeated the entire season, but she had won first place for the girl's high school mile. Both Alan and Annalisa were bursting with pride.

Later that afternoon, with the stands full of fans, reporters, and college coaches, it was Roger's turn at a record. The four minute mile had only been accomplished by a hand full of high school runners. A kid named Alan Webb from South Lakes High School in Reston, Virginia, had achieved the goal just two years previous. Ironically, almost thirty years ago, as a senior at Oakton High School, Alan had beaten everyone from South Lakes. Now, their runner held the national record for the mile. Granted, he ran it at a non-high school event, but even so, a 3:53.43 was incredibly fast for someone who hadn't even received his diploma yet. Alan was secretly hoping his own Roger Bellinger could once again set the record in order. It seemed reasonable to him that even though he wasn't there to beat the South Lakes miler's record, surely the runner he trained should accomplish it. He acknowledged it to be a very tall order though.

The stands were abuzz as the runners, fifteen in all, were called to the starting line of the mile final. Roger drew a position three runners from the inside curb. It was evident that each one was understandably nervous as they shook legs and arms randomly. Even Roger, who was the overwhelming favorite to win, appeared less confident than usual. He kept glancing at the runner from Apopka. This young man posed the biggest threat to Roger's victory, and Roger recognized that stranger things have happened in a high school state final. Like the time a few years back when a freshman sprinted past a senior in the last fifty yards to win the gold medal. Finally, the gun was up and with a loud pop, the pack of runners began charging around the track.

Roger completed the first lap in fifty-eight seconds with two other runners by his side. The half mile was done in a blazing one minute fifty-seven seconds, which meant his second lap clocked in at fifty-nine seconds. Roger was right on track to break the record, but as Alan was well aware; the third lap was always the most difficult. The time at the end of three laps was two minutes fifty-eight seconds. The third lap time clocked in at sixty-one seconds. Reaching out with its clutching tentacles, the curse of lap three had mercilessly grabbed ahold of Roger in a devastating way. Not only was the national record now out of sight, but if he didn't run a faster final lap, he wouldn't break the four minute mile either.

Darting back across the infield, Alan shouted his encouragement. With half a lap to go, he cheered Roger on with his time, and then ran back across the infield to beckon his protégé to fight for every second, "Run through the line, Roger, all the way through the line!"

Alan clicked his stopwatch to a halt just as Roger crossed the finish line. The time was 3:57.31. Alan Webb's national record was safe, but Roger Bellinger became the fifth high school miler to ever run a sub-four minute mile.

After the awards ceremony in which, first Julie, then Roger, both received gold medals and certificates for new Florida State High School records, their team gathered on the podium to receive the trophy for third place overall.

R. J. Graves, Jr.

While Alan and Annalisa were speaking with Roger's
mother, the track coach from the University of Florida
approached them. Julie and Roger proudly strode over with
their gold medals dangling from their necks. After Alan had
introduced the champions as his daughter and son, the
collegiate coach congratulated the two stars for their valiant
efforts.

The Florida coach shared the happy news that he had
been authorized to offer them both scholarships. Julie's
would be a half track and half academic grant. Whereas
Roger's was a full track scholarship. The entire Browne
family along with Roger's mother joined in a giant group
hug, even enveloping the collegiate coach in their joyous
embrace.

"Good news everywhere!" declared Alan to Annalisa on
their drive back home to Pensacola. "At every turn the Lord
is blessing us!" he smiled as he patted her leg.

"I know, honey, I too feel like we've turned a corner or
something."

"Yeah, and I hope it's a road we never have to travel
again. It will be very interesting to see where these new
speaking opportunities take us. Interesting days, you know,
honey?"

Little did Alan realize how true those words would
come to be. Having arrived home the following day, Annalisa
checked their answering machine in the kitchen. There were
nine messages: five from other track coaches offering
congratulations, two of them college coaches inquiring as to
his interest in coaching at the university level, plus three
from pastors asking if he had availability to speak at their

churches. The final message was from Annalisa's friend Rachel requesting a particular recipe for beef stroganoff.

"Alan," she shouted from the kitchen, "you're not going to believe this!"

"You know what this means?" asked Alan with a smile after listening to every message. "It means I could quit my woodworking business if I wanted to. Then I could coach and do speaking engagements at churches, retreats, and conferences. Just coaching and speaking, I think I could enjoy that lifestyle."

"Oh, I'm so happy for you, Alan. Seeing God bless you is amazing. I really can't believe it, you know what I mean?"

"Yeah, me, too . . . happy for us, sweetheart. For the first time in our lives I feel totally free in my heart. It is a most blessed feeling. I need to call . . . hey, did you mail that check to Joey and Pam?"

"Yes, I mailed a cashier's check before we left for Gainesville," she confirmed.

"Okay, thanks, honey, it's so very important that the right hand doesn't know what the left hand is doing,"[1] he nodded. "Sorry I forgot to do that. I guess with all the excitement over these last few days . . . wow, our daughter, a full ride to the University of Florida, un-be-stinking-lievable!"

"Yeah, well, I don't know about you, my dear sweet husband, but I'm not old enough to have a child in college," chided Annalisa as she slumped down on the living room sofa with a glass of iced tea.

"That's okay, you old battle-ax," he teased as he plopped down next to her. "This old man is going to put his feet up, watch some sports on television, sip on your iced tea . . . and then, he may even take a nice long nap."

Before he could get halfway through the plan for his Saturday afternoon utopia, the telephone rang. It was his best friend Joey. After the two exchanged pleasantries, Joey asked how Julie and Roger had done at the Track and Field Championships. Alan proudly and lavishly described in infinite detail how his daughter and Roger had each won their event in excellent fashion. The two laughed and joked for nearly an hour before agreeing to meet for lunch the following Thursday at one of their favorite spots, the Oar House seafood restaurant.

On Monday, Alan spent nearly the entire day returning phone calls, scheduling speaking engagements at churches, and planning campus visits for the possible coaching positions. He had a total of five Sunday messages to deliver throughout the Southeast before the end of July. The two campus visits were interviews for track and cross country coaching positions. The first one, scheduled for the second week of June, was at a small Christian college in Birmingham, Alabama. The second, a week later, would take him to a town outside of Jackson, Mississippi. Being considered for the next level was very exciting to Alan, especially after such a short time spent coaching high school. These wouldn't be his last opportunities either. Soon several other schools came courting.

Sitting at an umbrella table by the harbor on Thursday, Alan and Joey enjoyed a delicious seafood lunch together. Alan ordered the crab cake sandwich and Joey his favorite, a big basket of fried shrimp. Both had the Southern staple to drink, sweet tea. After some comments regarding the beautiful weather and a slick speed boat cruising by, Joey mentioned that he thought Alan was in an exceptionally good mood.

"Yes, I am, my old buddy," laughed Alan, referencing their age difference. "It is unbelievable all that God has done in my life lately. I was a bit of a basket case, you know, when we first met, what . . . almost ten years ago. Back then, I was all tied up in knots, worried about this or that, and feeling so insecure I could barely breathe. Yeah, Joey, now I feel totally free in my heart, a lightness, a liberty, a relaxation I have never felt before."

"That's awesome, Alan. What brought this on?"

"Oh, I don't know, everything from all the bills being paid, to a happy wife, to my oldest daughter getting a full ride to a major university. Life is good, my friend."

"Wow, that's great, Alan. Yeah, we too had an unusual blessing recently. Pam opened up the mail and someone had sent us a check for a huge amount of money. We fell to our knees right then and there and praised God for His help. I mean, we were on the ropes. Things had gotten really tight with the lack of work and trying to send the girls to college and all."

"That's wonderful news, Joey. So I guess you're feeling that freedom too, eh?"

"Well . . . I'm not sure what your definition of liberty or freedom is, but I can attest it's not money, my brother. The fact that my bills are all paid, and that I'm at peace with my spouse and my children are all good things to be sure. But it doesn't set me free on the inside, where it really counts.

Only the truth can set us free within.[2] Deep down inside where all our fears and aspirations lay hidden. All the intangibles reside there. These are what really control our lives, not these tangible things. I know you know that."

Seeking clarity, Alan asked Joey as Pontius Pilot had inquired of Jesus centuries before, "Truth? What is truth?"[3]

"Well, according to the Scriptures Jesus proclaimed, 'I am the Way, the Truth, and the Life; no one comes to the Father except through Me.'[4] He also told us God's Word is Truth,[5] and in one more passage, we find out the Spirit is Truth.[6] So Jesus is Truth, His Word is Truth, and the Holy Spirit is Truth. Combine those three and you have a pretty well rounded definition of Truth."

Just then, the waiter showed up with their lunch. The table conversation all but halted as both devoured their tasty seafood. Joey finished first.

"Look, Alan, we've been close friends for quite some time now, so I don't want to get into a discussion that would irritate you or have us part ways or something. I figure these are issues that we as men discuss, you know, 'like iron sharpens iron' in the Book of Proverbs."[7]

"Yeah, me either, Joey," agreed Alan with a smile. "In fact, I've been concerned about the very thing that you brought up here. I know these things don't set me free, but I do feel a very real sense of freedom within me. You know, it's a lack of worry or that awful insecure feeling I get. In that regard, I'm free."

"Well, kind of, but not really," admonished Joey. "God may bring times of quiet and calm. They are gifts from Him for us to enjoy. But they are not necessarily an indication that we are free on the inside. The things you mentioned are temporary. I mean, they can be taken away just as fast as they came. There's no real security or freedom in that. Not when it can all disappear at the drop of a hat. The only true freedom is based on something that never changes, that will always be there no matter what circumstances may come. What I believe you are expressing comes more from an emotional level, or maybe an ease of mind, or something. You know, what some folks call peace of mind. I've found that to be very short lived. True freedom dwells in our spirit and is the result or fruit of the Holy Spirit living there. However, He is so different, so other, so peculiar to us that it takes a great struggle of wills for us to finally come to the place of peace and rest in Him. The place of real security is where no storm of life is able to rock our boat and no manner of trial can disturb our inner joy and thankful hearts. Now, that is true freedom within you, my brother. "

"Yesterday, today, forever," Alan exclaimed softly. "Everything else changes but He doesn't."

"Yep, A. B. Simpson had it right when he wrote that hymn. He based it on a verse in the Book of Hebrews. God's Word never changes, neither does Jesus, nor the Holy Spirit. He is the truth. By basing your life on Him, you can have absolute peace and rest. Whatever tempest may come your way, He will be your solid Rock, your strong fortress,[8] and the anchor for your storm tossed soul.[9] He's not like the shifting sand under your feet, which is continually moving. No, He's steadfast, immovable, and never changing. You can cast your every concern upon Him for He cares for you."[10]

"I agree, Joey, and I know I'm a Christian, that I'm saved, but how will I ever know if I'm free from these burdens and cares that have plagued me nearly all my life? I don't always want to be looking around the next corner, so to speak, wondering what might happen or worse, watching over my shoulder to see what might be catching up. I can't express how much I truly despise that."

"Don't worry about it, Alan. God doesn't say we'll never have troubles in this life, but He does promise to be with us in those difficulties. If you're weak in faith, do things that will strengthen your faith. Spend time every day studying the Scriptures, soaking in them, praying and confessing before you do. When something jumps off the page at you, like God's really speaking to your heart, memorize that verse or passage. Then, think about it often. Chances are God will allow some test in the future and that particular Scripture will hold you steady . . . like an anchor for your soul. Remember, the primary way for faith to grow is through testing."[11]

"Testing, eh?" quipped Alan quietly. "I'm not too fond of testing."

"Well, it's for our best, my brother, and struggles are well worth the fruit it produces. It's like what you told me the vinedressers do in Napa, California. They prune so the vine bears more fruit. Well, He's pruning our vine, so we can bear more fruit,[12] spiritual fruit like love, joy, peace, patience, goodness, gentleness, kindness, self-control, and so on.[13] There's so much more spiritual fruit we can bear for Him. He's working on these hidden, intangible things, not the outward, tangible stuff." Joey paused a second because

Alan looked as though he agreed but also seemed to be having a bit of difficulty understanding how it applied to his own life.

"Look, Alan, you know what He says, if riches increase, don't set your heart on them.[14] You've been around long enough to know life is cyclical. One year you have plenty, even too much. Then, another year goes by and you have barely enough to make ends meet. However, you need to hold steady. Soon, there will be plenty again. He allows this because He loves us and wants us to stay close to Him."

"Man, I hope we don't have to go through being financially strapped again. I am so tired of that fight."

"Be careful what you wish for, Alan."

"What's that supposed to mean?"

"I mean . . . remember, I've seen tight times too. You know, there is not a person that walks this planet who will never suffer difficulty at one point or another. But if you have to go through something severe, then a lack of money isn't all that bad. There are a lot worse things to endure, I mean, other than eating beans and rice every day. We actually did that for almost five months one year. I thought we weren't going to make it, but we did. God met us and helped us along the way."

"Uh . . . I don't know, Joey."

"Alan, listen to me. Freedom is like faith. It has to be tested to assure that it is actually real and genuine. Don't worry about it; He never gives us anything that our faith can't handle.[15] But remember, He knows that freedom must be accompanied with law. There is no freedom without law. It's like fire without boundaries. When fire is in the fireplace where it was designed to be, everyone within the home may enjoy its glow and benefit from its warmth. But if it goes beyond its place, the peaceful abode soon becomes a dwelling of fear and terror."

"Yeah, I agree with all that. I just don't want to go through any more difficulties. I'm tired of the tests, the trials. I want to enjoy life a bit, you know, to do what I want to do . . ." breathed Alan.

"I completely understand, my brother. I'm not fond of troubles either. However, I recognize that God also provides seasons of quiet and calm. Even in these times He still has a purpose."

"I wish my whole life was quiet and calm," mumbled Alan.

"Look, maybe this will help; as a believer, this life on earth is as bad as it will ever get. Heaven will be much better than even the best day here. So keep your eye on the finish line, and it will make this all seem a bit easier," encouraged Joey with a nod.

"I agree. I tell my runners something like that, but . . ."

Joey interrupted, "Alan, freedom without law is anarchy. However, law without freedom is tyranny. True freedom is more than only an ability to do what you want or to feel lighthearted and good about yourself. True freedom is also the power to do what you should do. That very power is generated by resistance . . . and sometimes it's resistance to what I want to do. In other words, our sovereign Lord's gracious tests and trials provide the very resistance that increases our power to do what we know we should. And those same experiences which brought us the power we needed to endure and rejoice, act as the merciful boundaries wherein we are completely free. He designed it that way, and frankly, He designed us to live that way."

"Wow, I think I get what you're saying. It's spiritual, not natural. I was looking at it with the wrong eyes. That's quite profound, Joey," acknowledged Alan as they got up and headed for the parking lot. "I'm going to have to ponder this for a while. That was deep, brother. Where, uh . . . how did you learn all that?"

"School of hard knocks . . . of trials and errors, my brother, trials and errors," he smiled.

"Well, regardless, I have plenty of food for thought."

"Nah, just remember what God loves, that's all," propounded Joey as he patted Alan on the back.

"What? What do you mean, 'what God loves'?" quizzed Alan.

"God loves the heart of a volunteer,"[16] declared Joey. "He loves a cheerful giver.[17] He never forces His will on us. He is love,[18] and love, by His own definition, always seeks the best for others. He'll test us, Alan, but it's always for our best."

Alan quickly recalled those poignant words to mind while seated in their living room not six weeks later, when the next test came walking through the front door in the shape and appearance of his precious daughter Julie and her boyfriend, Roger.

"Hey, guys, what are y'all up to this afternoon," inquired Annalisa with a smile as Alan waved from the prone position he had assumed on the sofa, his head in her lap.

"Hi," greeted Julie quietly.

"Y'all doing anything tonight?" asked her mother with a cheerful tone. "We could play a game and pop some popcorn or something, interested?"

"Well, uh . . . we've been doing a lot of talking and we've decided . . . that is, Roger and I decided . . . that it would be best to go to school here locally instead of the University of Florida."

"What? Why?!" barked her father with more than a hint of confusion and indignation as he jumped up from his place on the sofa.

"Are you meaning to tell me that you are going to turn down those scholarships? You both have an all-expenses paid four year trip to a major university. What in the world are you thinking?" he refuted with a puzzled look on his face.

Sensing there was a deeper issue, something that had little to do with track scholarships; Annalisa put her hand on Alan's arm although she never took her eyes off her daughter's face. Alan glanced at Annalisa and slowly sat back down on the sofa next to her.

"What's the matter, honey?" Annalisa questioned her oldest daughter.

"Well," Julie swallowed hard and then took a long look at Roger, who was standing close to her with his arm around her waist. Then, looking back at her anxious parents, she began what sounded like a speech she had rehearsed several times, like a defendant in a courtroom, knowing the jury would remember and weigh each and every word.

"Mom and Dad, we have something we need to tell you."

-epilogue-

The first Wednesday of February 2017 was warm and sunny and my disposition matched the weather as I jogged up the long ramp at the popular Mobile, Alabama, seafood restaurant. I was very much looking forward to my visit with Alan and was prepared to present him with the second manuscript of his continuing story. As I had expected, having learned of his penchant for punctuality, Alan was early and stood waiting at the top of the ramp. Stretching out his hand to meet mine, his face stretched upward to accommodate a smile. His kind eyes welcomed me as a lone traveler would welcome a familiar face.

We sat down at a table by a window, which provided an unobstructed view of the bay below. An alligator was gliding along the surface, barely visible in the murky water. Our somewhat over enthusiastic waiter, with a distinct Southern accent, presented us with menus, then poured us some water. We both ordered glasses of half and half iced tea, and after performing his rehearsed sales pitch for the daily special, our server disappeared, apparently in search of our cool beverages.

"Well, here's the second book, Alan," I announced proudly as I slid the manuscript across the white linen table cloth. "I hope you'll find it an accurate portrayal of what you've shared with me and an enjoyable read."

"I'm sure I will," he responded with a smile. "You know, I still can't believe anyone would be interested in reading our story. However, I've learned over my sixty plus years that when it comes to walking with our God anything is possible and change is often on the horizon, so I might as well accept and enjoy it."

Laughing, I nodded my head in agreement. Although I was younger than my lunch companion, I recognized that change has been a large part of God's modus operandi in my life too. I was about to launch into a humorous story relating this fact when the waiter arrived with our iced teas and asked for our lunch orders. I deferred to Alan, who requested a bowl of this restaurants' famous She-Crab soup and a Caesar salad. I decided on the same with one exception, instead of the Caesar, I opted for a garden salad with extra tomatoes.

"You know," Alan posed, inadvertently preventing me from beginning my story, "ever since Julie and Roger dropped that bombshell on Annalisa and me, I purposed to seek first the Lord and His Kingdom.[1] Actually, I had initially set my heart to consider this years ago when a very dear friend and sister in the Lord passed away."

"Betsy Taft?"

"Yes. To me, she was the last of the great believers of that generation. Betsy will forever be in my Hall of Fame. But I remember thinking, 'I wonder if I'm in anyone's Hall of Fame? And if I'm not, why not?'"

Alan paused to let that thought sink in as he half-heartedly smiled across the table at me. The expression on his face faded to a blank stare, then a faint grimace as he slowly turned his head from side to side. Something he was remembering seemed to be troubling him.

He continued, "Freedom is one of the major themes in Scripture. However, it has an elusive quality, don't you think?"

"Uh, sure . . . I guess so," I shrugged.

"I believe it's one of the many and varied mysteries in the Bible. Did you know the word 'mystery' is used twenty-seven times in the New Testament, but only six times in the Old Testament? I think that is significant. In fact, the occurrences in the Old Testament are all in the Book of Daniel. In the New Testament, it's splashed throughout ten different books. I believe it is a clue that something had dramatically changed."

"I'm not sure what you're referring to, Alan."

"I think it's an indication that with the death and resurrection of Jesus Christ, something major shifted in the relationship between God and man."

"What do you think changed in our relationship with Him?"

"Well, many things actually, but I'm referring to the wonder of discovery," Alan proclaimed with a smile. "It's the joy and sense of purpose you discover within yourself as you search for truth, like a married couple revealing more of the depths of their hearts as the years go by. He loves us and woos us ever forward, teaching us how to walk alongside Him. He speaks, often in parables, every day to everyone. Can you hear Him? He's as quiet and gentle as a dove. Not forceful like our enemy," he nodded, looking for my acknowledgement.

"But remember," continued Alan, "God's focus is on our relationship with Him. His attention is always on the condition of our heart. His goal for us is oneness with Him. Look at Moses. Moses knew God's ways, but the Israelites only knew His acts.[2] There's a huge difference hidden in that little statement. And so many more mysteries are just waiting to be unearthed in the Scriptures. I believe God has concealed them on purpose. And the only way to find them is to have a relationship with Him, a continually growing, developing, close friendship with Him. He tells His secrets to His friends," smiled Alan. "And they're spiritually understood, not intellectually analyzed."

"What do you mean?" I questioned, still a bit confused.

"I mean, my brother, this eternal relationship with Him is a spiritual transaction, so don't get discouraged, don't give up, and don't ever quit. Unity takes time, a strong marriage takes time, and your intimacy with Him takes time. The understanding you seek may be just over the next hill or around the next curve. However, the answer or revelation you've been longing for oftentimes comes in a way you don't expect, like in the form of a trial or difficulty."

"What?"

"First the natural, then the spiritual.[3] In other words, He brings a circumstance across your path, perhaps a test or a trial, to teach you something spiritually deeper than you have learned to date. But you don't recognize it as an answer from God because it arrives as a very natural matter, like a flat tire on an unfamiliar road, a long line at the grocery store, or even a problem with a family member."

"Julie and her boyfriend Roger?"

"Yes," nodded Alan. "I desperately wanted to be free in my heart. Free from my worries about money, free from my fears, free from my bondage to feeling self-conscious and insecure. I had been so tied in knots for decades, and it had worn me to a frazzle. I was miserable and God knew precisely what I needed. So in response to my cry from the depths of my heart, He sent me a trial, which seemed so fleshly in nature, I almost missed the spiritual significance altogether."

"Really?"

"Yes. You see, I had told the Lord years previous, that I wanted to be one of those who sought after Him with all my heart. When we last visited with Betsy, Annalisa and I were having a serious conversation with her at the picnic table. She stated that it was extremely rare to find one who seeks first the Lord and His kingdom. As I was listening to her, my heart was burning within my chest. Although I made no profession with my mouth, I was shouting deep down within my heart, 'Yes, Lord, do that in my life—make me one among a million whose heart is completely committed to You.' And I really meant it."

"And?" I asked curiously.

"He answered my prayer, but not in a way I would have ever imagined. He responded by using Julie and Roger's situation to not only reveal to me what was in my heart, but also to deepen my relationship with Him. I know it sounds strange, but it's not. God knows what is hidden in my heart and how to get it out. All He needs is my cooperation."

Gratefully, at that moment the waiter showed up with our soups and salads. I was starting to feel considerably uncomfortable myself, recognizing Alan was sharing some very profound thoughts with me. I glanced across at him as he sprinkled some cayenne pepper on his soup. Thinking this was an opportune time to change the subject, I asked with a chuckle, "So you've really assimilated into the Cajun culture down here, haven't you? I mean the cayenne and all."

"Oh, I've always enjoyed a little spice with my food," he laughed. "Plus, I did read somewhere that peppers are good for your heart. Afterwards, Annalisa and I began growing a few varieties in our garden each year. This year we have some jalapenos, and pepperoncini, as well as a few red and green bell peppers. We just love them."

After pausing for a few seconds, Alan finished what he had started several minutes ago. "I don't want you to leave here without this one thing," he proceeded. "Even though I had proclaimed to Joey and several others that I was free . . . I wasn't. Yes, my circumstances had dramatically improved to a place where I felt freer than ever before. However, relief of difficulties isn't freedom. Those struggles can return as quickly as they departed. My daughter's announcement made that all too clear to me. It also showed me I wasn't really free on the inside. I still wanted to control others, to coerce them into doing what I thought was best. My friend, it was a startling and very disappointing revelation to me. But I knew God still loved me, and all I had to do was repent of my own ways and begin to seek Him first."

"Wow," I whispered under my breath as I gazed across the table at Alan.

"Yeah, wow, is right," he smiled. "It's not nearly as easy as it sounds. Nevertheless, by His great mercy and grace, He has enabled me to do that for nearly fifteen years now . . . with an occasional stumble here and there," he chuckled with a wink. Then his expression turned more sober. "I think the older I get, the more I realize my need for Him."

Nodding my head in agreement, I had little idea of the reality of what he professed. I had not known him as a younger man. The Alan I had become friends with was a wise and godly, older gentleman. So, like many times before, I found some of what he communicated about himself difficult to believe.

"Look, my brother," Alan continued. "If you are going to err, and we all do, then err on the side of faith, of believing Him, of leaving room for Him to act even right up to the last possible moment. Don't flounder in unbelief, doubt, and cynicism. Anybody can do that. Faith is powerful. The Bible tells us there are those who have what He calls 'little faith'[4], while others have 'weak faith'[5], but there are some with 'great faith'[6]. I would highly recommend making your life-long goal one of exploring how to become a Christian with 'great faith'. Now, there's a hidden mystery worth searching for," smiled Alan with a nod.

"Thank you for that," I affirmed.

"And there's one more essential thing I have discovered along those lines."

"What's that?" I asked as I leaned forward for the answer.

"How to fight the good fight of faith.[7] But let's save that story for another time."

My mouth dropped open when he declared those words. I knew then that it would be the main topic in the final installment of Alan and Annalisa's story. More significantly, it is the very thing I desire for myself. My face broke into a smile as I began to recognize God's magnificent kindness in sending me this dear, saintly man to teach me something I desperately needed at a time in my life when I needed it most.

As if he knew precisely what I was thinking, Alan smiled back at me, "Our God is so good, isn't He?" he expressed softly.

"Yes, I agree, Alan. He is so very good to us. Now, how about letting me treat you to a slice of their famous Key Lime Pie?"

footnotes

Chapter One:

1. Acts 14:22

2. John 21:3

3. Luke 17:21

Chapter Two:

1. Revelation 12:10

2. John 10:10

Chapter Three:

1. 1 Timothy 6:15;
   Psalms 103:19

2. John 3:16;
   1 John 4:10

3. Corinthians 13:13

4. Colossians 1:18

5. Job 1: 6, 7

6. John 10:10

7. Job 1:8

8. Job 1:1

Chapter Four:

1. Matthew 7:6

2. John 4:24

3. Hebrews 4:12

4. Peter 1:18, 19

5. Ephesians 2:8

6. Luke 7:47

7. 2 Corinthians 13:14

8. John 5:21;
   Revelation 1:18

9. Proverbs 18:21

10. Matthew 7:16

Chapter Six:

1. 2 Corinthians 1:4

Chapter Seven:

1. Hebrews 12:2

2. Romans 8:31

Chapter Eight:

1. Proverbs 27:14

Chapter Nine:

1. Psalms 37:25

2. 2 Chronicles 16:9

3. Matthew 6:33

Chapter Eleven:

1. John 20:14

2. Luke 24:13-35

3. John 21:1-14

4. 1 Corinthians 15:42-44

5. Matthew 10:39

Chapter Fifteen:

1. Matthew 18:16

Chapter Sixteen:

1. Malachi 3:10;

2. Jeremiah 31:3

3. Luke 12:1
4. Psalms 50:10
5. Proverbs 16:18

Chapter Seventeen:
1. Genesis 1:26
2. John 4:24
3. 1 Thessalonians 5:23
4. Galatians 5: 16, 17
5. Genesis 3:1-24
6. Romans 6:23
7. Romans 3:23
8. Romans 3:10
9. Isaiah 1:18
10. Romans 5:8
11. Hebrews 9:22
12. Hebrews 9:13, 14;
    Hebrews 10:12
13. Luke 1: 31-35;
    John 1:1-4
14. Philippians 2:5-8
15. Acts 2:22-24
16. John 3:16
17. John 3:6; 4:24
18. Revelation 3:20
19. Luke 15:10
20. Matthew 6:3
21. 1 Corinthians 9:11

Chapter Eighteen:
1. Matthew 6:3
2. John 8:31, 32
3. John 18:38
4. John 14:6
5. John 17:17
6. John 5:7
7. Proverbs 27:17
8. Psalms 31:3
9. Hebrews 6:19
10. 1 Peter 5:7
11. James 1:3, 4;
    1 Peter 1:6, 7
12. John 15:2
13. Galatians 5:22, 23
14. Psalm 62:10
15. 1 Corinthians 10:13
16. Psalms 110:3
17. 2 Corinthians 9:7
18. 1 John 4:8

Epilogue:
1. Matthew 6:33
2. Psalms 103:7
3. Corinthians 15:46
4. Luke 12:28
5. Romans 14:1
6. Matthew 15:28
7. 1 Timothy 6:12

about the author

R.J. Graves, Jr. and his wife, the lovely Mrs. Graves, met on the mission field in 1978, he a Virginian, and she from Northern California. They have been married thirty-seven years and have six wonderful children, three of whom are married and have blessed them, to date with three precious grandchildren.

Over the years, he has held many roles in church leadership, including teaching and preaching. However, he most enjoys leading interactive Bible studies. He believes, "Come, let us reason together," is every bit as pertinent today as it was centuries ago. He loves family gatherings and delights in walks with his wife Susie, and their dog Pumpkin. When he finds the time he likes to ride his bicycle and dabble in woodworking.

After college, R.J. began his career as a carpenter's apprentice. He quickly obtained journeyman status and also worked as a park ranger in California, being elected president of his police academy. He has held numerous management and executive positions throughout his more than forty year career mainly in construction. His gifts and calling are to exhort and encourage fellow believers to consider the greater possibilities and mysteries of a deeper life in our Lord Jesus Christ.

You can contact him on Facebook at www.facebook.com/rojocci or at: www.therojoccipapers.com if you have any questions or comments.

Look for the next book in

the rojocci paper

series

the rojocci papers

THE
KINGDOM
WITHIN YOU

R.J. Graves, Jr.